PRAISE FO

The Best Friend

"This is a well-constructed, compelling legal thriller that deals perceptively with guilt and retribution, all set on a firm basis of love."

—*Booklist*

A Matter of Will

"Business, blood, and deception help make this an exciting and fast-moving yarn. Fine fare for thriller fans."

—*Kirkus Reviews*

"[An] engrossing thriller from Mitzner (*Dead Certain*). The action never flags in this exciting cautionary tale."

—*Publishers Weekly*

"Mitzner is a master at making the complex understandable for the average reader while not letting the intricate details of the subject matter that supports his story weigh it down . . . *A Matter of Will* [is] a perfect vacation read."

—*Bookreporter*

"Mitzner really knows how to craft a page-turning mystery. A cover-to-cover read."

—*Press & Guide*

Dead Certain

An Amazon Charts Most Sold and Most Read Book

Authors on the Air Finalist for Book of the Year

"*Dead Certain* is dead-on terrific . . . It's an entertaining and riveting work that will more than hold your interest."

—*Bookreporter*

"Consistently compelling . . . Adam Mitzner is a master of the mystery genre."

—*Midwest Book Review*

"There are several twists and turns along the way . . . creating a big amount of tension."

—*The Parkersburg News and Sentinel*

"[*Dead Certain*'s] leading coincidence, which is quite a whopper, is offset by an equally dazzling surprise . . . It packs enough of a punch to make it worth reading."

—*Kirkus Reviews*

A Conflict of Interest

A *Suspense Magazine* Book of the Year

"A heady combination of Patricia Highsmith and Scott Turow, here's psychological and legal suspense at its finest. Adam Mitzner's masterful plotting begins on tiptoe and morphs into a sweaty gallop, with ambiguity of character that shakes your best guesses, and twists that punch you in the gut. This novel packs it. A terrific read!"

—Perri O'Shaughnessy

"Mitzner's assured debut . . . compares favorably to *Presumed Innocent* . . . Mitzner tosses in a number of twists, but his strength lies in his characters and his unflinching depiction of relationships in crisis. This gifted writer should have a long and successful career ahead of him."

—*Publishers Weekly* (starred review)

A Case of Redemption

An American Bar Association Silver Gavel Nominee for Fiction

"Head and shoulders above most."

—*Publishers Weekly*

Losing Faith

"Tightly plotted, fast-paced . . . Startling . . . A worthy courtroom yarn that fans of Grisham and Turow will enjoy."

—*Kirkus Reviews*

The Girl from Home

"An engrossing little gem."

—*Kirkus Reviews*

THE

PERFECT

MARRIAGE

OTHER TITLES BY ADAM MITZNER

THE
PERFECT
MARRIAGE

A NOVEL

ADAM MITZNER

THOMAS & MERCER

Published by Thomas & Mercer, Seattle

www.apub.com

Amazon, the Amazon logo, and Thomas & Mercer are trademarks of Amazon.com, Inc., or its affiliates.

ISBN-13: 9781542005760
ISBN-10: 1542005760

Cover design by Faceout Studio

Printed in the United States of America

For Susan, my partner in the perfect marriage

Owen had always assumed that the first funeral he would attend would be his own. Such a morbid thought would have been foreign to most teenagers, who invariably believed they were immortal. Owen's classmates were forever testing the thesis—driving while drunk, taking drugs of dubious origin, and vaping anything. They always lived to tell the tale, proving they'd been right all along: they could never die.

For Owen, however, there was no tempting fate in this way. Before he was old enough to grasp the indestructibility that other teenagers believed to be their birthright, Death had entered his inner circle. Once admitted, Death remained front and center in Owen's thoughts. So much so that Owen eventually thought of Death as a friend—a confidant. Someone who listened to him when no else did.

Everyone else in his life was always *talking*—about how it was all going to be okay, how brave or strong he was, or what a fighter he was. Even at thirteen, Owen knew it was a pack of lies. No one could predict whether he would live or die. He wasn't strong or brave or a fighter. In fact, some days he felt so weak that he couldn't get out of bed. He lived in a state of constant terror. More often than not, rather than fighting it, he succumbed to that dread.

Every time he did, Owen realized the one central fact of his existence: everyone was always lying to him.

Everyone except Death.

Death spoke the truth, whether Owen wanted to hear it or not. Death had no interest in Owen's feelings, in keeping his spirits high, or in stopping his mother's tears. Death didn't give two shits if he was having a good day, if it was his birthday or Christmas, or if he was up to handling bad news.

Death's only allegiance was to the truth.

What Death told Owen was simple: It had not chosen him because he was special or he could handle it or it would build his character. Death acted without any justification whatsoever, making selections at random.

In short, Death was unfair, and Death owned it.

And then, with no more warning than it had given when it entered his life, Death departed when the doctors told Owen that his cancer was in remission.

"You get to start your life all over again now," his mother said.

"Think about how lucky that is, O," his father said. "Most people would give anything for a second chance, and you have one, buddy."

In the years that followed, Owen was surprised at how much he missed Death's company. He was more than happy to forgo the chemo sickness, of course, and God knew he enjoyed having his hair back. But still he longed for that sense that, amid all the lies he encountered on a daily basis, someone close by was willing to speak the truth.

Of course, Owen knew that Death would return. It came for everyone, after all. It was only a matter of when.

And then, in the winter of Owen's eighteenth year, Death came back into his life. Much to his surprise, however, Death bypassed him, coming for someone else. And Death's modus operandi this time was not cancer, but homicide.

PART ONE

1

James Sommers considered looking at his wife in her wedding dress irrefutable proof that there was no relationship between virtue and happiness. It had been a year and four days since they'd married, and the simple sight of Jessica still made him smile like an idiot at his good fortune.

"Too much?"

James knew his wife was asking whether rewearing her wedding dress was overkill for their anniversary party. She had posed the question before—several times, in fact. He had always answered honestly, telling Jessica that she looked perfect.

This time, however, he decided to flirt.

"I do prefer you naked."

She smiled at his joke. "There'll be time for that later. But seriously, do I look okay in this?"

"Perfect," he said.

Jessica rolled her eyes. "I don't even know why I ask."

James did not consider himself a particularly introspective man. He certainly wasn't a religious one, having no faith in a higher power. Still, he had always tried to do the right thing. He'd be the first to admit that he wasn't perfect in that regard, but all things considered, he thought he'd more or less walked the line. It was not an easy thing to do in his profession, where most art dealers believed that if you weren't cheating someone—the buyers, the sellers, the artists, the IRS—you weren't trying hard enough.

Much to James's surprise, keeping to the straight and narrow had led him to unhappiness, and only after detouring had he found the contentment he'd previously thought unattainable.

He owed all his happiness to Jessica, but at times he felt like a thief. As if he had stolen the happiness meant for someone else, and at any moment he might be apprehended and forced to give it back. That was why, like any good criminal, he took care to keep his haul out of public view.

It was for that reason that James had initially expressed concern when Jessica proposed this party. Gathering everyone they knew for the purpose of celebrating their first anniversary seemed like tempting fate.

"You know my view," James said. "You can have either a big wedding or a happy marriage, but not both."

The line had become a recurring joke between them. At first to justify James's resistance to a big wedding, then to explain to friends and family why they'd elected to elope.

Regardless of whether there actually was any relation between the number of guests invited to watch nuptials and the happiness of the marriage to follow, James could not deny that after their elopement, their first year together had been nothing but pure bliss. Before Jessica, he had imagined happiness in the form of exotic trips and grand romantic gestures. But in reality, it was the smallest moments that he had come to cherish most: the way Jessica talked about the characters in novels as if they were friends and how she could throw her whole body into a laugh brought on by something he found only mildly amusing.

"Nothing over the top," Jessica had assured him about the anniversary party. "Fifty people, no more. No sit-down meal. We'll cater in some low-key food. Sushi, maybe. Or even just order in some pizzas."

James had responded to this request the way he did to most things Jessica asked of him. He'd agreed. Which was why he was now staring with a big idiot grin on his face at his bride of a year and four days wearing her wedding dress.

For his own attire, James had decided to follow Jessica's lead and wear the suit he had donned to get married, a navy crepe that he'd had custom-made for the occasion. It was a tad lightweight for late January in New York, but he didn't intend to leave the apartment tonight. He'd briefly considered pairing the suit with a different tie than he'd worn at the wedding, but in the end, he reached for the same solid silver Kiton sevenfold that had served him so well the first time.

James's father had been killed in a car accident, going on fifteen years ago now. For months after, James had considered how the world would be different if his father had not been driving across that intersection at exactly the same moment the truck had entered it. What if his father had been delayed even thirty seconds before getting behind the wheel? What if he hadn't made a light ten blocks north? Or if the truck driver had started his journey five minutes later? All the infinite variables that could have been different. But because none of them were, his father was dead.

Afterward, people said it was meant to be. That nothing could have been done to change it. It was no one's fault. Some things were beyond anyone's control.

For years he wondered if that were true. If the world actually worked that way, with the onslaught of sudden inalterable cataclysmic events.

And then he met Jessica. And he finally believed.

The same way that fifteen years earlier nothing could have been done to change his father's fate, Jessica's entry into his life was similarly preordained, and he was powerless to alter it.

———

Despite her husband's repeated assurances, Jessica still couldn't help but wonder if her dress was too much for a house party. She had initially justified the garment's exorbitant price tag with the thought that, because it wasn't so wedding-y, she'd get more than one use out of it. In reality, few occasions were appropriate for a knee-length off-white silk dress. She couldn't wear it to anyone else's wedding, and the art openings at which she served as James's plus-one usually required something understated and black.

Her final assessment met with her approval. She looked good. Forty-one years old and everything still more or less where it was supposed to be.

Then she shifted her gaze toward her lawfully wedded husband. James looked better than good, the way some men—the very lucky ones—were at their most handsome in their forties and fifties. She'd seen pictures of James as a younger man, all chiseled features, six-pack abs, and that hair—Jim Morrison from the cover of the *Best of the Doors* album, which she'd listened to on repeat in her teenage years, thinking it made her edgy. But James had grown into his looks over the years; now he had gravitas. Not only a pretty face, but a serious one too.

Sometimes she considered how close she had come to never seeing that face and therefore not living the life she now considered to be nothing short of perfection. Like a fairy tale, except that instead of leaving behind a glass slipper, she had forgotten her wallet at work. By the time she'd returned to retrieve it, it was past six and her office was a ghost town.

She'd been ready to leave her office for the second time that night when her phone buzzed with a text from Lisa Rollins, her boss at the real estate agency.

URGENT: CAN ANYONE BE AT THE LOFT IN 10 MINUTES?!!!

Jessica texted back—I CAN!!!—mirroring Lisa's use of all caps and exclamation points.

Her phone rang a millisecond later.

"Thank God," Lisa said. "There's a serious buyer interested in the loft. He's already got an offer in on this other place, but I convinced him to take a look at ours before deciding. Problem is, he's only available to see it tonight. After that he's heading to Europe or Asia or somewhere. So I need someone to be down there with the key in ten minutes."

Although the agency had numerous listings, Jessica knew which one Lisa was referencing. It was the crown jewel of their portfolio at the time, described as a *True Artist's Loft* in the glossy brochure Jessica had helped write, even though everyone in the office knew that a banker would likely buy it.

The loft was only a five-minute walk from the office. When Jessica arrived, James was waiting outside. She was immediately drawn to him—tall and well built with a face that seemed vaguely Italian in its dark-featured, straight-nosed way.

"I'm Jessica, the broker. Lisa Rollins asked me to show you around."

"James Sommers," he said, smiling in a way that Jessica would never forget.

So many times in the past year she'd used the phrase "love at first sight." It sounded corny, but she had no other words to capture the overwhelming sense of inevitability of meeting James. Time and again she thought of that quote from *Wuthering Heights*, how Catherine described Heathcliff as more herself than she was, and that whatever souls are made of, theirs were the same. That's how Jessica felt within thirty seconds of meeting James.

She led him through the space, trying to remember the tear sheet's description of the origin of the marble surrounding the fireplace and the brand of tile in the master bath. Fortunately, the place sold itself; their walk-through lasted less than twenty minutes. During that time, however, the heavens had opened outside. By the time they returned to the street, it was hailing, chunks of ice hitting the pavement hard enough to activate car alarms into a cacophony of wails.

Jessica suggested that they escape the weather by going inside the Starbucks next door. When the hail let up an hour later, they parted ways. Jessica couldn't sense whether James was seriously considering the loft and had no reason to think that she had made any personal impression on him. But two days later, he called her and made no pretense about his interest in both.

———

Wayne wasn't nearly as naïve as people thought. He knew that attending a party to celebrate his ex-wife's first year of wedded bliss with another man made him the marital equivalent of a sideshow freak. And yet, here he was, all dressed up on a Saturday night, leaving Forest Hills, Queens, and riding the 7 train into Manhattan for that very purpose.

Wayne's mother often said that her husband was "a hard man." Wayne supposed it was a more charitable description than "angry alcoholic," although the latter was more accurate.

Somewhere along the line, Wayne's father had decided that the world had betrayed him. Archibald Fiske was smart enough to know that his true adversaries—his boss, the man at the service station who told him their Buick needed a new transmission, or the neighbor who didn't pull his garbage cans in from the street quickly enough—would never stand for his abuse. So, rather than risk a counterpunch, ole Archie took out his frustrations on people who would not fight back: his wife and son.

"He's just a man of his time" was another of his mother's efforts to justify her husband's rage, as if every male born in the decade after World War II thought nothing of striking the woman he had sworn to love until death, or striking a child who had done nothing wrong but be born. "You'll be different, though," Wayne's mother always said to him.

Wayne's entire life had been an effort to fulfill his mother's wish and be nothing like Archibald Fiske. It was only recently that he had come to understand that by pursuing this quest with such single-mindedness, he had failed to devote the necessary time to being Wayne Fiske.

The irony was not lost on him that, by making this mistake, he had inadvertently become hard himself. Sometimes he even drank too much. In fact, at his low points, Wayne believed that the only meaningful difference between him and his father might be that Wayne hid his demons better. Whereas his father would lose his temper over nothing at all, Wayne couldn't remember the last time he'd *not* been in control.

It was a skill he would need to call upon this evening. In fact, he could barely think of a more un–Archibald Fiske thing to do than smile and drink a toast to Jessica and James's happiness.

———

Owen's mother had told him that he could invite a friend to the party. "A boy or a girl," she'd said in that I'm-so-woke way that she sometimes tried on.

Owen said he'd think about it, the phrase he used whenever he meant no but didn't want to engage further on the topic. It was inconceivable that he would subject any of his friends to the spectacle taking place this evening. Instead, he would fly solo for an hour, smile at his parents' friends, and then retreat into his room the moment his mother granted him such dispensation.

He was mentally preparing for the evening by blasting Pop Smoke's "War" through his headphones when a knock on his door interrupted the jam.

"What is it?" he said.

His mom stepped inside. "Just checking on you." She looked him over approvingly. "My, my. You clean up nice, Owen."

In point of fact, Owen thought he looked ridiculous. The blazer his mother had bought for him to wear for the occasion was way too big across the shoulders and too short in the sleeves. On top of that, his hair didn't go well with a sports-jacket-and-trousers look. It was now past his shoulders, long with tight curls, making him look like a seventeenth-century French monarch. In tonight's outfit, the overall effect was like when people put hats on dogs: it just didn't make any sense.

"Nikes? Really?" she said when she noticed his feet.

"The shoes I wore to Aunt Emma's wedding were too small."

"James's shoes will probably fit you," she said. "He'll give you a pair of loafers or something."

"Please, Mom," he said, in the whiny voice that sometimes worked.

She considered his plea for a moment, then smiled, settling the issue. "Okay. If wearing sneakers is going to make you happy, far be it from me to stand in your way."

He was tempted to tell her that his choice of footwear was not really going to make him any happier. He didn't want to attend this party no matter what he wore. Instead, he said, "When do I have to be out there?"

"By nine, please. And you don't have to stay long. Just until after the toasts."

With that, his mother leaned over and kissed him on the top of his head.

"Mom, I'm not six."

"I love you, Owen," she whispered, as if he hadn't said anything at all.

———

Reid Warwick loved a good party—the feeling that the night ahead contained unlimited possibilities. That anything could happen.

He did not expect James Sommers's anniversary party to be a *good* party, though. James was one of the few truly respectable people Reid knew. Maybe the only one, come to think of it. To Reid, that meant that James and his new bride's friends were also respectable people, and therefore the party would be a bunch of stiffs sipping chardonnay while they discussed their children's school achievements or swapped home renovation stories.

There were other places Reid could have gone if debauchery were his true objective for the evening. In fact, when he received the invite, Reid had assumed that he'd be at one of his usual haunts while James and Jessica celebrated their anniversary. But two weeks ago, Reid had the good fortune of being presented with a business opportunity that required James to consummate it.

That meant that, as far as Reid was concerned, tonight was more akin to a business meeting, which was why he had decided to wear a suit, pairing it with a plain white shirt. A tie would be trying too hard. He did shave for the first time in several days, though.

Tommy Murcer called for the second time that day while Reid was getting ready. Reid pressed decline on his phone. He'd fill Tommy in on James's response once he knew it. The Pollock sketches were now firmly in Reid's possession, so there was nothing Tommy could do to screw him over at this point.

The last Jackson Pollock canvas to come to auction had fetched $40 million, and that was nearly a decade ago. The record for a sale of his work was approximately $200 million, made in a 2015 private sale.

Unfortunately, Tommy didn't have paintings. What he'd entrusted Reid to sell were preliminary sketches. Unsigned too. That meant the price per sketch would be below a million.

On the bright side, Murcer had four of them. And Reid's take was 35 percent.

To make this payday happen—for himself as well as for Murcer—Reid needed James's connections in the art world. It was a fairly small universe of people who could afford to shell out the price of a McMansion for a piece of paper with some paint splatter on it. Reid didn't know even one, but James's contact list was chock-full of such people.

Even if he had to cut James in for half of his take (and he was hoping it wouldn't come to that), Reid would still end up netting somewhere in the neighborhood of half a million bucks. And he'd do his best to keep James's take below that. Either way, it wasn't a bad day's business, considering that he was doing little more than introducing a guy with access to some Jackson Pollocks to another guy who knew people who could afford them.

———

Haley Sommers was already two glasses into the bottle of chardonnay she had opened as her evening's plans. A Saturday night spent drinking and feeling sorry for herself had become almost the norm these days.

Sometimes she wondered how she could have fallen so far, so quickly. Two years ago she was a married investment banker, and now she was . . . a cautionary tale. Closing in on thirty, divorced, no children, and unemployed. Not to mention bitter to the core.

All too often, Haley felt the hate burn within her. A fire that could be extinguished only with alcohol, of all things. And then only temporarily.

All of her and James's friends had long ago chosen sides. Some took longer than others, pledging pious promises to keep loving them both, but it was only a matter of time before loyalties were tested and battle lines inalterably drawn.

Even though lunch invitations and movie nights with James's social set were now a thing of the past for Haley, his friends still cared enough about their friend and follower counts on Facebook and Instagram that they had not blocked Haley on social media.

Mandy's feed had been especially helpful. Tonight's entry captured her in a full-length shot wearing a little black dress and posed to show that she barely had a rib cage. In the caption she wrote: *Anniversary Party at James and Jessica Sommers' Loft. #truelove.*

James and Jessica's first anniversary had actually been last week. Haley had commemorated the occasion with a series of thinly veiled tweets about how certain people were destined to burn in hell. As the evening had worn on and her alcohol intake had increased, she'd upped the ante—calling James and hanging up, just so he knew she was thinking of him. Then, around midnight, when she was well past drunk, she left him a voice mail. In the morning she could no longer recall the exact words she'd used, but the gist of it had been that she was looking forward to his death and sincerely hoped it was preceded by immense suffering.

Her admittedly juvenile shenanigans violated the restraining order that prohibited Haley from engaging in any direct contact with James or Jessica. It also required that she stay fifty yards away from Owen. Haley knew the restraining order had been Jessica's idea. And, sure, showing up at Jessica's son's school for the sole purpose of telling him that his mother was a gold-digging whore might have been over the line, but that didn't make Haley's comment any less true. Besides, she'd been drunk . . . though that excuse was running a bit thin at this point.

The thing about restraining orders, Haley had learned, was that they really weren't worth the paper they were written on. For James to complain about any violation, he'd have to file something in court. So far, he hadn't. Nonetheless, Haley's divorce lawyer had repeatedly warned her that if she kept flouting the injunction, James's patience with her would end.

Staring at the Instagram photo of Mandy's bony arms, Haley poured herself another glass of wine and began to contemplate what offensive she could launch to ruin James and Jessica's celebration of their love. Calling in a bomb threat required minimal effort, but James would know it was her, and her efforts would be for naught.

That didn't mean that she couldn't report, anonymously of course, some other type of suspicious activity that the police would be required to investigate. *Yes, Officer, I'm seeing some very shady-looking characters entering the building. I think one of them is carrying a gun.*

But even assuming that was enough to warrant a police drop-in, it still wouldn't dampen the festivities. With Haley's luck, it would only add to the merriment. She could imagine Jessica laughing in her Jessica way. *We were having such an amazing time that the police thought something illegal was going down!*

Back to the drawing board, then . . .

The more she thought about it, the more it seemed that this occasion required her personal intervention. James's loft had a crap security system: a buzzer alerting the residents that their guests had arrived and enabling them to unlock the door remotely. Haley could wait behind some other invitee and follow them in. It would have to be someone who didn't know her . . . but most of Jessica's friends only knew *of* her—James's batshit psycho of an ex-wife—and wouldn't recognize her on sight.

Once she got inside, Haley would be behind enemy lines, which meant that she needed backup for this mission. She mentally scrolled through a list of potential accomplices before realizing Malik would be perfect. He was ridiculously handsome, and big too: six three, with a basketball player's biceps. Even an armed security guard would think twice about forcibly removing Malik from the premises.

He'd come with her too, even though it was late notice. She'd make Malik an offer he couldn't resist: hang there with her for fifteen minutes, after which they would go back to her place, and he could do whatever he wanted to her for as long as he desired.

2

James glanced at his watch. He was one of the last people he knew who still wore a timepiece rather than check their phone every thirty seconds. It was all part of the persona he'd meticulously cultivated. If you were in the business of selling people million-dollar pieces of art, you needed to establish that you were a person of impeccable taste. In this case, James did so with a Patek Philippe chronograph.

That horological symbol of Swiss precision told him it was still nearly thirty minutes before the first guests were slated to arrive. He stepped out into the living room. The calm before the storm, as it were.

Few of tonight's attendees had ever been to his home before. Those who had were mainly Jessica's friends. James's contributions to the guest list were by and large work colleagues and clients. The loft would undoubtedly impress them, so different from the limestone town houses, Upper East Side classic sixes and sevens, and new-construction penthouses they called home.

He still could not fathom what he'd been thinking back then, but he distinctly recalled that when he'd first set foot in this place, he'd known he'd live in it with Jessica someday. The fact that he was married to Haley at the time somehow hadn't entered into the equation, even though it had been her idea for them to find a new place rather than continue to live in her bachelorette apartment, as she had called their home on Riverside Drive.

By the time the renovation work on the loft was finished (new kitchen and new master bathroom), so was his marriage to Haley. She'd never lived here. Instead, Jessica moved in only a few months after James.

Before beginning his affair with Jessica, James had never been unfaithful to a partner; he'd never even thought cheating was something he was capable of doing. Nor had he ever been "the other man," always staying clear of married women, even when they offered him no-strings-attached sexual relationships in his single days.

James was forty-two when Jessica came into his life, and by then he'd had more than his share of experiences with women. *Much* more than his share, all false modesty aside. But within minutes of being in Jessica's company, he realized that he'd previously been completely ignorant about love. It was like how he'd thought he understood the Sistine Chapel because he'd studied it in school. But when he finally stepped into the Vatican and looked up at the ceiling, he realized he'd never comprehended it at all.

He knew it was somewhat twisted logic, but James was convinced that everything had transpired exactly as he'd predicted from the outset because the universe's imperative to bring Jessica to him could not be denied, just like nothing could have stopped the universe from taking his father in that accident. Of course, that did not mean he was blameless. Or that he wouldn't someday pay a price for his sins.

———

Tonight the loft looked even bigger than its three thousand square feet because nearly all their living room furniture had been put into storage, replaced by rented bistro tables and chairs. The fact that everything in the space was white—the chairs, the tablecloths, the tulips, and the vases in which they stood—gave the place an even more cavernous feel.

Even the waitstaff charged with walking around and serving the hors d'oeuvres wore uniforms consistent with the alabaster theme.

The decor didn't seem the least bit monochromatic, however. That was because the perimeter of the space was adorned with more than thirty pieces of art, each bursting with color. The largest was roughly the size of a queen bed, the smallest hardly bigger than a postage stamp. James rotated the pieces from time to time, as one would in an art gallery. Regardless of which pieces were on display, the room provided something of a kaleidoscopic experience. At times, Jessica felt as if the art were actually swirling around her.

She found Katerina, the caterer recommended by one of James's clients, in the kitchen. Katerina was a sculptor when she wasn't creating menus for parties, and she was beautiful—a common denominator of most, if not all, of the women in James's orbit.

"You're an absolute vision, Jessica," she said.

"Thank you. How's everything going?"

"Like a well-oiled machine," Katerina said. "No . . . no," she told a woman placing unfilled champagne flutes on a tray. "The champagne's always poured here."

"Anything I can do?" Jessica asked.

"Just have the time of your life, my dear."

———

Not five minutes after Owen's mother's visit, James knocked on his door.

His stepfather looked as if he'd been born in a suit and tie, wearing it with an ease that Owen was near certain he'd never achieve at any age. He took after his father, Wayne, in that regard, possessing a healthy bit of skepticism about the 1 percent.

"Just checking on you, Owen," James said.

"I haven't run away yet."

James smiled. "Yeah, I hear you. But tonight's party is going to make your mother happy. That's why we're doing it."

This was a common refrain from James: "It'll make your mother happy." Owen tried to think of instances in which his father had uttered the same sentiment, but his mind always came up blank. He knew that wasn't the reason his parents had split, or why his mother was now with James, but he didn't think it was necessarily *not* the reason either.

"The jacket looks good on you," James continued. "And I like pairing it with the Nikes. Very *GQ* of you."

"Thanks. I do it all for you, James."

This made his stepfather laugh. "I'm lucky to have you, Owen."

"Right back at you, James," Owen said with a laugh of his own.

———

Wayne's plus-one for the evening was Stephanie Cunningham, a thirty-nine-year-old physician's assistant he'd met online. She had never been married but was quick to point out that she was not a commitment-phobe, having lived with a man for much of her thirties.

She and Wayne had been seeing each other for about four months—that in-between period of a relationship among people their age in which overnight stays were a given on those alternating weekends when Owen stayed with his mother, but it was still too soon to talk about the future.

For the subway ride from Queens to Manhattan, Stephanie had her overcoat buttoned to the top. Beneath it was a dress she'd gotten from Rent the Runway, a burgundy velvet number held up by spaghetti straps with a nearly nonexistent back. It was sexier than anything Wayne had seen Stephanie wear before. He was smart enough not to make that observation audibly, of course. He knew why his plus-one was dressing as if this were some type of competition: because for Stephanie, it was.

It was also a contest Stephanie could never win, no matter what she wore. Jessica would always look better because his ex-wife was movie-star beautiful, while, on her best day, Stephanie was merely pretty in a supporting-role way.

Wayne felt justified in making that assertion because he knew full well that the same analysis applied to the comparison between James and him. All of which meant that, on first sight, Wayne's ex-wife and her current husband made a much more obvious pair than Wayne and Jessica ever had.

"Are you okay?" Stephanie asked.

His expression must have betrayed that he was not okay. Wayne had told Stephanie all about his breakup with Jessica, how it hurt at first but that he was over it now. It was the kind of thing he was expected to say, whether it was true or not. The reality was that it hurt every day, almost as acutely as it had when Jessica had told him that their marriage was over. Worse, even now he wished for nothing more than a chance to be with Jessica again. He still loved Jessica the way you only get to love once, and it absolutely shattered him that she now loved James in that way.

"I'm fine," he said.

3

Jessica greeted the first few guests at the door. Soon enough they were coming in too quickly for her to provide such personal attention. As the room began to fill, it no longer looked as empty as she had feared, and the champagne trays were circulating without a hitch.

"Everything looks magical," James said to her as he surveyed their home.

"It did all come together rather nicely," Jessica replied.

"Thank you."

She laughed. "You didn't even want this party. I should be thanking you."

"Not for the party," he said. "For my life."

"I should be thanking you for that too," she said.

She had declined James's original overture, two days after their Starbucks "date."

"I'm married," she had said. "And so are you."

He'd said that he understood.

And she'd assumed that would be the end of it. After all, she'd done nothing to lead him on. In fact, over the next few weeks, as they closed on the loft, she had been all business. Even when James told her that he thought someday they'd live in the loft together, she smiled and said that she didn't think his wife, or her husband, would approve of that arrangement.

"I'm going to leave Haley," James confided. "It has nothing to do with you. We're just not right for each other. Sadly, I've known that for some time. Maybe since the beginning. But I didn't listen to that little voice inside my head that told me not to marry her. And now that same little voice is shouting at me that *we're* destined to be together."

She tried to inject some reason, but her "you barely know me" protestations fell on deaf ears.

"I'm not one of those love-at-first-sight believers," he said, "but I'm as sure about this as I've ever been about anything in my life."

Jessica never questioned James's over-the-top pronouncements as anything but sincere. Although other men tended to tell Jessica whatever they thought would get her into bed, she somehow knew it wasn't like that with James.

The only explanation she had for her lack of skepticism was that she believed him. And the only reason she could attribute to her conclusion was that she felt the same way.

After the sale of the loft closed, Lisa Rollins invited Jessica, James, and his wife to a group dinner. A thank-you for the rather sizable commission her firm had earned. James accepted for him and his wife but showed up at the restaurant alone.

"My wife's working late," he said.

Before they ordered, Lisa's phone rang. "A family emergency," she explained, apologizing for having to leave so suddenly.

As soon as Lisa left, James looked at Jessica with a smile that made her wonder whether he had orchestrated Lisa's sudden departure.

"Did you create her family emergency?" Jessica asked.

"No, but I do plan to take full advantage of it," he replied.

They stayed in the restaurant until the maître d' told them that the staff had to go home, at which point James suggested they go to a bar he liked so the night didn't have to end.

She told him she had to go home. But when he put her in a cab, they kissed, and from that moment, she knew that everything he'd said about their future would come true.

———

Owen heard the first guests arrive. That was also the time that the party music abruptly changed from the crap his stepfather liked—Sinatra and other crooners from a million years ago—to the crap that his mother favored—soulless Top 40 pop.

He stayed sequestered in his bedroom until the moment the clock on his computer read nine, then stepped into the living room to keep his promise to his mother.

Jessica and James were on opposite sides of the crowded room. James was in the company of a woman whose dress was a size too tight, whose hair was dyed a shade too blonde, and whose body language—the way she tossed her hair over her shoulder when she laughed or touched James's arm when he laughed—was a little too desperate. His mother was talking to some guy with tennis-player hair.

A girl not much older than Owen approached with a tray of champagne flutes. He was tempted to grab one, but out of the corner of his eye, he saw his mother shaking her head.

"No, thank you," he told the girl.

"Are you in college?" she asked.

Owen's first thought was to lie. She was obviously in college. And once he told her that he was still a year away, he knew their conversation would be over.

But he wasn't the type to lie to a girl. To his parents, sure. But not to a girl.

"Next year. I'm a senior in high school now."

"Cool. Where do you go to school?"

"LaGuardia."

"Nice. I had a friend who graduated from there. What's your . . . do they call them majors?"

"Yeah. I'm instrumental. I play the violin."

"You must be really good. My friend was a vocal major, and I swear, she sings like an angel."

"I'm okay. Where are you at school?"

"NYU. Freshman. So we're practically the same age. Is this your parents' party?"

"Mom and stepdad. First anniversary. So you can only imagine how much I really want that drink. Unfortunately, my mother is watching me like a hawk."

The server laughed, a lovely sound.

"I'm Owen, by the way." He thought about extending his hand, but realized that she was holding the tray, so that wouldn't work.

"Emily," she said. "You know, I can hide some rum in a Coke and nobody will know."

"Yeah?"

"For you, sure."

Owen was trying to think of something witty to keep Emily with him a few seconds longer when out of his peripheral vision, he saw his father enter the loft. That was par for the course. The first, and probably last, moment of the party that Owen was actually enjoying, and now it would be cut short.

"Oh, great. My dad just got here," he said.

"Wait . . . your father's coming to celebrate your mother's anniversary with some other dude?" She laughed that sweet laugh again. "I better get you that rum and Coke. You're gonna need it."

He watched her walk away, feeling the ache that he sometimes did when things weren't the way he wanted them to be. The party had now joined the ever-growing list of things his father had ruined for him.

———

"You look stunning, Jessica," Reid Warwick said.

He kissed Jessica on both cheeks, European-style.

23

"Thank you. I'm so glad that you could make it."

He didn't expect Jessica to return the compliment. Not because he didn't look stunning too. Jessica wasn't blind, after all. But Reid knew that he had yet to win her over. He would, eventually. He always did. Especially when it came to the fairer sex.

"Wouldn't have missed it for the world. It's like every major player in the New York art scene is here. If there was a fire in the apartment and everybody died, the value of the art market would triple."

"Isn't that a lovely thought."

Reid laughed. "But mainly I'm here to pay homage to my best friend being the luckiest sonofabitch in New York City."

"Is that right?"

"It is from where I'm standing," Reid said, looking hard at Jessica.

Even with the mood lighting, Reid thought he saw the slightest flush color Jessica's cheeks. A pregnant pause hung between them. Reid was leaning in closer, about to comment on Jessica's dress, when she said, "My son has apparently decided to grace us all with his presence."

This pushed Reid back a step. He turned to take a look.

"He's getting big."

"Tall, yeah. Still skinny as a rail, though."

"How's he doing?"

"Okay, all things considered. I think sometimes he can't wait to go to college just to get away from the circus of a life I've thrown him into."

Reid looked around the space. "It doesn't seem like such a bad life."

"You don't remember being seventeen, do you?"

Reid turned back to Owen, and Jessica followed his sight line. Owen was now speaking to a younger attractive woman, one of the caterers. She appeared to be enjoying the conversation.

"I remember seventeen all too well," Reid said.

Jessica shook her head. "I can only imagine what you were like at that age, but I assure you that Owen is about a million miles away from being *that* kid."

"Trust me. All seventeen-year-old boys are the same."

"Trust *me*, they're not. Not at seventeen. Not at forty. There are good ones and bad ones."

Reid held his tongue. He had little doubt on which side of the divide Jessica believed he fell.

"If you'll excuse me, I need to mingle a bit," she said.

Reid returned to the bar, where he got himself another Johnnie Walker Black, neat. Drink in hand, he surveyed the crowd. He had decided to come stag with the fleeting thought that he might not leave alone. Based on the attendees, that seemed unlikely. Most of the women were coupled up and about his age, which was a good ten years older than he favored. The caterer chatting up Owen had caught his eye, though. Maybe later.

He reminded himself to focus. Tonight was about business, not pleasure.

———

Wayne and Owen had reached that awkward stage in a father-son relationship where neither knew how to express affection. Owen was too old to hug, and Wayne felt ridiculous shaking hands with his son like they were about to close a business deal.

"You look really good, O," Wayne said, placing his hand on Owen's shoulder.

Stephanie kissed Owen on the cheek, which Wayne noticed made his son wince a bit.

Wayne scanned the room, looking for Jessica or James, but he couldn't spot either in the crowd. "Not too shabby," he said, taking in the room.

Owen didn't answer, which was nothing new. In fact, it surprised Wayne when his son actually responded to something he'd said.

"You having fun so far?"

"Not too much. Mom said I could go back in my room after the toasts."

"I suspect we won't stay much longer than that either. I mainly came to see you."

Owen had just finished his sophomore year of high school when Wayne and Jessica told him that they were getting a divorce. Like so many things with his son, Wayne couldn't decipher how Owen actually felt about what was undoubtedly a sea change in his life. At the time, Owen was two years removed from his cancer diagnosis and it had been a year since he was told he was in remission. Perhaps compared to such an existential threat, his parents' divorce was of lesser importance. On the other hand, Owen could often be a black box. Teenagers keeping their emotions hidden from their parents was nothing new, of course, but Owen seemed to elevate it to an art form. Wayne almost could never tell how Owen felt about anything, good or bad. But the one thing Wayne was near certain about was that Owen had not been surprised by the news that his parents were no longer in love, as if his son had somehow seen coming what had so blindsided him.

Wayne originally resisted Jessica's request that Owen live with her in Manhattan and visit Wayne only on Wednesdays and alternating weekends. He claimed he was thinking about Owen's best interests, but that hadn't been his true motivation. He'd simply wanted to push back about something. Make Jessica pay some price for destroying him. The way he saw it, even though he couldn't stop Jessica from leaving him for James, he could at least deprive her of Owen for as many nights as possible.

So he told her that she was being selfish. That she should think of Owen.

"I *am* thinking about Owen," Jessica had fired back. "Maybe you should too. He's going to high school in Manhattan already, so it's actually easier for him to spend most of his time with me."

In the end, Wayne had acquiesced. He liked to think that it was because he had elevated his son's well-being above his own, but deep down, a part of him knew that he'd done it for Jessica—to make her believe that he was the kind of man who'd elevate his son's interests above his own. And that revelation made him hate himself.

———

"So, you in or what?"

James had lost the thread of the conversation about thirty seconds before. He knew Reid was presenting him with a business opportunity. It had something to do with a friend of Reid's who had access to some Jackson Pollock sketches.

"How'd this guy get the Pollocks again?" James asked, if only to show that he was paying attention.

"The guy is Tommy Murcer," Reid said, emphasizing his name to convey that he wanted James's undivided attention this time through. "Like I said, he was fucking Lee Krasner back in the day. She gifted them to him."

Lee Krasner was a first-rate artist in her own right but even more well known for being Jackson Pollock's widow. She'd died in 1984, almost thirty years after her husband.

"How old is this Murcer guy?"

"I'm not sure exactly, but my guess is he's closing in on eighty. That's why he wants to sell now. He knows that after he kicks, provenance is gonna be much harder to come by."

Provenance. The bugaboo of the art market and the bane of every dealer's existence. Proof that what you were selling was the work of one of the greats and not a well-executed forgery.

There were experts who opined on the authenticity of works, and certain artists' estates set up commissions to be the final arbiters when forgery questions arose. A signature was all but worthless in this regard because anyone talented enough to replicate the brushstrokes of a Rothko or a Picasso, or the splatter of a Pollock, could easily copy the scrawl of their signature on the back of a canvas. For that reason, one of the best ways to establish provenance was to link the work's chain of custody back to the artist. While Murcer was still alive, he could attest that Lee Krasner had gifted him the pieces.

"My take is twenty-five percent," Reid said. "I'll cut you in for half of my end. That's twelve and a half percent for you. A lot better than a typical finder's fee."

"You know this really isn't my sweet spot."

"Maybe I can get Tommy to do a little more."

"It's not about the money."

"Then what?"

Although Reid was acting like he didn't understand the basis for James's hesitation, James knew it was only for show. Whatever weaknesses Reid possessed, being naïve was not one of them.

"I'm sorry, Reid, I'm just not your guy."

"Do me this favor, will you? Come out to East Hampton with me on Monday and let me show them to you. You'll see that they're authentic. Maybe that'll change your mind."

"I've got some things on my schedule . . ."

"Cancel them. C'mon, James, do me a solid on this, will you? Just take a look at them. No obligation."

———

"If I can have everyone's attention, just for a moment," Jessica yelled above the din of the party. Some of the guests began to strike their silver against their glasses, and the crowd quieted. "Yes, this is the time for toasts," she said. "So, if you're a little low, fill up. I'll wait. And James, that means you need to join me."

One or two people took Jessica up on her offer and made their way toward the bar. James stepped away from Reid Warwick. When he reached Jessica in the middle of the room, he took his wife's hand.

"James and I want to thank all of you, our dearest friends and family, for sharing this moment with us," she began. "There is absolutely nothing I would redo about my first year of marriage to James, and that includes our decision to elope. But I must confess that, at times, I'm a little sad that I missed out on the joy of sharing my wedding day with the people I love most in this world. Now that you have all allowed me that by being here today, I can truly say that everything about marriage to James is one hundred percent perfection. If you'll indulge me for a moment more, I would like now to say a few words directly to my husband."

She turned to look at James. He was beaming at her.

"James, the last year has been the happiest of my life. It's the kind of happiness that I thought existed only in fairy tales. But with you, I feel like the person that I was always destined to be, and I cannot imagine wanting more out of life than that." She paused a beat, and then upon turning back to the guests said, "Please raise a glass and drink a toast to my wonderful husband, James."

As soon as Jessica finished her sip of champagne, James took up the toast duty.

"I promise I'll be short, and not as charming as Jessica," he said, which elicited a few chuckles. "I would also like to thank our friends and family for being here tonight. It means so much to Jessica and me that we have such incredible people with whom to share our lives. And I want to especially say directly to my bride how much I love her. All of you who know Jessica are well aware of what a wonderful person she is. Smart, kind, thoughtful, and of course, absolutely beautiful. But I can say that she's so much more of all of those things than you can even imagine. This past year has already been the best of my life, and at the same time, I have no doubt that next year will be even better. In fact, I'm quite certain that every year will be better than the last, for as long as we both shall live."

"Or until you decide to fuck someone else behind her back, you mean, don't you, James?"

Haley watched James's eyes search the room, looking for her. He clearly recognized her voice. Finally, he spotted her. She could tell by the look in his eyes.

"Really, everyone, you do all know that is the genesis of this great love story you're all toasting, don't you?" Haley shouted, loud enough that she was certain everyone could hear. That point was further driven home by the slack-jawed expression of the guests around her.

Out of her peripheral vision, she saw Malik looking as dumbfounded as anyone. She hadn't told him about her connection to the happy couple, for fear that even the promise of sex wouldn't be enough for him to join her if he knew her intentions. Poor guy . . . he thought they were making a courtesy visit to an old friend's party, then going back to her place for the night. He hadn't realized that the arrangement was more transactional than that: sex in exchange for being something of a human shield.

Now that she had the floor, Haley was not about to yield. "James and Jessica, the patron saints of romance, thought the vows from their first marriages were shit, and decided that fucking each other behind their spouses' backs was a good thing. So long as they were happy, they didn't give a fuck about anyone else. Let's all drink to that, shall we?"

"Ladies and gentlemen, it's not a party until your ex-wife breaks the terms of her restraining order to shout profanity at you," said James. "Am I right?"

Haley heard zero laughter in response to James's retort. She had won.

"Fuck you all, and fuck you the most, James," Haley shouted. "And you too, Jessica, you slut whore," she added for good measure.

With that said, Haley took Malik's hand and led him to the door. When she opened it, she turned back to James and flashed her best fuck-you smile before exiting.

4

"Who was the blonde?" Jessica called out to James, who was in the bathroom with the door open.

It was 2:00 a.m. The caterers had just left, and she was in bed.

"What blonde?" he asked.

"What blonde," she repeated, all sarcasm.

"Oh," he said, a chuckle in his voice. "Sarah Roth. She owns a gallery in Chelsea. Don't worry, she's harmless. Her bark is much worse than her bite."

"It wasn't her bark that caught my attention, my dear."

Plenty of people had questioned how Jessica could trust James after he cheated on his first wife. Some said it without even the slightest sense that James should be wondering the same thing about her.

Jessica had been propositioned before. Men never tired of trying to seduce married women, and real estate agents were a particularly inviting target. But she had never thought twice about any of these overtures. And not because the men weren't interesting or attractive—often they were both. Instead, she thought of herself as a good person, a moral person, and her marriage vows meant something.

Why did she break those vows for James? That was a question that she had never fully been able to answer. A part of her liked to believe she had simply been overwhelmed by their connection and rendered incapable of resistance.

James enabled this narrative by saying that it was precisely what had compelled him.

"I was brought up a Catholic," he told her once, after their affair had begun. "I was an altar boy, the whole thing. But I never believed. Not the way some people claimed that they did. But I wished that I had faith that there was something out there that powerful. Something that made you feel safe, that banished all your fears and made you feel loved. And then I met you, and suddenly, I believed."

James said that he had not been tested in that faith since. In fact, he sometimes joked that he was Jessica's disciple. Like the original twelve, he would follow her anywhere.

"You know what happened to their leader," she said once. "And then they all turned. Some of them thrice."

"Not me," he said. "Never. I promise you that."

Did that mean that James would never stray? Jessica didn't know, of course. No spouse ever knew that for sure. They might assume they knew. *Oh, my husband, he's not that kind.* But Wayne would have said the same about her, once upon a time. The truth was that all you could ever know for sure about your spouse was that you never really knew what they were capable of.

The one thing she did know, however, was that she was a different person from the woman who'd been with Wayne. She was happy now, and in love. Why would such a fortunate woman ever be unfaithful? And if that was true of her, she had every reason to believe it applied equally to her husband.

James stepped out of the bathroom wearing only pajama bottoms. He looked good. Too good, Jessica sometimes thought.

His smile made clear he was thinking exactly the same thing about her.

"You like?" she asked, referring to the lingerie she had purchased for tonight—black lace and hardly there.

"Oh yeah," he said. "Enough that I'll be very careful taking it off you."

33

———

After the fireworks created by James's ex-wife, Owen's mother had tried to talk to him, but all he'd wanted to do was go back into his room, shut the door, put on his headphones, and escape into the world of his computer. She let him go, but James came into his room a few minutes later. He told him that what Haley said wasn't true. That she would say anything to hurt James, and he was sorry if Owen had been upset by her lies.

Owen said he understood. No big deal.

The truth was that he had long known about his mother's affair. They'd all tried to keep it from him, even his father. After his mother moved out, she went so far as to rent a small apartment in Forest Hills for three months as part of the subterfuge. She claimed she'd met James during that summer.

Sometimes they slipped up. His mother would mention some interaction she had with James that winter, which could not have happened if they'd met in June, as she claimed.

Even though his mother was the unfaithful one, Owen blamed his father for the divorce. To his way of thinking, his father should have done more to keep his mother happy. Owen recalled their fights, which, more often than not, were over nonsense: his mother's desire to see her siblings, not his, over the holidays; his father's refusal to close the kitchen cabinet doors after opening them; or his father's failure to buy her a birthday or Valentine's Day gift because, according to his stupid joke, he treated her specially every day.

Why couldn't Wayne have made Owen's mother happier? Done the things she wanted?

That was part of the reason that Owen had decided to go with his mother when the choice was presented. He simply couldn't imagine living with a man as weak as his father.

———

Reid hated fake tits. He had decided to overlook it because Sarah was so very willing, and he thought that there might be some business upside in it for him. (She claimed she was involved in the art world somehow, although he couldn't remember how, exactly.)

As soon as he unhooked her bra, he began having a serious case of buyer's remorse. *Let that be a lesson to you,* his mind (okay, maybe not his mind) told him. *Never go for the sure deal when there's a better transaction that requires more work to close.* In this case, he was kicking himself for not making a play for the hot young caterer.

At least Sarah got the hint that his place wasn't a bed-and-breakfast. After they were done, she gathered up her clothes and did the walk of shame. He told her that he'd call, but she looked like she knew he wouldn't, which was just as well because he had no intention to.

All in all, he had been right to attend the party. The evening's carnal activity had been a bonus, but the primary objective had been to whet James's appetite for the Pollocks. On that score he could declare mission accomplished.

He had expected James to hem and haw a bit. James was that way. Like a woman needing to put on a show of resistance so you wouldn't think she was too easy. That kind of performance had never made any sense to Reid. Everybody wanted the same things—sex and money. Why not embrace it?

———

"Was it everything you had hoped for and more?" James asked.

They were basking in the afterglow. Still a bit sweaty.

Jessica looked at him with a sly smile. He got the joke without her having to say a word.

"I meant the party. I could tell that you enjoyed the other thing quite a bit."

"Oh, the party," she said with an exaggerated laugh. "To be honest, when I imagined it in my mind, it didn't include your ex-wife calling me an adulteress in front of my seventeen-year-old son and all of my friends."

James had wanted to be a good and faithful husband to Haley. Truly he had. And he could recite chapter and verse why he had failed in the objective, a litany of complaints about Haley—how she wasn't exactly who he thought she was when he proposed; her workaholism; her anger issues. Or he could turn it around and argue that their split had nothing to do with her at all. Excuses ranging from his own miscalculation about his readiness for marriage to his simply being unable to resist his attraction to Jessica.

In the end, however, he knew that all these things were just that—excuses. He had consciously decided to cheat on Haley with Jessica, while a more honorable man would have found a way to refrain. In other words, Haley was right: he'd made a vow to be faithful to her, then treated that vow like shit.

"I'm so sorry about that," James said for about the millionth time this evening.

"And you thought my inviting Wayne was going to be the low point. But you know what they say—if the second marriage is successful, the first one wasn't a failure."

"I actually didn't know that's what they say."

"Well, they do."

James reflected on whether there was any truth to what they apparently said. "I prefer the Hemingway approach."

"Oh yeah? What's that?"

"That the first draft is always shit."

"That's certainly the better quote," Jessica said, laughing.

"I talked to Owen about it afterward. I think he's okay with it all."

James had initially expected nothing but hostility from Owen. Even though Jessica did her best to pretend that James's arrival into his life had nothing to do with Owen's parents' divorce, James assumed that Owen knew better. Still, and much to James's surprise, he and his stepson had quickly formed a bond of their own. Not like father and son, because Wayne filled that space. Fun uncle and nephew, perhaps. The guy who'll slide a fifty to the youngest server at the party to be extra nice to his stepson.

"I talked to him a little bit too," Jessica said. "Maybe I should just tell him the truth. He's almost eighteen. I think he'll understand."

"What would Wayne think about that?"

"As if I ever knew what that man thinks about *anything*. I was pretty sure he wasn't going to come tonight, but there he was. With a date, no less."

"Jealous?"

"Trust me, not even a little bit. Wayne's love life is the least of my worries."

"I didn't think you had *any* worries, my dear."

He kissed her. At first softly, then with her encouragement, more deeply. When he rolled on top of her, as his body pressed against hers, he was ready to go again.

———

After bearing witness to an evening celebrating the perfect wedded bliss that his ex-wife was now sharing with another man, Wayne had hoped for a little attention in the bedroom from Stephanie. He'd thought they were on their way when Stephanie agreed to stay over, but as soon as they got to Wayne's house, she announced that she was tired, which signaled that he might as well not even try.

"I thought Owen didn't seem so good," he said once they had gotten into bed and the television was on.

"He seemed okay to me," Stephanie answered.

"Tough position for him to be in. First, hearing his mother telling the world that she was never happy with his father—that she's finally found true love with this other guy. And then that she was cheating on me."

"You never told him?"

"No. Why would I?"

"Because it's the truth."

"No teenager wants to think about his mother that way, whether it's true or not. Makes you wonder, though, what James did to that woman."

Stephanie laughed. "I would have gone the other way on that. It makes me wonder what's wrong with James that he ever married such a nutcase."

"I don't know what's crazier—showing up uninvited and making a scene so you can tell off your ex-husband and the woman he cheated on you with, or raising a glass to toast your ex-wife's happiness with the guy she cheated on you with."

Stephanie offered him a soft smile. "Thanks for saying that. Sometimes, you get so defensive about your relationship with Jessica that I don't understand what's going on between the two of you."

"I'm just . . . trying real hard not to be like James's ex-wife, is all."

"I get that. I also think that what you did tonight was good for Owen. Not to mention very brave of you. I wouldn't have done it. I'm not sure I know many people who would have."

"Thanks, I guess."

"Yeah, well, I don't mean that you should do it again. In fact, let's make a pact right now that we don't go to their second anniversary party."

"Even money they don't make it to next year."

"What makes you say that?"

"Nothing really. Just a feeling. Did you see the way James was talking up that blonde who looked like she might tip over?"

Stephanie's shrug said more than words.

"What?"

"If anything, I thought that Jessica was pretty engrossed with that guy with the shaggy hair."

Wayne had to laugh at that. "I guess I'm the last person on earth who'd know what Jessica looks like when she's cheating on her husband."

Among Wayne's many self-recognized shortcomings, he believed this to be the worst. How could he have been so blind that he didn't realize his wife was sleeping with another man? In hindsight, the signs were glowing neon. The late nights she claimed to be working, her newfound dedication to the gym, her loss of interest in sex (at least with him).

It had been easy at the time to attribute it all to Owen's cancer. That first year, they had been in shock, not themselves at all. Even after Owen was in remission, when Jessica first met James, her extracurricular activities had seemed a legit way of finding positive outlets to cope with the trauma of almost losing Owen.

He realized now that he had been all too willing to let Jessica grieve and process on her own. He simply hadn't had the bandwidth to be there for her while grieving and processing it himself.

Had they been better partners, they would have helped each other get through it. Instead, they retreated into their separate spaces. Jessica's, apparently, had been too empty, so she'd invited James in.

But the real blame, he knew, lay only with him. It was his weakness that directly led to his wife's infidelity. A stronger man—a man, dare he say, more like his father—would have protected what was his. Indeed, if there was one thing Wayne knew for certain, it was that Archibald Fiske would have made damned sure that no man broke up his family.

———

Somewhere along the line, someone must have told Malik that being able to have sex for a long time was the same thing as being good at it. Haley was certain that there were many women who enjoyed his combination of a chiseled body, larger-than-average equipment, and commitment to an hour of intercourse, but Haley would have preferred that he be a little more attentive to her.

Almost as soon as they were finished, Haley told Malik that it was time for him to get going. "Busy day tomorrow, love. But you were great, as always."

She didn't think Malik wanted to hang around anyway. He wasn't the kind to stay for breakfast.

After she hustled him out the door, Haley relit the blunt they'd been sharing for the few moments before the undressing began. As she inhaled deeply, a smile came to her face. Her plan had been perfectly executed. Even as she imagined the angry call from her lawyer on Monday, she was still glad that she'd called out her cheating sack of an ex-husband in front of his new wife and their friends.

PART TWO

5

The intake nurse was pretty. Her name was Sasha. She was seated behind a glass partition like a bank teller.

Sasha always seemed happy to see Owen, as her smile that morning confirmed. "Cool tee," she said.

Owen had worn the shirt for her, so he was pleased that she'd commented on it. During last week's visit, she had told him about liking *Batwoman*, the TV show on the CW. He tried it but found it unwatchable. Still, he'd decided to wear his Batman and Joker split-face graphic T-shirt today.

"I see that this is a redo," Sasha said. "So sorry about that. I know it's no fun to come here two weeks in a row because we didn't get a good read from last week's sample. Why don't you meet me at the door, and I'll take you in. With any luck, you'll be in and out real fast."

"I'll be right out here, Owen," his mother said.

She had a way of making it seem like she was sending her baby off to war, rather than to a routine blood test.

The brief walk from the waiting room to the exam room was the only time Owen would spend with Sasha. Sometimes she was still at the front desk when he scheduled his next appointment, but last week she hadn't been, and some old guy with a disgusting beard had done the honors.

"So, I watched that show you mentioned," he said as soon as they were alone.

Sasha looked momentarily confused.

"*Batwoman* or whatever," he said.

"Right. *Batwoman*. What did you think?"

"It was okay."

"That bad, huh?"

"I just mean . . . I don't know. It took a little more suspension of disbelief than I thought made sense."

"It's a show about a woman who pretends to be Batman, Owen. It's not a documentary."

"It's not?" he said, trying to hold back a smile. "In that case, maybe it wasn't so bad."

She laughed and then stopped in front of exam room three. Owen preferred exam room eight. The rooms were identical, but going farther down the hallway meant he got to spend another thirty seconds with Sasha.

She opened the door. "You know the drill," she said. "Strip down to your shorts. The doctor will be in—"

"Whenever he damn well feels like it," Owen finished for her.

"That's about right," she said, laughing again.

"Hey, how old are you?" he asked.

"Twenty-two."

"Perfect," he said.

"That's enough for today, Owen. Now get in there and get naked."

———

Jessica considered the fact that she was annoyed to be a good sign. When she and Owen first started going to these blood work appointments, they filled her with dread. After enough visits in a row ended with good news, they felt more like a terrible inconvenience. Why were the doctors making them hike out to Queens once every other month to check his blood for whatever they were checking it for when it was obvious to her that Owen was now perfectly healthy?

The waiting room contained the usual hodgepodge of child cancer patients in various stages of illness. Jessica still vividly remembered their first visit. Back then, Owen had looked so healthy, and they'd sat beside a boy a few years younger than him, bald as a cue ball. *Dear God,* she had prayed, *don't let that ever be Owen.* And yet, within a matter of weeks, it was; then it was Jessica watching the other mothers with their hirsute children silently utter the same prayer. Weeks later, she saw that those other mothers' prayers had not been answered either.

But then, the pendulum swung. Owen went into remission. Whereas he had once epitomized every parent's worst nightmare, his presence in the waiting room today was a beacon of hope. With hair flowing past his shoulders, he had become the poster boy for answered prayers.

"Ms. Fiske," someone said.

Jessica was used to being called Ms. Fiske, especially by Owen's doctors and teachers. She looked up to see Dr. Goldman in the waiting room.

She hadn't set eyes on the doctor in some time. He looked older than she recalled from the chemo days. A little grayer, perhaps. Maybe a few more wrinkles too, even though she didn't think he was yet sixty-five. She took some comfort in the fact that enough time had passed since she'd last had an audience with him that he'd actually changed.

"Would you mind coming back for a moment?" he asked. "There's something I would like to discuss with you."

All Jessica's alarms went off at once. She couldn't imagine Dr. Goldman had anything to discuss with her that she wanted to hear.

———

The trip to East Hampton from Lower Manhattan took most people close to four hours, more if they hit traffic along the Long Island Expressway. But Reid prided himself in making it in three, although that required he keep his Porsche above ninety miles an hour and weave in and out of traffic.

Today, however, he abided by the speed limit. Not exactly, as he still went ten miles an hour faster, but the last thing he wanted was for his passenger to think he was reckless. He needed James to think he was the very epitome of responsibility.

Reid's father had been part of the East Hampton art crowd, although he'd shown up at the tail end of the scene, in the late 1960s. By then, the most famous of its members—Willem de Kooning, Robert Motherwell, Franz Kline, not to mention the undisputed king of the New York school, Jackson Pollock, and his wife, Lee Krasner—were already name brands. But while Reid's father might have missed the heyday of the art scene, he was lucky enough to get in on the ground floor of the East End real estate market. He paid something like $35,000 for his "cottage," which Reid had inherited a decade ago.

"Quite the party the other night," Reid said. "That Sarah Ross is insatiable."

"Roth," James said.

"What?"

"The insatiable woman to whom you're referring is actually named Sarah Roth."

Reid shrugged. "I can only imagine Jessica was none too pleased with Haley's one-woman show."

"No, she was not. At least she didn't blame me for it. But that reminds me, I do need to call my divorce lawyer and see if there's anything that can be done to prevent another such performance in the future, although I highly doubt there is. Short of murder, of course."

Reid laughed. "That, my friend, is why I've never married."

"And here I thought it was because no woman would have you."

"Sarah Roth had me. Twice, in fact," Reid said, taking his eyes off the road to smirk at James.

"It's easy to get into a woman's bed for a night. It's being allowed to stay that's the challenge."

"Not a challenge I plan on taking up in this lifetime."

"You'll be missing out then. I can tell you that there's nothing like being married to someone you truly love."

"Aww," Reid said. "Check back with me in ten years and see if you still feel that way. Meanwhile, the woman I'll be with then is in elementary school now."

"You are truly disgusting."

"Just speaking my truth."

———

David Kaplan called a few minutes before noon. Haley was in her apartment, more or less waiting for her divorce lawyer's call.

Even though it had been less than two years, she could no longer recall how she had come to retain her attorney. He must have been a referral from someone. She hadn't found him on the internet, that she knew, although when she did google David's name, she was pleasantly surprised to find that he was a Super Lawyer, whatever that meant. Then again, so was James's mouthpiece, a woman whose name Haley tried to banish from all recesses of her brain, though occasionally it came through like scratches on a chalkboard—Angela or Andrea or Abigail. Some *A* name.

That was the way it went in divorce these days; the men hired women to make them seem more understanding, and the women hired men to make them stronger.

Then she remembered who'd made the introduction to David. It was her financial adviser, Arthur Cochrane. Of course, she'd asked him for the referral. The symmetry to it all had been weirdly pleasing, as it was Arthur who'd introduced her to James.

Four years before, her financial adviser had suggested that Haley spend some of her recent bonus money on artwork. "Even though I won't see a penny on commissions for it, you might get some psychic satisfaction at seeing your bonus money hanging on your walls, as opposed to being digits in a brokerage account."

He'd recommended James Sommers, claiming that he was one of the best art dealers in the city. "Trust me," she remembered Arthur saying, "you'll be in excellent hands."

She met James at his office, which was actually an apartment that he worked out of on Madison in the seventies, a few streets north of the Met Breuer museum, which most New Yorkers still referred to as the Whitney, and a few blocks south of the Met and the Guggenheim. She had expected James to show her some pieces to choose from. But he told her that was how people bought furniture; buying art was more akin to falling in love.

"You need to date a little bit, see what you like, what you don't," he said. "Then, when you come upon that piece that you just know you can't live without, then, and only then, are you ready to buy art."

It felt a bit like a come-on, but Haley didn't mind. She hadn't had much time to date since joining Maeve Grant, the investment bank that employed her in its mergers and acquisition department. The men she did make time to go out with quickly proved that they weren't worth it: man-boys who spent most of their time bragging about the things they owned and fretting about losing their hair. She could envision worse ways to spend an evening than in James's company, looking at beautiful objets d'art.

He took her to a downtown gallery that specialized in photography. The show on display contained a lot of staged pieces, most of which struck Haley as contrived.

"I gather you're not falling in love with anything here," he said after they had taken their first lap around the room.

"A few I might fuck, but none I'd marry," she said.

"Well put. Because something you're going to look at every day has to justify its existence every day. It's easy to like something for a while just because it fills a blank wall, but over time, you're going to resent paying so much for it if you're not in love with it."

"How can someone who knows so much about love still be single?"

"Precisely," James answered.

"So you're a cynic, are you?"

"Let's just say that I've found my share that I'd fuck, but none that I'd marry."

"Well said, James," she replied.

That night, they fucked. Slightly less than a year later, they married.

She was twenty-seven when they tied the knot. James was forty-one. That should have been a red flag. Her mother made no pretense about expressing such concerns, wondering aloud how a man who was as successful and handsome as James had managed to stay single for all these years, then suddenly became eager to marry.

Needless to say, Haley saw her mother's concern as an insult. Another way for her to convey that her daughter wasn't good enough.

A little more than a year after their vows, James told her that he was in love with another woman and wanted a divorce.

By then, it had already become clear to her that her marriage to James had been a mistake. Her long hours at work were not always out of necessity but just as frequently to avoid facing that reality. When they were together, she could feel James drifting from her. Sex, which had always been plentiful, had become less so, and on those nights when she wasn't working late, he often was.

Another woman might have been relieved that James was doing the dirty work of ending it, but Haley wasn't that woman. She had never before failed at anything, and her marriage was not the place she intended to start.

She begged him to stay. She swore she'd do whatever he wanted to make him happy. She offered to quit her job, to start a family if that's what he wanted. Anything.

James told her it was not about her. He would never love Haley in the way he loved Jessica. It was not her fault. It was just a fact. He actually used the words *soul mate*.

She had never believed that soul mates existed. But even worse, she didn't think James believed it either. The fact he was invoking the term to describe his adulterous lover told Haley that this was a fight she could not win.

At that point, she'd figured that James leaving her for Jessica would be her rock bottom. Then she learned that there was actually no such thing. Given the opportunity, you can always descend further.

"David, to what do I owe the pleasure of a Monday morning phone call?" Haley said.

She imagined the scene playing out in real time. James had called his shark of a lawyer first thing, which for Manhattan lawyers meant 10:00 a.m. After receiving James's call, Angela or Abigail or Applesauce must have spent the next hour and a half drafting a cease-and-desist letter. That letter had just arrived in David Kaplan's email, and he'd wasted no time in calling Haley to start his meter running.

"One question: What could possibly have possessed you to show up at James's house—at his anniversary party, no less?"

"I assumed he wanted me there and my invitation got lost," she said.

Like all men, David was not immune to her charms. Of course, his professional life was devoted to helping women at their most vulnerable, so he was accustomed to clients flirting, and he'd never suggested he would cross any line with her. Still, men go the extra mile for women they want to sleep with, even when they know it'll never come to pass.

David sighed. "Haley . . . we've been over this before. These types of shenanigans are serious. Not only does it cost you legal fees every time you engage in one of these stunts, which you no longer can afford, but sooner or later, James will take real action."

"Is this one of those times?"

Another sigh from David, but louder. That meant *no*.

As Haley suspected, this was all for show. In order to placate Jessica, James could now report that he'd sicced his lawyer on Haley. But James must have also instructed Abigail or Angela or Artichoke to heel as soon as she delivered her threat.

"The impression I got was that if you send James an email promising to stop and apologize for the other night, he'll drop this thing for now without a court filing."

"Let me think about it," Haley said.

She felt sure David knew what that meant—*never gonna happen*.

———

Reid had always struck James as something of a man of mystery. Part Jay Gatsby, part John Galt from *Atlas Shrugged*. Self-confident to the point of cocky, an incorrigible womanizer, and rich without a discernible source of income. That said, there were times in James's life when the same description could have been fairly applied to him.

Reid's East Hampton house was at the end of a long pebbled driveway, tucked away from the ten-thousand-square-foot behemoths that surrounded it on all sides. It looked as if it had been designed from a Beatrix Potter illustration, with shake siding and sloping roofs. The interior elaborated on the theme—grandfather clocks, English antiques, and large windows overlooking manicured grounds.

Reid led James into the first-floor study. A Louis XVI desk was in the center of the space, an English secretary standing against the wall.

Reid pulled open the center drawer of the desk, retrieving an old-fashioned skeleton key. "Not the greatest security system, I know," he joked. He carefully lifted the few items that were on the desk and moved them to the floor. With his shirttail, Reid cleaned the desk of any dust, then made his way to the secretary.

From it, he removed four sheets of paper, careful to hold them from the underside so as not to mar them. Then he laid the pieces on the desk.

James excused himself to wash his hands. When he returned, he looked at the first, then the second, and finally the last two drawings on the desk.

"So, what do you think?"

"I think you've got one of two things here." James lifted his eyes from the artwork. "One possibility is that your friend Tommy Murcer is a forger. Or that he knows some forgers."

"They're authentic. I know it."

James thought so too. The genius of Pollock was both undefinable and unmistakable. How many times had he heard that someone's kindergartener could create a piece that rivaled some modern masterpiece? He had always been tempted to respond that if they could, they should, because the world needs more beauty, and their five-year-old would be paid handsomely.

"That doesn't completely solve your problem, though. Because if they are, in fact, Pollocks, then I'm pretty sure what you have here is some stolen art."

"No way. Tommy's on the up-and-up. He knew Lee Krasner. He's got photos of the two of them together."

"That may be, but it's still possible that at some point in this lovely relationship—which by the way, assuming Murcer's eighty now, means that he was having sex with a seventy-five-year-old when he was in his early forties—ole Tommy decided to help himself to some of the master's work while Lee was looking the other way . . . or after she died."

Reid shook his head. "Why can't you just believe what Tommy says?"

James laughed. "Because I'm an art dealer. And if you did so much as a Google search on Lee Krasner, you'd know that she jealously guarded her husband's legacy. She would never in a million years have gifted to anybody what seems clearly to be unfinished work. Much less four of them."

"Then why did she keep them?"

"I don't know. People keep gum wrappers their husbands left in their pockets, Reid. She was probably sentimental enough about his work that she didn't want to throw them out. Or maybe she intended them to go to a museum or something for study about his work. She died in the mideighties. By that time, she knew full well that her husband's doodles on napkins were worth the price of a house. Maybe she gave one away to a friend. Hell, the Springs section of East Hampton is chock-full of stories about shop owners and tradesmen with original Pollocks they received as barter. But those were one-off deals. I'm sorry, but there's just no way Lee Krasner gives anyone but a museum four unfinished pieces. On top of which, unless your friend Tommy lives under a rock, he would have been smart enough to know he'd need some type of authentication. Certainly Lee Krasner would have known that. So, at the time of the gift, she would have given Tommy a notarized letter or something to prove that they were a gift."

"I asked him about that. He said that Lee didn't want the tax implications of gifting it through her will, or any gift tax that would be associated with her giving them away before she died, so they didn't do any paperwork."

"I've heard that story before," James said. "In fact, it's the art-world equivalent of 'the check's in the mail.'"

"Well, that's what Tommy said. And I believe him," Reid said defiantly. "You going to help me on this or not? Because it's just too big an opportunity for me to pass up. I thought, to be honest with you, that I was giving you a gift. But if you don't want to do it, no worries. There are lots of other guys I know who would jump at the chance."

———

Wayne taught biology at the Sheffield Academy, where the elites of New York City sent their offspring. For fifty thousand dollars a year, these princes and princesses could hobnob without interference from anyone whose parents couldn't afford the tuition. Wayne had risen to become the chairperson of the science department, and from that perch he ruled over the biologists, the chemists, and the physicists, exercising all the fake authority with which high school teachers are imbued.

Wayne had attended an elite Manhattan high school too. Stuyvesant High School was the crème de la crème of the New York City public high schools. Acceptance was by test score only. Thirty thousand kids took the entrance exam, and about eight hundred made the cut, for a 2.67 percent acceptance rate. Harvard accepted 5 percent, for comparison's sake.

Even among this group, Wayne rose to the top, almost to the very top. He graduated second in his class, a distinction that his father had mocked, of course. *Salutatorian—does that mean you're the smartest of all the idiots?* Wayne had his choice of colleges, and his heart was set on MIT, but Archibald Fiske once again intervened.

"You think I got the tuition money coming out of my ass?"

"I can get loans for most of it. It probably won't cost that much more than a SUNY in the end."

"Did you say it was the same cost of a SUNY?"

"Not the same, but maybe close."

"Well, I'm not bankrupting this family for you to tell me that your shit don't stink because you went to some fancy Ivy League college."

Wayne likened his matriculation at SUNY Buffalo as a detour, determined that after four years he'd arrive in the same place as if he'd gone to MIT. Sure enough, it played out exactly that way, and Wayne was accepted at Harvard Medical School. This time, admission came with enough financial aid that Archibald Fiske couldn't say boo about it.

Ole Archie still ended up with the last laugh, though. He died during the second semester of Wayne's first year, leaving Wayne's mother without even enough resources to cover the funeral expenses, much less keep her in her apartment and fed.

So instead of his second year in medical school, Wayne took a job teaching biology at Sheffield. He told his mother that it was only another detour. He'd teach for a year, maybe two, and then go back to medical school. Deep down, however, he knew that this time was different. Archibald Fiske had finally kept Wayne down. He had given up his life to do it, but Wayne imagined his father would have considered it a fair trade-off. Winning was winning, after all.

About ten years ago, Wayne's students had started calling him Heisenberg, a reference to Bryan Cranston's character in *Breaking Bad*. Jessica had thought it was disrespectful and told Wayne that he should put a stop to it, but Wayne rather enjoyed the comparison. It told him that even his students knew that, given the opportunity, he could be a man like Walter White. A man whom other men feared.

6

Dr. Goldman had a small office. It was crammed with textbooks that Jessica assumed he had not opened in years and suspected he might have kept from his medical school days. His diplomas hung on the wall, which she always thought was tacky, suggestive of some type of intellectual insecurity. But perhaps for doctors it was different.

"I'm sorry to have to tell you this, but Owen's cancer has returned," Dr. Goldman said without emotion. "The blood tests we did last week came back positive. We're doing a new set today, but we expect the same result."

Even though Jessica had known this was coming in the waiting room, she was still floored by the news.

At the beginning of Owen's ordeal, she had steeled herself against the possibility that the chemo wasn't going to work. Not completely, of course, because no one could truly mentally prepare for losing their child, but she at least considered the possibility of a bad outcome. Once Dr. Goldman declared the treatment a success, however, and then when he later used the term *remission* and ultimately proclaimed Owen cancer-free, she had cast away all negative thoughts.

Of course, Dr. Goldman always hedged Owen's prognosis, telling her about recurrences and five-year survival rates, the obvious implication being that there were those who survived two, or three, or even four years, but not five. But that was more information than Jessica could absorb. To her way of thinking, you either had cancer or you did not.

Owen had it. He might die. Then he didn't. Which meant he would live. For Jessica, there was no in-between. There couldn't be.

Dr. Goldman had stopped speaking, apparently expecting Jessica to say something. Or at least to respond to what he'd said by crying.

That was how she had responded the first time he had given her this same news. Even before he told her the type of leukemia, she was sobbing. Wayne had been sitting beside her. She buried her face in Wayne's chest, wanting only for the doctor to stop talking. As if his words were the cancer eating away at her son.

This time, however, was different. Jessica sat there alone, and when she heard the diagnosis, she remained mute and still, as if in a catatonic trance. The words reverberated in her head. She understood their urgency, of course. Yet at the same time, she knew that the moment she acknowledged them, Owen would, once again, be dying.

"I know that this is not the news you were expecting," Dr. Goldman continued, "but you shouldn't lose hope that Owen can still go into remission again. There is an experimental treatment in Manhattan, at Memorial Sloan Kettering, and I think he'd be a very suitable candidate. They've been having great success over there."

If hearing the word *cancer* made Jessica sick to her stomach, *experimental treatment* made her want to vomit. Still, this was some sliver of hope. She grasped it with all her might, like it was a branch overhanging a raging river, knowing it was the only thing preventing her from going over the falls.

"Okay," Jessica said, surprised at the sound of her own voice, almost as if she were hovering above the office, watching the scene unfold. "When can that start?"

Dr. Goldman pursed his lips. Jessica could not imagine that there was still bad news to come, but she recognized this tell. Even the slim branch he had extended would not keep her from the plunge ahead.

"It's a process, I'm afraid. First we'll need to do some more tests to confirm that Owen is a viable candidate. I think he will be, but I can't be sure without the lab results to back it up. But the greater hurdle, I'm sorry to say, will be the cost. Because it's an experimental protocol, insurance won't cover the treatment."

"What's the cost?"

"It's significant. I don't know precisely how much, but at a minimum, it will be in the low– to mid–six figures to complete the entire protocol."

Jessica found it pretentious to talk about money this way, like dropping foreign words into a conversation. Everyone in the real estate world did it, though, and even James sprinkled his art talk with the same lingo. It always forced Jessica to translate the amount in her head. If six figures meant it cost at least $100,000, then low– to mid–six figures meant anything between $100,000 and . . . what? Half a million?

Jessica understood why Dr. Goldman was using such imprecise language. He was saying that no matter what the final tally ended up being, it was beyond her means.

———

Haley was late for her 10:00 a.m. appointment with Dr. Rubenstein. She had no excuse for her tardiness, of course. She had no job and no other place she had to be.

As always, when she arrived after ten, Haley immediately apologized. And as was his custom, Dr. Rubenstein told her that she should seek not his forgiveness, but her own.

"I get paid for the full session whether you use it or not. You're only hurting yourself by being late."

Dr. Rubenstein was a hard-core Freudian. He insisted that these sessions take place with Haley supine on the couch. *Insisted* was strong, as he said it was her choice, but he made it clear that he thought his approach was better. "To block out anything that might interfere with our work," he'd explained.

So that morning, Haley did what she did each Monday at 10:00 a.m. (or a few minutes after). She removed her shoes, lay on his sofa, and stared up at the ceiling tiles.

She had been under Dr. Rubenstein's care for almost a year. Oddly enough, it wasn't James's leaving her that sent her to therapy, but a work crisis.

Shortly after her marriage ended, Haley was assigned to a deal in which Maeve Grant was advising the acquirer in a huge merger between two aerospace conglomerates. The transaction involved the usual complex structure of share swaps, leverage, and cash. It was the largest deal in Maeve Grant history, and no fewer than seventy people had spent time on it during its various phases.

The closing was scheduled for year-end, tax considerations requiring that it be finalized before January 1. Haley worked through the Thanksgiving holiday—which suited her fine, given that she had no one to spend it with now that James was with Jessica. Afterward, however, she often thought that if James hadn't dumped her for Jessica, she would have been eating turkey with him instead of discovering the problem that would ultimately end with her being unemployed and unemployable.

Amid the millions of pages of due diligence documents that she had pored over, Haley saw that some of the target's defense contracts would be invalidated after the merger for some arcane regulatory reasons having to do with joint ownership. The loss would be in the $300 million range, which even on a deal this size was meaningful for Maeve Grant's client.

Haley brought the problem to the attention of her direct supervisor, Lawrence Chittik. He told her that she was wrong, that she didn't understand the regulations like he did. That he'd actually worked on the Senate subcommittee that had drafted them.

But she knew she was right. So she put her analysis down on paper and sent it to Chittik, copying the partner in charge of their team, Sean

Keener, and pretending that this was the first time she'd raised the issue so as to not make Chittik look bad with his boss. She even claimed that Chittik had asked her to look at the question, so he could share credit in her discovery.

Keener called Haley and Chittik into his office a minute after the email hit his in-box. "What the fuck?" was literally how he started the meeting.

"I didn't know she was sending it to you," Chittik said, immediately throwing Haley under the bus.

"I'm sorry," Haley said, unsure why she was apologizing for doing her job well.

"Get out," Keener said to Chittik.

Chittik didn't need to be asked twice and scurried away like a frightened bunny. Once they were alone, Keener asked Haley, "Who else have you told?"

"No one."

"If you're lying to me, I'm going to fire you and make sure that no one ever hires you. Understand?"

"I'm sorry. I don't know what I did wrong. The analysis is right. I'm sure of it."

"I don't fucking care. What I do fucking care about is the $100 million fee Maeve Grant gets at closing. Every penny of that vanishes if this deal craters. Do you have any idea what that would mean to our bonus pool?"

The deal closed on time, without the client ever becoming the wiser of the land mine that awaited them with the regulators. At the closing dinner, the client's CEO toasted Maeve Grant's dedication to the cause and thanked them profusely for their hard work. Champagne flowed. Caviar was consumed. In February, bonuses were paid. Instead of a bonus, Haley was fired. "Restructuring," they told her. But if she signed a release promising never to sue, they'd pay her a bonus.

After her sacking, Haley dutifully did all the things the recently unemployed are supposed to do. She reached out to her contacts, asking for leads. When that ran dry, she sent out résumés. First to the blue-chip firms, then broadening her circle, until there was hardly a financial institution she hadn't contacted. She made it to the final interview stage twice, but in each instance, after contacting Haley's references, the head of HR called back to say that they couldn't extend an offer. When Haley asked why, she was told both times that they were not at liberty to say. Haley knew that was corporate-speak meaning that Maeve Grant was blackballing her.

Within twelve months, she'd lost her husband and her career. That's when she started seeing Dr. Rubenstein. She'd been having self-harm fantasies, she admitted to the shrink straightaway, and worse.

"I think about how happy I'd be if someone flew a plane into the Maeve Grant tower and killed them all," she told him once. "Or I construct these elaborate scenarios to kill James or Jessica. Sometimes I even fantasize about killing Jessica's ex-husband, which makes absolutely no sense because he's a victim like me in all this."

Rubenstein said that type of misplaced rage was perfectly normal, although he was quick to point out that it was important for her not to act on the feelings but instead to rechannel them.

"They're telling you something important, Haley," he said.

"And what's that?" Haley asked.

"The anger you feel to the people who wronged you—your bosses, James, even Jessica—that's straightforward enough and understandable at face value. You want to hurt them the way that they hurt you. It's your rage toward Jessica's ex-husband, however, that, as you acknowledge, doesn't fit that pattern. What do you think that means?"

"I don't know. That's why I come here," Haley said.

Of course, she did know. On some level, at least, she knew. Still, she waited for Dr. Rubenstein to say it aloud.

"It suggests that you think that Jessica's ex-husband also bears some blame in all of this. That if he had been a better husband, perhaps Jessica wouldn't have started an affair with your husband. So what it's really telling you is that you think *you* bear some blame for James being unfaithful to you too."

She wondered if that was true. How much of her anger at James was fueled by her own self-loathing? Then again, *she* hadn't broken her marriage vows. James had. It wasn't her fault. Neither was what had happened at Maeve Grant. She had done everything right—in both instances—only to be the one devastated by people with zero concern for honesty or integrity.

And yet, she was still the one seeing a shrink once a week. She was certain that neither James nor Jessica, nor even Lawrence Chittik or Sean Keener for that matter, had lost a moment's sleep about what they'd done. Still, she couldn't deny that she was in a downward spiral, with self-destruction seemingly at the top of her daily routine.

"How has your week been?" Dr. Rubenstein asked, once Haley had assumed her position on the sofa.

"Well, let's see now," she said. "Pretty uneventful. No job leads. Stayed inside. Drank a lot." She paused. "And, oh yeah, I offered some guy sex in exchange for him accompanying me to James and Jessica's anniversary party, and once I was there, I screamed profanity at them during the toasts in front of all their friends and family." Another pause. "So, pretty much just a regular week in the life of Haley Sommers."

———

Owen knew almost immediately something was wrong. During the subway ride home from the doctor's office, his mother looked like she might faint at any moment, white as a ghost and holding on to the pole for dear life.

All of which made Owen sick to his stomach too. There are a limited number of options for what constitutes bad news when you're visiting a pediatric oncologist, after all.

A few minutes after they returned home, his mother knocked on his door. He heard the knock through his headphones but didn't turn around.

When his mother found him in this position, she sometimes shouted his name or touched him on the shoulder to get his attention. But other times, when the point wasn't to engage him but to ascertain whether he was occupied, she'd quietly retreat from his bedroom, as if she wanted her entry to go unnoticed.

Which was why Owen's most prized possession was not his computer, despite what his mother thought. It was his Beats noise-canceling headphones. He liked the way they enhanced the audio when he was playing *Call of Duty*, but what made them so dear to his heart was that whenever he wore them, his mother assumed that he was hearing impaired.

Which made them almost akin to an invisibility cloak. When he wore them with the sound off, they weren't *canceling* outside speech but *amplifying* it.

This was apparently one of those times when his mother didn't want to engage him. Her visit was to ascertain that he was busy. She did that when she wanted some privacy of her own.

After retreating from his room, his mother entered her own bedroom, and the door shut behind her. He gave her a few minutes to settle into whatever she was doing, then left his bedroom to do some eavesdropping.

He pressed his ear against her closed door. At first, he couldn't hear words. Only sobs.

When the words came, they were halting.

"I know. I know. I'm trying. It's just . . . I thought this was all over." More crying. "Yeah . . . I know. They said that there's some experimental

treatment . . . No. Not covered by insurance . . . 'Low– to mid–six figures,' is what the doctor said . . . I'm not sure. I think we should wait
until they confirm it. So next week, I guess . . . I don't know . . ."

Owen had heard enough. He went back into his room, shut the
door behind him, and put the headphones back on, turning the volume
up high.

But instead of losing itself in his game, his mind ran through what
his mother's side of the conversation meant. The cancer had returned.
That was obvious, and he had surmised as much by his mother's behavior on the subway. While they were poking him with needles, someone
must have told her about the recurrence.

The other part was about money. Owen didn't know how much the
chemo had cost the first time around, but his parents were always going
on about drugs that cost $100 a pill, and he'd taken seven of them a day.
He remembered his father saying that getting treated for acute myeloid
leukemia was more expensive than four years at Harvard.

If it weren't for health insurance, Owen knew he would have died
that first year. And from what he could piece together from his mother's
call, insurance wasn't going to help this time around.

His father was always going on about how the important things
in life couldn't be bought. But like so many things his old man said, it
was wrong. The most important things always came with a price tag.

———

Wayne's lunch break was between noon and 12:50 p.m. One of the
perks of his seniority was that he got to eat at a normal time. The new-
bies found themselves having lunch as early as 10:30 a.m. or as late as
2:00 p.m.

The faculty lounge was a windowless space, furnished with the same
type of Formica picnic tables that the students used. But whereas the
main cafeteria must have had thirty tables lined up in rows, the teachers

had two, side by side. As the joke went: one for the cool teachers and one for the losers, although which was which was also a point of dispute.

Wayne was about to tear open the cellophane surrounding the turkey and cheese sandwich he'd packed for himself five hours earlier when his phone rang. The caller ID identified his ex-wife.

Jessica had never called him at school, not even when they were married. That she was calling now meant two things. First, it was about Owen. And second, it was important.

There was a general rule among the teachers that you didn't take phone calls in the lounge. But an exception was made if the call was short, in consideration of the fact that even teachers weren't allowed to be seen in the hallways with a phone, and it could take ten minutes to walk outside, which meant that a two-minute call would take up nearly half your lunch break.

"Everything okay?" he whispered, conserving his words so as to not disrupt the other teachers.

"No. Everything is definitely not okay."

Jessica began telling him that Owen's cancer had returned and something about a possible experimental treatment. As soon as she did, the air left his lungs. He felt as if he might pass out.

Jessica did nearly all the talking, and for most of it, she sobbed. Their call ended in less than five minutes, which was still long enough that Wayne got the stink eye from Ed Weston, who had been old when Wayne joined the faculty twenty-two years ago.

Wayne knew that Owen had never been cured—that you never were cured of leukemia—but it had been easy to accept Jessica's assurances to the contrary. The few times he had made a comment that hopefully Owen would be well enough to go to college, Jessica had glared daggers at him, suggesting that it was Wayne's pessimism, rather than the cancer, that was making their son sick.

In the end, like so many other things, he'd been right, and she'd been wrong. It reminded him of all the times he'd said that something was not right in their marriage, and that maybe counseling would help, and she had gaslighted him into believing their problems were all in his mind. Right up until the day she left, in fact.

He tried to focus on the one positive thing Jessica had said: the experimental treatment. But just as quickly he remembered that health insurance wouldn't cover it and that it would cost several hundred thousand dollars.

Wayne calculated the maximum amount of money he could beg, borrow, and steal. He had no assets to sell. In fact, he was in debt up to his eyeballs. He had used every last nickel he could get his hands on—which included getting cash advances on his credit cards and taking a second mortgage—to fund the $50,000 he needed to buy Jessica out of her half of the equity they had in their house during the divorce. The housing market dropped even before the ink on the divorce decree was dry. If he sold the house now, he doubted he'd net much more than thirty grand after transaction fees and paying off both mortgages, and he'd still have to find a new place to live.

His 401(k) had less than $20,000, his savings account less than $2,000.

Wayne still had thirty minutes left for lunch but no appetite to go with it. He decided that his time would best be spent out of view of the other teachers.

He didn't stop back at his locker to get his coat and felt a shiver the moment he left the building. Still, he found the fresh air helpful to break him out of the daze he'd been in since answering Jessica's call.

An empty bench was a few feet away, overlooking the football field. Wayne sat down, covered his face with his hands, and began to cry.

———

Reid had not even tried to hide his annoyance at James's rejection of his proposal, suggesting that James take the train back into the city under the rather transparent ruse that he needed to conduct some business out of East Hampton for the next few days.

The train back to Manhattan was delayed outside Bay Shore. Some type of track problem, the conductor said. The end result was what should have been a four-hour trip took nearly twice that long. James called Jessica and told her to have dinner without him, his own evening meal a slice of pizza he grabbed in Penn Station.

By the time James finally got home, he expected Jessica to already be in the bedroom. Instead, he found her in the living room, sitting almost completely in the dark but for a small reading lamp beside her. The television was off, and he didn't see a book or anything else that could have been occupying her time.

"Sit down, James," she said. "There's something I need to tell you."

He knew at once that whatever it was, it was serious. He did as she asked.

"I got some terrible news at Owen's doctor's visit," she said. "It wasn't a redo of the blood test, after all. The last test showed the cancer was back. They wanted him to retest, but they're sure it'll be the same result."

Jessica was trying to keep an even keel about this news, but James knew it must be devastating her. By the time he'd met Jessica, Owen's cancer was something spoken about in the past tense. Like a movie he had walked into in the middle, after that particular plot point had already been resolved. Still, he knew that this very possibility had always hung over Jessica like a black cloud.

"Oh God, I'm so sorry, Jessica. What . . . what's the prognosis?"

"It depends on if you're a glass-half-full type or not, I suppose," she said, trying to eke out a smile that didn't quite appear. "The doctor wants to put Owen on this experimental treatment. He said that if Owen qualifies for it, there's a good chance—actually the doctor said a *very good* chance—that the cancer would go back into remission."

"That's good news, then, right?" James said.

He was trying to sound upbeat, even though he knew that anything short of a guarantee of survival still sounded like a death sentence when it pertained to your child.

"Not great, though. It's going to cost a lot."

"What about insurance?"

"It's not covered because it's experimental."

James now understood. Jessica's hesitancy was because she was asking him for money.

"I know that you didn't sign up for this when we got married. But it means Owen's life. The doctor said that there was no point in going back to any of the insurance-approved protocols because they were unlikely to work. So it's this or . . . Owen's going to die. I'm sorry to be so dramatic about it, but that's the truth."

Jessica began to cry. James got up and sat on her chair's armrest, holding her hand until the sobbing subsided.

"How much?" he asked at last.

"The doctor said low– to mid–six figures."

Jessica knew that they were not nearly as well off as they seemed to the outside world. Before they had married, James had explained that it was an occupational requirement that he present as rich so that his wealthy clients respected him. That meant he lived well beyond his means. The purchase of the loft had taken every penny he had. So much that he'd had to use the money Wayne had paid Jessica for her half of the house in Queens, plus a second mortgage, to settle up with Haley.

"You know how tight things are now, Jessica. We don't have anything to speak of in the bank, and with the slowdown in the art market, I haven't made a decent commission in six months."

"What about selling some of the art?" she said, looking at the walls as if they were a life preserver that could save her from going under.

"I don't own any of it. It's all consigned. And I can't even sell them at fire-sale prices to raise money because most of my deals have a contractual minimum."

"Don't we own anything that we can sell?"

James sighed. "Yeah. My watch might fetch fifty grand, and if I cash out my life insurance policy and my very modest retirement savings, maybe I could pool together . . . I don't know, seventy-five grand?"

She let go of any resolve. Jessica's entire body seemed to fail, and she fell onto him.

Of course, James did have one possible solution. Their sudden need to raise money fast made Reid's earlier offer of a quick score seem heaven sent. Of course, that was true only if God trafficked in stolen art.

"There is a way," James said.

It was as if she had been given an antidote to a poison. Jessica's head snapped up. "What?"

"The deal Reid wanted me to do. I think I can raise the money that way."

Jessica's entire face lit up. "I . . . I don't know what to say, James. You're not only saving Owen's life but mine too. I mean that. And I'll borrow the money from you. That way, if anything ever happens between us, I'll pay you back."

"Nothing is ever going to happen between us, Jessica. I love you and always will. Let's just worry about getting Owen healthy. That's all that matters now."

———

"You look like the cat that ate the canary," Haley said, still in bed. "I'm a little insulted that fucking me didn't put a smile like that on your face."

Reid put the phone down and debated whether to tell her the truth. On the one hand, Haley fucked better when she was angry at James. On the other, he couldn't guarantee she wouldn't call the cops if she knew James was involved in a deal with him.

"It was business," he said. "You're pleasure."

"I'm not pleasure, Reid. I'm . . . I don't know what I am to you, actually. It's never made any sense. I know that something must go on in your head, because every once in a while it makes you decide we should do this, but for the life of me, I don't know what it is."

"Right back at ya. I never know what possesses you to agree to come over when I call."

Their affair—if that was the right word, which it wasn't—had begun shortly after James left Haley. She called Reid one day, spilling out a sob story about how all their mutual friends had chosen James over her. He reminded her that those people were James's friends to begin with.

"We met *you* together," she said. "You're friends to both of us. Please, don't abandon me."

Reid didn't really have friends. The people in his life were there for a reason: family, business, pleasure.

He'd seen an opportunity for Haley to serve as pleasure. And she certainly had served. Each and every time. And all he'd had to pay to be the recipient of the most off-the-wall sex of his life was to listen to Haley rant about James doing her wrong and how she'd get even with him someday.

"I think you know exactly why I come over to fuck your brains out whenever you call," she said.

"Yeah, why's that?"

"It's my way of getting some small measure of revenge against James. Because I know he'd be absolutely incensed if he knew. Which begs the question: What did James do to you this time to make you want to fuck me?"

"You're crazy," he said. "Why can't I just enjoy the company of a beautiful woman?"

"For the same reason that a cigar can't just be a cigar."

She was right, at least in part of it. Truth be told, Reid didn't think James would care in the least if he knew that Reid and Haley sometimes went at it. "Better you than me," he'd probably say. But Haley was undoubtedly correct that, for her at least, their encounters had much more to do with James than with him. It didn't take an advanced psychology degree to realize that Haley was hate-fucking James with Reid's body. For her, it was like a drug—she got the positive reinforcement that she was desired, with the added benefit of believing that James would be apoplectic if he found out she was screwing Reid.

"That just makes me feel cheap, Haley."

"Then it's good you got that phone call, I guess. Sounds like you'll be feeling richer any day now."

7

It wasn't until three days after their doctor's visit that Owen's mother came into his room, sat on the edge of his bed, and finally told him what he already knew.

"I've got a good news–bad news situation to share with you, Owen. The bad news is that there's been a recurrence of the leukemia. But the much more important good news is that there's a treatment that will cure it. You're going to get a transplant in which your bone marrow is replaced by someone else's that doesn't create leukemia cells."

The whole time she was talking, his mother managed to maintain a smile. Owen knew that there was nothing to be happy about. Since the moment he left the doctor's office, Owen had been googling like crazy the possible treatments for a recurrence of AML.

It took him a beat too long to realize that if his mother were actually imparting new information, as she thought, then he should have said something or at least changed his expression.

"Who's going to be the donor?" he asked.

"That's still to be determined. Your father or me, hopefully. If not, we'll go to the national database. But don't worry. We'll definitely find someone compatible."

The American Red Cross, or whatever the website was where he had read about this, had a contrary view. According to them, it wasn't easy to find a donor, and the best chance was a sibling, which he didn't have.

"Okay," he said, largely because he didn't know what else to say.

"You, me, and Dad are going to see a new doctor tomorrow. The doctor in charge of the treatment program. So, you'll miss school. Another piece of good news, right?"

He actually didn't want to miss school. The orchestra was rehearsing for the opera, and he was in the running to be first violin. As soon as this thought hit him, however, he realized it would never come to pass. A bone marrow transplant meant he'd be missing most of the rest of the school year. All those things that seniors had to wait four years to achieve—final concerts, the senior prom, hanging out with your friends—were not going to happen for him. Nevertheless, he smiled, because he knew his mother was trying.

The next morning, Owen sat between his parents in Dr. Cammerman's office at Memorial Sloan Kettering, which his mother had already told him several times was the premier cancer hospital in the country, if not the world. If their new doctor was as big a deal as Owen's mother claimed, he certainly didn't have the office to back it up. There was barely enough space for the third chair to fit across from the desk.

The man himself didn't look any more impressive than his surroundings. Bald, with a goatee and oversize glasses. If it weren't for the fact that his white lab coat had DOCTOR stenciled above the pocket, Owen might have assumed he was a janitor.

"The procedure is going to be difficult, Owen," Dr. Cammerman said. "So let me apologize in advance for the things we're going to be putting into your body and the way it's going to make you feel. But know that it's all for the good. We do it so, at the end of the process, you can go on and live as normal and productive a life as you would if you'd never heard the word *leukemia*."

His mother smiled at him, and his father nodded approvingly. Owen wanted to scream at them to cut the shit already. He was *so* beyond tired of the lies that people peddled in an effort to make him reject reality. But he kept his emotions in check, a frozen, neutral expression on his face suggesting that he believed the doctor's every word.

"I'm sure you want to know what this is going to look like," Dr. Cammerman said, now with a smile of his own. "First step is we need to do some more tests to confirm that you're eligible for the transplant. I'm not going to bore you with all the things we're looking for, or seeking to rule out, but I can say that I'm almost certain that when we're done with that process, we're going to conclude that you're a good candidate. But as you'll hear me say a lot, there are no guarantees on any of this. So, I can only tell you something after I know it. I can't predict beforehand."

"Okay," Owen said, even as he was thinking that the first thing the doctor had said—that if he underwent the treatment, it would all turn out okay in the end—was precisely the type of prediction he'd just said he'd never make.

"Good," Dr. Cammerman said with another smile. "So, let's assume that you're a viable candidate. What comes next is we put in a central venous catheter, which we call a CVC. It can be done as outpatient surgery, which means you will not have to stay overnight in the hospital. It won't hurt. The CVC allows us to more easily draw blood and give you medicine. It stays in you during the entirety of your treatment, and even for a little bit after it's all over. We take it out once your new stem cells are firmly in place and starting to reproduce the way we want."

"Okay," Owen said again, wanting this entire thing to be over.

"Good. It's easiest to think about the procedure as occurring in two phases. Stage one has a fancy name called *myeloablation*."

Owen knew all about myeloablation too. The internet had practically made him an AML specialist.

"The myeloablation process is basically another round of chemo," Dr. Cammerman continued. "The intent is to remove the cancer cells in your body and to make room for the transplant we're going to do in phase two. Now, I know you're a chemo veteran, so you're familiar with the drill. It'll be like it was the last time, except the regimen will be shorter. About a week, give or take. It's a different type of chemo, different medicines than the last time, so I can't guarantee—there's that word again, right? But I can't predict whether you'll tolerate it better or worse or about the same as you did the last time. Also, you're older and stronger than before, so that might help, but it's a high-dose regimen, so that makes it more likely the side effects will be more severe, I'm afraid."

Owen touched the ends of his hair out of reflex. It had taken him three years to get it to this length, and now it would be gone in a matter of weeks. As if reading his mind, his mother reached over and caressed his shoulder.

"Okay, now we're done with phase one," Dr. Cammerman continued. "We give you a day or two to rest. Then, after forty-eight hours of downtime, the main event occurs. The transplant. Here's how that works: you'll be under sedation, so all you have to do is sleep, and my team does the work. The transplant takes only a few hours. We'll be placing donor stem cells into your bone marrow. Sounds like fun, right?"

That smile again. Out of his peripheral vision, Owen saw his parents wearing stupid grins too.

"Now, I said that there were two phases," Dr. Cammerman continued, "but I'm going to add a third one: posttransplant. There are some strange side effects to the procedure that you may or may not experience. For instance, you might have a strong taste of garlic or creamed corn in your mouth. Sucking on candy or sipping flavored drinks during and after the infusion can help with the taste. I know, not pleasant. I'm sorry to say, your body will also smell like this."

"So that might be a little bit of improvement for you, huh?" his father said with a chuckle.

Dr. Cammerman laughed. "Don't worry. The smell fades after a few days, but this is something that most patients tell me about, and I don't want you to worry if you experience it. You're not becoming a vampire or anything like that."

Owen wanted to tell him that vampires were repelled by garlic; they didn't smell like it. Instead, he smiled while silently praying that the doctor would stop talking already.

But Dr. Cammerman still wasn't finished. "So, at this point in the process, posttransplant, we're waiting to see if the transplanted stem cells engraft and start to multiply and make new blood cells. That usually occurs within a few weeks. Unfortunately, you're in the hospital this entire time. No exceptions."

Owen knew this from the internet too. Still he asked, "How long am I going to be in the hospital? I mean after the transplant?"

"Anywhere from three to six weeks. During this period, you'll be highly susceptible to infection, which is why we require the hospital stay. Your visitors will be limited to your immediate family, and everyone else who comes in contact with you will have to wash their hands before entering and then wear surgical masks, glasses, and gowns. What we're looking for before we send you home is that you haven't run a fever in a few days, you're feeling relatively good, and your blood counts have hit a certain level. It varies from person to person how long that takes. But like I said, it'll most likely be a month or so."

Owen timed it out in his head. If the first stage took two weeks, and the second anywhere from three to six weeks, he was looking at about two months from start to finish. And for most of the time, he'd be in the hospital.

As he had predicted, there'd be no opera performance in his future. No final orchestra recital. No chance at first violin. Likely no prom either.

"We'll get you a tutor," his mother said. "That way, you'll still be able to graduate on time."

Owen smiled again. The timing did permit him to attend graduation. Of course, that would only be true if he didn't die before then.

———

Haley sat at the bar at Sant Ambroeus, an upscale Italian restaurant on Madison Avenue. In her previous life, she would stroll past the bar area, take a table inside the restaurant, and order the Dover sole. But now the bar was as far as she dared go. For one thing, she could no longer afford the prices at the tables. For another, she was here not for the food, but the view.

In the morning, her order was a cappuccino. In the afternoon it was a martini, extra dirty. Usually more than one.

It was somewhat disconcerting that this morning the barista nodded when she took her seat. He was about her age, but not handsome enough for Haley to think his gesture was a come-on. More likely, he remembered her as a regular.

Sant Ambroeus was the ground-floor tenant of the building where James worked. By sitting at the bar, Haley had an unobstructed sight line to Madison Avenue, which allowed her to see her ex-husband enter and leave his office.

These stalking measures did not always bear fruit. Far from it. Haley estimated that she saw James less than half the times she visited. Then again, he never spotted her, which was more important.

At 10:15 a.m., Haley finally got the payoff for which she had been so patiently waiting. James was wearing a tie, which he did only when he was meeting a client. Her heart skipped a beat when he stopped directly in front of Sant Ambroeus. She thought that maybe he had seen her, but he was instead checking his look in the window's reflection, which gave her a few extra seconds to stare.

A man quickly approached, placing his hand on James's shoulder. It took a moment before Haley realized that it was Reid Warwick. He wasn't wearing a tie, but his wolfish grin suggested that money was on his mind.

James had always said that Reid was fun to have a drink with, but he'd never do business with him because he didn't trust him. Then again, he'd also told her that he'd love her until death parted them, forsaking all others, so James was hardly the gold standard of reliability. Still, she couldn't help but connect Reid's phone call from the other night—the deal he said was going to net him "a few mill"—with his sudden presence at James's place of business this morning.

So that's the call that made you smile, huh?

Quickly, another thought hit her: What if they're planning something criminal? And what if she could find evidence that led to James being locked up?

That was another fantasy of hers. Most often, she imagined killing James. Sometimes it was an elaborate, Rube Goldberg kind of torture device. Or she played the part of Goldfinger, with James strapped to a table and a laser slowly moving up between his legs while he begged for his life.

"Do you want me to say I love you, Haley? That I love you more than Jessica?" he'd scream out.

"No, James," she'd respond. *"I want you to die."*

But other times the fantasy was far simpler. Just a gun, a short speech about how she was evening the score, and then James's shocked expression. She even had one that involved sex, like in that Sharon Stone movie when she plunged an ice pick into a man's back as he climaxed.

But putting James behind bars was the best. In that fantasy, she'd come to visit him in the pen. He'd be expecting Jessica when the guards shouted, *"Sommers! Visitor!"* But as he approached the glass divider separating inmates from their visitors, he'd see her face behind the glass partition.

"Surprised?" she'd say on her end of the phone.

"Wh-what are you doing here?" he'd respond.

"I came to see how prison's treating you. I figured it was the least I could do, seeing that you're in here because of me."

Then she'd stand and, like a badass, turn her back on him, and walk away. She wouldn't look back while he screamed silently from behind the partition.

During the divorce, she'd told her lawyer to look into tax issues or anything else that might put James in criminal jeopardy. "That's not in your interest, Haley," David had told her. "In fact, it's the last thing you want. James will spend all of your joint assets on lawyers. Or he'll settle by paying the IRS money that otherwise would be marital property."

She didn't care. At the time, she hadn't needed James's money; she only wanted him to suffer. In the end, her lawyer and his battery of forensic accountants never found anything shady about James's business dealings.

Dr. Rubenstein knew about her stalking . . . kind of. After a few months of therapy, Haley mentioned that she *sometimes* sat at the bar at Sant Ambroeus in the hope of catching a glimpse of James but was quick to add that she also liked their coffee, and besides, she and James often had gone to that restaurant when they were married, so it had sentimental appeal for her too.

"Tell me what it feels like before, during, and after," Dr. Rubenstein had asked.

"When I know I'm going to do it, it's something I'm looking forward to, and there isn't much of that in my life nowadays. But I'm also afraid he'll see me. When he appears, it's like this huge wave comes over me. Almost as if I feel invincible or something, because I can see him, but he can't see me. And then, when he walks away, I feel stupid for being there. I vow that I won't do it again, but that never holds. Within a day or two, I'm there again."

"Does that remind you of anything else you do?"

"What?"

"The sequence you just described. Does it fit any other activity you engage in?"

She thought for a moment. "No, not really."

"It's actually not such an uncommon pattern. It is the progression that often is described by people suffering from addiction, be it drugs or alcohol or something else. They all share a commonality regarding the anticipation, combined with the fear of getting caught, the thrill of the act in the moment, followed by guilt, then a powerful need for more. Which, of course, is what makes it such a vicious cycle."

It had now been nearly two years since James had left her, and her hope that time would heal the wound was becoming more tenuous every day. She had experienced some obsessive behavior in the past over failed relationships, sometimes lasting long enough that her friends expressed concern, but it had always eventually passed. By now, she knew the fallout from her divorce was not going in that direction. If anything, things were getting worse. Her need to crash the anniversary party was prime evidence of that.

As was the fact that, as she left Sant Ambroeus that morning, she was already planning her return later that evening. She wanted—no, *needed*—to know what Reid and James were doing together.

"Tell me about this guy," Reid said.

Reid sometimes got this feeling. It wasn't quite a tingling of the hairs on the back of his neck, but it was a sixth sense of sorts that something wasn't right. He wasn't sure he was experiencing that feeling now, but he might be. Maybe it had nothing to do with the deal. Maybe it was a sign he had chosen the wrong business partner.

When he had asked James to help, Reid had expected a little pushback. There was something too holier-than-thou about James for his taste. Then again, being a Boy Scout in the art world was akin to being the world's tallest little person. Even the most scrupulous art dealers cut corners when real money was on the line. Which was why Reid was taken aback when James initially turned the deal down. Then when James called him back to change his mind later that day, Reid wondered whether his original disinclination was all for show, although that seemed a bit over-the-top for even James to demonstrate his scruples.

Reid might have let that go without a second thought if it hadn't been for the fact that immediately after James said he was in, he suddenly had a buyer. Like some guy was just waiting to buy an unsigned Pollock, and all James had to do was add water.

Reid wasn't one to look a gift horse in the mouth, but it seemed a little too good to be true that, in less than twenty-four hours, James had not only changed his mind about doing the deal but also found an all-cash buyer. Could James be setting him up somehow?

Reid shook the thought away. James wasn't that way. Besides, what would his angle be?

No matter how much he tried to assuage his fears, Reid couldn't completely dispel them, however. It all seemed a bit hinky. Even for a semiclandestine art deal.

"His name is Noah Reiss," James said. "I sold him a Miró a year or two ago."

"And what's his business?"

"Not clear. He's a No Footprint Guy."

A No Footprint Guy meant that the client had no internet footprint. Google his name, nothing would come up. No Footprint Guys kept their business interests under the radar.

No website. No social media presence. No press about them at all.

It made sense that a No Footprint Guy would buy a Pollock of dubious provenance in an all-cash deal. But Reid still thought it was hinky.

"Why not sell him all four?"

"That'll scare him off. You want every buyer to think they're getting the only one."

Though Reid talked a good game about art, that's all it was—talk. He didn't know much about actually selling it.

The buzzer to James's office was too loud, startling Reid. As soon as it went off, James walked over to the intercom to tell Mr. No Footprint Guy to come up.

"It's showtime," he said to Reid.

———

To James's surprise, two people entered his studio. One was his expected buyer, Noah Reiss. Beside him was a woman James might have thought was Noah's wife except for the fact that she was a ten and Noah Reiss was a three, tops. He was a lump of a man, practically the same size around as he was vertical, and his face was largely hidden by a scraggly beard under a pair of beady eyes. By contrast, Reiss's companion was James's height, with the slender figure of a ballerina; she carried off a pixie cut as only an exceptionally beautiful woman could. Still, money made for strange partners, so maybe the woman was Mrs. Reiss.

"Noah, good to see you again," James said heartily while shaking Noah's hand. "This is my partner on this deal, Reid Warwick. Reid, meet Noah Reiss."

While gripping Reid's hand, Noah said, "This is Allison Longley. Allison's an expert in midcentury modern American art. I asked her to come along to give me some comfort that everything is kosher. No offense, James. It's not that I don't trust you, but you know how it is. Trust, but verify."

"Of course," James said with a big smile. "I wouldn't have it any other way. So, come in. Have a seat on the sofa, and I'll bring the guest of honor over. Normally I would offer you something to drink, but I'm sure you understand that I don't want an irreplaceable piece of art to be ruined by a knocked-over cup of coffee."

The viewing area was four leather armchairs around a four-foot-square table made of glass and steel. James put on a pair of paper gloves and retrieved a sheet of paper from his credenza, placing it in the center of the table.

"As you can see, this is truly an extraordinary piece," James said. "It shows Jackson Pollock's thought process in crafting his larger canvases. The owner of this work, who would like to remain anonymous, was a very close friend of Lee Krasner's, Pollock's widow. She provided this piece to him more than thirty years ago as a gift."

Noah couldn't hide a Cheshire cat grin. No doubt he was already mentally composing the tale he'd tell his friends about how he'd acquired this bit of art history. For collectors, the story was sometimes more important than the art itself.

Allison, however, looked far from sold. She examined the work closely, her eyes within a few inches of the paper. "No signature, right?"

"As I have already explained to Noah, it is an unfinished piece, which is why Jackson Pollock didn't sign or number it."

"That's also why provenance is going to be difficult to establish," Allison said. "And that reduces the piece's value considerably."

James caught Reid's pained expression out of his peripheral vision. He tried to show the opposite to Allison.

"I'm not a hard-sell kind of guy, Allison. As you know, if the piece had Jackson Pollock's John Hancock on the reverse, it would be up a few blocks at the Met. This is a preliminary work, which undoubtedly formed the basis for one of the master's larger canvases. If that's not what you're interested in purchasing, then this isn't for you. But this is an extremely rare opportunity to own something that Jackson Pollock actually put his hands on, without shelling out eight or nine figures for the privilege."

As much as James liked to fancy himself an art expert, he was first and foremost a salesman. He knew a lot about the art he was selling, but he knew even more about the art of persuasion that went into closing a deal. Right now, he knew that Noah Reiss was sold. It was Allison he had to convince that everything was on the up-and-up.

Or even better, convince Noah not to follow Allison's advice.

James touched his pants pocket and quickly removed his cell phone. "Excuse me. I need to take this call. I'll be quick."

He walked into the other room, shutting the door behind him. James waited for two minutes, which was as long as he thought a phone call with another prospective buyer would take, if he had actually received such a call.

"Apologies," James said when he returned to the others. "I don't want to rush you, of course. Unfortunately, that call was from another buyer. I had originally planned to meet with him tomorrow, but he's had a change of plans, and needs to return to Dubai this afternoon. He wanted to come by now to see the piece. I told him that I needed another fifteen minutes or so and would get back to him. So, if you're not interested, I really do need to take that meeting."

Reid was smiling as if trying not to break into laughter. James hoped his own expression better concealed the ruse.

"You can tell your Arab guy happy trails back to the Middle East," Noah said. "I'll take it."

"As I told you over the phone, the purchase price is $750,000," James said. "That's firm."

Noah extended his hand to seal the deal. "I'll wire the money as soon as I get back to the office."

———

After the doctor's visit, Wayne suggested that they all get lunch together. Jessica declined, claiming that she had already made lunch plans with James.

Wayne doubted that was true, and her lie made him feel worse than if Jessica actually had plans with James. At least that way it didn't necessarily mean that she didn't want to spend time in his company.

He and Owen stopped in the first restaurant they saw that didn't seem to cater exclusively to billionaires. It was a diner, but because it sat in New York City, the chef's salad still cost twenty-one dollars, even though everything else about the place looked cheap. Cracked vinyl booths, scratched tables, fake Tiffany tulip chandeliers in pink.

They settled into a booth in the back. Owen ordered a grilled cheese and french fries. Wayne selected the overpriced salad.

"How you feeling about everything we heard today?" Wayne asked.

Owen's response was a shrug.

"Yes, that makes sense, and I agree with your logic, but would you care to elaborate a little?"

At least that got a smile from his son. "It is what it is," Owen said.

"I think you know that statement is the verbal equivalent of a shrug. I'm asking you to talk to me, Owen. Here's the thing, and I'm not under any illusion that you're going to believe any of it, but I swear to you that what I'm about to say is the one hundred percent God's honest truth. In your life, you'll meet lots of people. Some you'll like. Some you'll love. Some will like you. If you're lucky, some will love you. But no one is going to love you the way your mom and I do. And that's not bragging. It's just . . . a fact, is all. Everyone else you ever meet, their love for you is conditional. And by that I mean you could do something to make them stop loving you, or you could just fall out of love with them, or vice versa. I guess your mom and I are Exhibit A on that one. But it doesn't work that way with your children. There is nothing—and I mean *nothing*—that you could ever do that would change the way your mom and I feel about you."

He had composed this little speech while in the Sloan Kettering waiting room. It had come out even better than it sounded in his head.

So much so that Wayne's only regret was that Jessica hadn't been present to witness it.

"Why are you telling me this, Dad? Did the doctor say something?"

Wayne had intended this pep talk to cause his son to trust him more. But like so many things he did these days, it seemed to have had the opposite effect.

"No. Nothing like that," he said, backpedaling. "What I'm trying to say is that you should know that you can always tell your mom and me the truth. Because there's nothing you're going to say to us that'll change the way we feel about you. So, long story short, talk to me, Owen. I won't judge. And maybe, just maybe, I'll come up with something helpful. Or, even if I don't, you'll surprise yourself and feel better just for sharing."

If Owen was moved by his father's sentiments, he hid it well. "Thanks for saying all of that, Dad. I just . . . I really don't have much to say about it. Honest. I'm bummed about missing school. Senior year and all, especially because I had a real shot at being first violin. But in the big scheme of things, that stuff isn't important. What matters is that I get accepted into the treatment, and they find a donor, and all the rest. I figure that's all going to happen because, you know, there's no real benefit to thinking about the worst-case scenario all the time. So, I might as well have a positive attitude, right? And if all goes well, then, like the doctor said, it'll suck for a while, and then I'll be okay."

Wayne stared hard at his son, trying to comprehend the jumble of contradictions that could reside in a seventeen-year-old mind. Owen rarely displayed any emotion, giving off the vibe that he didn't care much about anything. But all it took was listening to him play the violin for two minutes to realize that wasn't true. With a bow in his hand, Owen gave voice to feelings more deeply held than Wayne imagined possible. Last year, when Owen was rehearsing Vivaldi's *The Four Seasons* for hours on end, all he could think about was that no one could play it like Owen did without fully experiencing the range of emotion those pieces called for—joy, sadness, anger, love.

Yet, away from the concert stage, Owen ran on a completely even keel. Today was a perfect example: his calm, considered reaction to what would be the scariest time in most people's lives.

In this way, Wayne understood his son perfectly. For Owen had undoubtedly learned from him how to hide his anger from the world.

———

Jessica's mother had been a high school teacher. She always said she taught history, but the curriculum called it social studies and included things like geography and basic economics. She claimed that as a girl, she had wanted to be a lawyer or a college professor but had to put aside such ambitions because those opportunities were not available to girls of her generation. Jessica knew that wasn't entirely true. Two of the women on the Supreme Court were younger than Linda Terry, as had been many of Jessica's college professors.

But in her mother's telling of her life, her options were limited by her gender, the times in which she lived, and her own mother's low expectations. "My mother—your grandmother—made it very clear to me that finding a husband was my only real job," she'd told Jessica more times than she could count. "Anything else I wanted to do ended when I got married, which meant pursuing something that required a long-term payoff made no sense. Thank God women today have more choices."

Many of Jessica's classmates ended up in high-powered fields, but those women weren't reared by Linda Terry. While Jessica's mother claimed to be an equal-rights disciple, the subtext of everything she had ever told Jessica was no different from the pearls of wisdom her own mother had imparted a generation earlier—that you were nothing unless you had a man. Over and over again, Linda Terry made clear to her daughter that women were divided into two categories: those who were able to attract men—life's winners—and those who, in her mother's words, "never had a date in their lives."

Jessica had been determined not to be a loser in her mother's eyes. So she made sure that she had plenty of boyfriends. Even if it required she barely eat a meal for ten years after she got her period. Even if it meant not pursuing a JD or MD or PhD because by the time she got out of school, she'd be too old to attract a man.

Wayne was the first of those men who asked her to marry him. She said yes because she feared that there would never be another one who would ask.

Linda Terry died two years before Jessica's marriage did. Wayne always said the two were connected. That so long as her mother was alive, Jessica would have stayed married, but the moment she didn't have to face Linda's disapproval, she could have the rebellious adolescence she'd denied herself back when it was age appropriate.

Jessica knew that explanation was too pat. Her mother had died six months after Owen's diagnosis, and Jessica saw the potential loss of her son as a far greater proximate cause of her need to rethink her life choices than the subsequent death of her mother.

But this much was true: Jessica had wanted a brand-new life. Not just wanted. Had to have.

The first step in that renaissance was to be with a man she loved and not the one she had accepted out of fear that no one else would have her. And then, while that thought was beginning to take root, fate handed her James.

In the last months that she was living with Wayne, when her affair with James was all-consuming, Jessica sometimes heard her mother's voice in her head, trying to talk her out of the path she had begun to think of as inevitable.

Think about Owen, Linda Terry's voice would say.

"I am, Mom," Jessica would say back. "This will be good for him too."

You know that's not true, her mother would answer. *Divorce is never good for kids. It teaches them that love can end, and they fear that might be true of your love for them too. Why do you think I stayed with your father all those years?*

"Hopefully, by leaving an unhappy marriage, I'll teach Owen that he has the power to make himself happy. To show him what a loving marriage looks like," she answered.

Jessica never for a second believed that she'd persuaded her mother in this imaginary debate. But the rightness of leaving Wayne for James was reinforced every time she saw James, including early that afternoon when she paid him a visit at his office.

"What a pleasant surprise," he said. "And your timing is impeccable. My last appointment just left, and it ended very well."

"Is that so? Well, I was, as they say, in the neighborhood. I thought we could get lunch. And now there seems to be something to celebrate."

"Sadly, I'm not hungry," he said with a smile that told her exactly what he meant.

"Then how will we ever fill the time?"

8

Allison Longley called James later that afternoon, while he and Jessica were in flagrante delicto in the bedroom in James's office. He phoned her back after Jessica had left and he'd showered.

"I think there are some real opportunities for you and me," Allison said, sounding much more like a character out of a 1940s femme fatale movie than an art expert.

"Is that right?"

"I have clients. You have access to Pollocks. What's the phrase? This sounds like the beginning of a beautiful friendship."

"Like I told you, your client bought our entire inventory of the Pollocks."

She laughed. "Yes. That's what you told me. What kind of an art person would I be if I believed that? But, look, if you have the other Pollocks earmarked for other buyers, then there's no need for me to take you for drinks so we can talk further about making some serious money."

He paused for a moment. Jessica was cooking tonight. She wanted to have a family dinner to cheer Owen up. Still, landing this business opportunity would be far better for Owen than lasagna.

"I never turn down an offer to make serious money," he said at last.

"Good. Meet me at the Flora Bar. Let's say six."

He was about to hang up when she made a second request. "Just you, James. Don't bring your partner."

The Flora Bar was the newest place to be seen among the players in the New York City art market. It was located in the basement of the Met Breuer. Happy hour began at 5:30 p.m., and everyone certainly looked happy when James walked in. He immediately saw Allison at a table in the corner, a drink in her hand.

She had changed her outfit. This morning she'd worn a suit—gray flannel, if James recalled correctly. There was nothing remotely business-like about this evening's ensemble, however. Black, tight, and low cut.

"Twice in one day," James said as he approached.

"I'm tempted to say, 'That's what she said,' but I won't."

"But you just did."

She laughed. "Touché."

A waiter was on them fast. "Can I get you something from the bar?"

"Jack Daniel's, neat," he said.

As soon as the waiter left to fetch his drink, James said, "I trust that Noah's over the moon with his new acquisition."

"He is. Not every day you have an original Jackson Pollock to call your very own."

"How'd you two meet, anyway? Last time I dealt with Noah it was . . . I don't know, a year, maybe two years ago. I sold him a very nice Miró. I remember he said it reminded him of his dog."

"Yes, that about sums up Noah's art expertise right there."

James took note that she had not answered his question about how they'd met. That likely meant that they had been at one time lovers, or still were.

The waiter returned with James's whiskey.

"To Jackson Pollock," he said, raising his glass.

"And to making money," she answered before clinking.

"You're quite direct and more than a little mercenary," James said. "Most of the art dealers I encounter like to talk about the beauty of the pieces before getting to the real reason we're meeting."

"Well, you should learn this about me right now: I'm not a beat-around-the-bush kind of girl. I tell it straight. And when I want something, I go straight for it. No hesitation."

It was becoming readily apparent to James that the Pollocks weren't the only thing that Allison Longley wanted out of this meeting. "Cheers to that," he said, and they both took another swig.

She was nearly finished with her drink. "Catch up, will ya?" she joked. "I never talk business until the second drink."

She flashed a temptress's smile if ever James had seen one. Openmouthed and inviting, with a subtle show of tongue between the teeth.

"Then you're going to have to make small talk because I never rush a glass of whiskey."

"Challenge accepted. Let's start with you. I see you're married," she said, looking down at his wedding band.

"Yes. Just celebrated my one-year anniversary last week, in fact."

"So does that mean that there are no children yet?"

"I have a seventeen-year-old stepson."

"You're already surprising me. Why did I think your wife would be in her twenties?"

He laughed. "Because you're apparently the type of woman who jumps to unfounded conclusions about men. And you? I don't see a ring on your finger."

"And you never will. I'm not the marrying kind. But don't get me wrong. I have nothing against married men. In fact—"

"Some of your best friends are married men?"

She laughed. James finished his drink. She called the waiter over and asked for two more.

Allison segued to business as soon as the second round arrived. She said that she had other buyers interested in paying top dollar for an original Pollock like the one they'd just sold Noah Reiss and pressed

James about how many he could get his hands on. James did his best to be nonresponsive without seeming evasive, but he suspected that Allison saw through that act.

"How'd you get them?" she asked.

"I told you at the meeting. Our client had a relationship with Lee Krasner before she died."

"I know that's what you told me. But who *is* this mystery lover of the now more-than-thirty-years-deceased Lee Krasner?"

"I told you that too. His name is Anonymous."

"Strange that so many sellers of high-priced art were named the same thing by their parents, isn't it?"

"No odder than every butler being named Jeeves," James said with a sly smile.

She touched his hand. "Funny. You're very funny, you know that?"

"I have my moments."

"Moments," she said, as she finally removed her hand from atop his. "That's what life is really comprised of, isn't it? These spectacular moments without which the rest of it would be completely unbearable."

"You mean like selling a Pollock?"

"No. That is entirely *not* what I mean."

A long silence followed. James could see where this was going. Before Jessica, he'd closed many a high-priced deal not with a handshake but with intercourse.

"Here's the thing, James. I'll wager you cannot show me another Pollock this evening."

She looked at him hard. A challenge in her eyes.

"What are the terms?"

"Whatever you want them to be."

James hesitated for a moment, as if considering whether to take that bet. The truth was, he was already all in.

Haley still had a key to James's office. It had been his home back when they'd met until after they'd wedded, at which time he'd moved into her place. When they got divorced, James moved into the loft, and likely had forgotten that he'd ever given Haley a key to the office because, if he had remembered, he would have certainly changed the locks.

She didn't use the key very often. Maybe once a month. Okay, sometimes twice. But she knew that frequency was hardly the issue. That was why it was her secret. She hadn't even told Dr. Rubenstein about it.

She had googled "is it breaking and entering if you have a key," and the unequivocal answer was *yes*. No loophole. If your presence was not permitted—and hers was certainly not—then it was illegal to enter. A criminal act, in fact. Although whether it was the misdemeanor of criminal trespass or the felony of burglary depended on whether she intended to commit a crime, which was never clear, even in her own mind.

She took precautions to avoid detection, of course. She only ever entered after James left for the day. Even then, she waited at least thirty minutes in case he had forgotten something and decided to double back. And her visits were usually brief. She'd use the flashlight in her phone to see what was on James's desk. Sometimes, if he hadn't logged off his computer, she'd read his emails, hoping to see evidence of a fight with Jessica, or better yet, proof he was cheating on her. So far, at least, she hadn't. To the contrary, the emails between them were so saccharine they made her want to vomit. How much they missed each other. Or lamer, what kind of wild sex they were planning.

Today she was looking for evidence that whatever deal James and Reid were cooking up was illegal. Unfortunately, James's computer was locked. She wondered if he had done that because he and Reid were engaged in something shady.

She moved straight to the credenza. If James was hiding something, it would be there.

It too was locked. Normally it was not. To Haley, that was tantamount to a smoking gun. James was definitely hiding something.

Haley doubted that she'd find any answers in the bedroom, but now that she was here, she couldn't resist entering the inner sanctum. It was pitch dark, but she didn't dare risk turning on the light. Instead, she positioned the flashlight on her phone to guide her.

That was when Haley heard the most frightening sound of her life.

The front door was opening.

James had come back.

And he wasn't alone. A woman's laugh followed him in.

Not Jessica's. Haley had that woman's cackle committed to memory.

Haley hid in the bedroom closet, petrified. What if he found her? Would he prosecute her? Would Jessica insist on it?

But then she realized she had it all backward. Yes, it was perilous, but she was not the one in peril. James was. He would have to explain to Jessica why he was in his office after business hours with another woman.

From her vantage point inside the bedroom closet, Haley could not see what was going on in the main room. She could hear them, though. The sound was garbled, but foreplay always sounds the same, even without the words.

The credenza door clicked open. James reaching for a bottle of wine, perhaps. Then their voices went silent. They must have started kissing.

Haley knew that meant that they'd enter the bedroom shortly. She reached for her phone, ready to video the entire scene through the crack in the closet doors. Even in her wildest fantasies, she hadn't imagined procuring a sex tape starring James and the woman he was cheating with. She was nearly salivating at the thought of Jessica's face when she clicked on the email Haley would send her and saw a video of James doing to her what he'd done to Haley.

A few minutes later, the light from the other room allowed her to make out the contours of a person entering the bedroom. Not James, but the woman.

Haley couldn't see her face, but that didn't mean that she was unable to draw certain assumptions.

Not Jessica—confirmed.

James's latest conquest was thin, almost to a childlike degree. Apparently, James had opted for a little variety for this round of infidelity.

Haley tried not to breathe. The toilet flushed. The faucet ran, then didn't. The bathroom door opened.

When the woman emerged from the bathroom, Haley finally saw her from the front. She was a bit flat-chested for James's taste, and her hair was short, like a boy's. But she was still the type to turn Haley's ex-husband's head. And the way she was dressed suggested she was fully committed to the task at hand.

James must have heard the bathroom door open too because he had made his way to the bedroom. Just Haley's luck—he had positioned himself in front of the closet. Now all she could see was the back of his suit jacket. She strained her eyes and focused her hearing, trying to block out the sound of her beating heart.

Were they kissing again? Was that why she couldn't hear anything?

"Shall we?" James said.

It seemed an odd way for him to suggest that they should have sex, but maybe that's what James considered gallant these days. She imagined him extending his arm over the bed, like a game show model showing off a new car.

"Yes," the woman said.

Haley checked to make sure the camera side of her phone didn't emit any light. Once satisfied she would go undetected, she pressed the record button and pointed it at James's back.

James moved a step forward. Haley waited for them to fall onto the bed. It would be any moment now.

Then, everything changed. James stepped aside so that the camera captured the woman. In a flash, however, she moved out of the frame too.

They weren't heading to the bed, after all. They had returned to the main room and were there only briefly. A few seconds later, Haley heard the front door open, then shut behind them.

———

Jessica had a strict no-phones-at-the-dinner-table policy. But the moment she heard the ring, she jumped up to answer it.

"It might be James," she said to Owen by way of explanation.

Once the phone was in her hand, however, she knew that was not true. The caller ID was from a number outside of her contacts.

Jessica thought for a second about letting it go to voice mail, then changed her mind.

"Is this Jessica Sommers?" said a man's voice.

"It is."

"Ask your husband how he enjoyed fucking that short-haired, skinny bitch," he said.

"What?"

"You heard me. Just ask him."

"Who is this?"

The connection went dead.

Jessica assumed it was Haley. Not the voice, obviously, but that she was behind the call. There had been other calls like this in the past. *Just want to tell you that your husband fucked me so good last night* kind of things.

More often than not, James had been home when the supposed fucking had occurred, and so there was no reason for Jessica to be concerned that it might be true. But there hadn't been a call like this in a few weeks, maybe a few months. It was the specificity with which the caller described the other woman—short-haired and skinny—that Jessica found most alarming. If Haley were going to make some woman up, why call her short-haired and skinny? Wouldn't a twisted mind like Haley's conjure up a more threatening image—big breasts and wild hair?

"Who was that?" Owen asked.

"No one."

"You don't look like it was no one."

"It was no one for you to concern yourself about," she said.

Jessica hated to admit it, but Haley had achieved her purpose. All through dinner, she couldn't get the mental image of James with a short-haired, skinny woman out of her head.

As the hours passed without James coming home, Jessica's imagination began to get away from her, and as it did, her anger bubbled closer to the surface. At ten, she went upstairs and got into bed. She knew she wouldn't go to sleep until James arrived home, but she might as well not be sitting up in the living room with her arms folded when he did.

A half hour later, he was standing in the bedroom. Even though the room was illuminated by only her bedside lamp, she could tell that his cheeks were flushed. His hair even seemed slightly tousled.

"I'm so sorry I'm late," James said. "The traffic was ridiculous tonight. The president's in town, and for some reason that means that they have to close off the entire FDR or something."

He began to undress. As he unbuttoned his shirt, Jessica wondered if he was trying to get out of his clothes quickly so she wouldn't see some telltale sign of his infidelity. Lipstick on his collar or the scent of her perfume.

"How was your dinner?" she asked.

"Good."

Jessica had been hoping for a more informative response. She remembered how, back when she was living a double life, she'd adhered to the mantra that "less is more" when parceling out info to Wayne.

"Where'd you go?"

"Eleven Madison."

Eleven Madison Park was among the most expensive, to say nothing of romantic, restaurants in the city. Dinner for two would clock in at about $1,000.

"That must have cost you a pretty penny. Is your client buying the entire Museum of Modern Art?"

"Actually, it didn't cost me even a penny. She paid."

"Oh, she did, did she?"

"And she's not a client. Not really. She's more of a broker. Remember I told you that I sold her the Pollock today? Well, I sold it to her client. Then, after you left this afternoon, she called and said that if I could get more, she had other buyers. So it's possible that I can raise enough for Owen's entire treatment with just her clients."

The righteous indignation that had gripped Jessica since she'd answered the phone at dinner immediately dissipated. She was being foolish. James's dinner was a business meeting. The purpose of which was to raise money for Owen. Even if it was with a woman at a romantic restaurant and ran late, that didn't mean he'd slept with her. Besides, James had seemed plenty sated when she'd left him that afternoon.

She watched her husband continue to disrobe. When he was wearing only his boxer shorts, he rolled back the comforter and slid into bed beside her.

"I've been thinking lately that I might be psychic," she said.

"Is that a fact?"

"It is. And right now, I'm getting the very strong psychic vision that your dinner companion tonight was short-haired and thin?"

An odd smile came to James's mouth. "Were you at the restaurant?"

"No."

"Then who told you?"

"Your *other* wife."

His smile disappeared. "What did Haley do this time?"

Jessica sighed. "While Owen and I were having a lovely lasagna dinner, I received a phone call. A man's voice on the other line told me to ask my husband how he enjoyed fucking the thin, short-haired bitch."

"Jesus," James said. "I'm so sorry, Jessica. That's terrible."

"It is now that I know you were at the most romantic restaurant in Manhattan with a thin, short-haired woman."

James rolled closer to her until their faces were only inches apart. "Of all the gin joints in all of Manhattan, right? What are the odds that Haley would be at Eleven Madison on the same night I was? But it doesn't matter. There's no excuse for her calling you. I'll reach out to Amanda tomorrow and see about getting her to file something in court. This craziness has got to stop."

"Just tell me that I have nothing to worry about, James. Please."

He kissed her on the lips. "Jessica, I love you. You have nothing to worry about. Not now. And not ever."

He certainly looked sincere. Then again, so had Jessica when she made the same promises to Wayne.

9

Owen thought it was odd that, when he exited his bedroom on the way to school the following morning, James was sitting at the dining table. His stepfather almost always slept later than anyone else. Owen might have assumed that James had an early meeting had it not been for the fact that he was still wearing pajamas.

"You got a few minutes to have some breakfast?" James said. "I'm having a delicious and nutritious bowl of Cap'n Crunch. Fix yourself one and join me."

Owen was usually pressed for time in the morning, but as luck would have it, today he was running early. Besides, Cap'n Crunch actually sounded good. Owen poured himself a bowl of cereal and sat down beside James.

"Your mom told me that you all had a good doctor's visit yesterday. I know that it's a tough road ahead for you, but I also know that you can handle it."

Owen's usual comeback when someone said something in this vein was to point out that he didn't really have much choice in the matter. Inside, he wondered if he really could handle it.

Neither response seemed right here. He hoped that he could go without replying, but when it seemed as if James was waiting for an answer, he offered up, "I guess."

"I don't need to guess. I know."

Owen was glad that James, who would not lose his hair or feel sick as a dog for weeks or spend more than a month in the hospital, had such confidence that Owen could endure all those things. Another lie from someone who had no idea what the truth was.

James took a spoonful of cereal. Before he had finishing chewing, he said, "I understand your mom got a very disconcerting phone call last night."

This was undoubtedly the reason James had gotten himself out of bed early this morning. "Yeah. She seemed upset by it."

"I know. It came from Haley. Or at least Haley asked some poor sap to make the call for her. Haley's crazy. I'm sorry to say it like that, but, sadly, it's just a fact. I don't know if anyone ever told you this, but Haley used to be an investment banker. She worked at a top-tier firm. After she and I got divorced, totally unrelated to our split, she had this problem at work and got fired. She says she's unemployable now because of it. I don't know if that's true, but I do know that she blames me for every bad thing that's happened in her life since we split up. Probably blames me for climate change at this point too."

James chuckled, but Owen could eke out only the smallest of smiles. He was still waiting for James to get to the purpose of this tête-à-tête.

"Anyway, she's so filled with hate these days she's become unstable," he continued. "Like what she did at our anniversary party."

Owen nodded. "Yeah. That was messed up."

"Messed up seems to be Haley's specialty lately. Anyway, I wanted to tell you that I'm really sorry that she's been so intrusive. It's not fair to you and your mom. Me either, really, but I can take it, and besides, I was fool enough to marry her. But you and your mom, you're just collateral damage. I'm going to talk to my lawyers to make sure this stops, once and for all. And finally, and far most importantly, I wanted to tell you what I told your mom last night. What Haley—or her boy toy—said is just not true. The short-haired woman Haley saw me with last night is named Allison. She's just a business colleague. We're doing a deal together. Your mom and I are solid. Trust me on that."

So that was what the call was all about. Some guy claiming James was cheating.

And now James wanted Owen, who had known him for barely two years, to trust him when he claimed he was faithful, while his own mother was still lying to him about her own infidelity.

"Okay, thanks for telling me," Owen said. Then he scooped a spoonful of sugary cereal.

———

James still wasn't sure that he had convinced Owen that everything between him and Allison was on the up-and-up when his phone rang. Speak of the devil—it was Allison.

He looked at Owen, still eating his Cap'n Crunch.

"You're going to really love me now," Allison said.

James mouthed to Owen, "Work." Then he began making his way into the kitchen for some privacy. "Why am I really going to love you now, Allison?" he said into the phone.

"Because I've got the perfect buyer for the Pollocks. The guy's been my client for about ten years. When I told him that I could get him some original Pollock sketches with paint splatter, he said, and I quote, 'I don't care about the price.' And get this, I told him that you're asking a million per, and that still didn't spook him. When we meet, I'll counter at eight hundred grand, and then we'll shake hands at nine."

That was the way the art world worked. It was the Wild West. Every broker was out for him- or herself, and the clients had no clue. It wasn't like your broker was your lawyer, with a fiduciary duty to represent your best interests. It was more akin to a real estate transaction. There might be brokers on both sides, but they were loyal only to the deal.

Allison got paid a percentage of the purchase price from the buyer, and James took a percentage from the seller. Or in his case, half of Reid's percentage. The higher the price, the more found its way to them.

Given that incentive structure, brokers never cared about fairness. Their first duty was to close the deal. Their second duty was to do it at the highest price possible. There was no third duty.

"He wants to meet today," she said. "Just tell me when and where."

"How about four at my office?"

"Perfect. I actually think we can run the table with this guy. The remaining three in one deal. I'll tell him that the more he owns, the more each piece is worth. Kind of like how having a monopoly increases the value of each property."

James thought the analogy fitting. Who wouldn't be convinced to buy millions of dollars of art based on the logic of a board game?

———

Reid arrived at James's office at a quarter to four. Despite the fact that he was about to be a million dollars richer, he was hopping mad.

"When did you and Allison arrange to sell *my* Pollocks?"

James smiled at the implicit accusation.

The reaction made Reid angrier by confirming that he was on the right track. James was screwing him over.

"Last night. We had dinner, and she told me she might have this other buyer. She called me this morning and said her guy wants all three of them today, and is willing to pay nine hundred per. The first thing I did after hearing that was to call you. So, unless you have an objection to making some serious money, I don't see the problem."

"The problem is you don't fucking meet with her behind my back to discuss *my* deal—a deal that you're only in because of my good graces. That's the fucking problem, James."

"I'm sorry. She wanted to see me alone."

"Oh, *she* wanted to. Makes it easier to fuck her, I assume."

"Let's keep our eye on the ball, shall we? I thought you were in this to make some money. Not to get laid. And not to keep tabs on my love life. So stop worrying about whether I'm fucking Allison, and start thinking about how you're going to spend the money we're going to earn on this deal."

"I don't care who you fuck. I care if the two of you are going to fuck me."

That's when the buzzer sounded. Allison was there.

"Take a deep breath, Reid. No one is fucking you. But if you want to turn away three million dollars because you're jealous, just say the word and I'll send them away."

Reid wasn't one to cut off his nose to spite his face. Especially when money was on the line. A lot of money.

Still, he didn't like the way this was going.

And then things only got worse when Allison arrived. She was alone.

"My client couldn't get out of DC," she said. "His instructions are for me to look at the merchandise. If I give the okay, he wants me to deliver them to him in DC this evening. As soon as I get there, he'll make payment in cash to me."

"No fucking way," Reid said. "You think I'm going to trust you with three Pollocks? Not to mention nearly three million dollars in cash after you sell them?"

"Thanks for the vote of confidence. But I wasn't proposing doing it alone. James can come. In fact, I want him there."

"No. They're mine. I brought James into this. I'll go with you."

"No offense, Reid, but I'm not doing that. I trust James, and I don't know you. I'm not going to be alone with some guy I don't know with a suitcase filled with cash. I'm sorry, I just don't feel safe doing that."

Reid did not like this. Not one bit.

He was getting that hinky feeling again. In spades.

———

"Jesus, James, really? Why can't Reid go?" Jessica said.

"I suggested that. She said she knows *me*, not Reid. I'd rather not go either. But remember why I'm going, okay? If all goes well, I'll be coming back with enough money to pay for the rest of Owen's treatment."

He was right. With effort, Jessica put her suspicions aside.

"Are you coming home to get a change of clothes?"

"No time, I'm afraid. I'll have to wear the same suit for tomorrow's meeting. Maybe I'll buy a shirt on the way down."

"Okay," she said, then debated how much nagging she wanted to do. One more, she told herself, and then she'd stop. "Just promise me one thing, will you?"

"Anything, Jessica."

"You'll be home first thing in the morning."

"Yes," he said with a chuckle. "I swear to you that, come hell or high water, I'll be on the first Acela in the morning. Reid will be angrier at me than you if I'm not, believe me. He wants his money yesterday."

"Okay. You have a safe trip. I'll miss you."

"I'll miss you too, Jessica. I love you."

"Love you too."

———

Haley ordered her second martini even though it was not yet four. For reasons that she was certain Dr. Rubenstein could make sense of, nearly being caught the other night had scared her to the core, but not enough to keep her away from Sant Ambroeus to see what today might bring. Her appetite whetted, she was craving more.

Not a minute after she arrived, Haley saw Reid enter James's office building. A few minutes after that, the skinny, short-haired woman from the other night went in.

Haley was trying to make her drink last when she saw Reid exit the building. She caught only a glimpse, but he looked angry. About a half hour after that, the woman left. In sharp contrast to Reid, she had a self-satisfied smile on her face.

"Another round, miss?" the bartender asked.

"Yes, please." She smiled at him. "It looks like I'm gonna be here awhile."

———

Wayne was uneasy. He tried to calm himself, but he knew that was a losing proposition. Even a couple of beers had done nothing to ease his nerves.

Owen arrived exactly when the pizza did. At dinner, he barely said a word, no matter how Wayne tried to engage him. Wayne knew it was because of what awaited his son tomorrow at Sloan Kettering, a final determination as to whether he'd be admitted into the protocol. Other kids his son's age were worried about their college acceptances, whereas Owen was waiting to hear whether he would live or die.

"Can you text me as soon as you hear?" Wayne asked. "I wanted to be there tomorrow, but we have this mandatory faculty thing. I tried to get out of it, but—"

"It's fine. Yeah, I'll text you as soon as I know."

"And not like you texted me as soon as you got on the subway tonight, right?"

Owen offered a sheepish smile. "No. I'll actually do it tomorrow. I promise."

Wayne began clearing the table, but when he reached Owen's seat, rather than grab his son's plate, he placed his hand on Owen's shoulder.

"I love you, Owen. I'm so proud that you're my son."

Wayne had said such things countless times to Owen in the past. He assumed that such expressions of affection were like white noise to a teenager. Owen certainly never reciprocated the sentiment, but Wayne didn't care about that. He wanted his son to know that he was loved and valued, something Archibald Fiske had never thought important to convey to Wayne.

Owen averted his eyes, his usual reaction to any effort at intimacy. He looked, if anything, embarrassed rather than loved. Still, Wayne was glad to have said it. He wanted his son to know that he would do anything for him.

PART THREE

10

Haley awoke momentarily confused. It was still dark outside, and even though she could not see a foot in front of her, she knew she was in a foreign place. Then she saw Malik's chiseled bicep above the blanket, and it all came rushing back.

Little more than twelve hours earlier, she had been at Sant Ambroeus, sitting at the bar. She got there at four, and although she hadn't checked the time, she assumed it was hardly past five when she went inside James's office. She'd fled like a bat out of hell no more than five minutes later.

Her plan thereafter had been simple: go to Malik's apartment, immediately get him into bed, and when they were done, try to confuse him about what time she had arrived. Her hope was that after enough carnal activity, he would believe she'd shown up an hour earlier than she actually had, and therefore would later tell the police that she'd been with him from five o'clock until morning.

Malik worked what he called "freelance." She thought that was a euphemism for *not too often*. He did something computer-related but was never too descriptive about how he spent his days, and she'd never had any reason to care. She did have a reason last evening, of course. If he hadn't been home or was on his way to work, her entire plan would've been shot to hell.

She'd assumed Malik's walk-up building north of the Grand Concourse in the Bronx had limited security, but she didn't take any chances. She'd pulled her hood over her head and kept her face down. Then she'd pressed the buzzer and uttered a silent prayer that he answered.

It took longer than she imagined it should for Malik to cross what she knew to be a small apartment. But she eventually heard his voice coming through the intercom.

"Who is it?"

"It's Haley. Can I come up?"

"What you doing here, girl?"

"Wouldn't you rather me show you than tell you?"

As she had expected, getting Malik to drop what he was doing to have sex with her had not been difficult. After, he'd fallen right to sleep. When he awoke an hour later and asked what time it was, Haley answered quickly: "Time to go again."

That ended the conversation for the next hour. Malik's slumber the second time was marked by the deep guttural sound of his snoring, which signaled that he was down for the count.

Sleep was to be only intermittent for Haley, however. Every time she shut her eyes in hopes that darkness would erase her thoughts, she was brought back to the images she feared she'd never shake.

In an hour, it would be sunrise. Haley wouldn't be able to continue to hide in Malik's apartment. The new day required that she go on with her life, as if she had no knowledge of what had transpired in James's office last night.

———

Owen had an 8:30 a.m. appointment at Memorial Sloan Kettering.

He got there before eight and took a seat in the hospital waiting room, which was officially designated as the Clinical Cancer Trial Family and Friends Area. His mother arrived less than five minutes later.

"Looks like we're both early worms," she said.

"Birds," he said.

"What?"

"Early birds. They're the ones who catch the worms. Worms are always there, I think."

She laughed. "Before caffeine, my brain doesn't work."

The space must have been recently remodeled. It looked more like a hotel lobby than a hospital waiting room. The furniture had virtually no signs of wear. Two imposing Keurig machines filled the room with the aroma of coffee.

His mother was in the process of making herself a cup when the receptionist called Owen's name.

"Good luck." His mom looked as if she wanted to hug him, but he moved quickly to avoid any physical contact. "I'll be here when you're done," she called after him instead.

A nurse met him on the other side of the door. She was older, with a cheerful smile that Owen assumed was standard issue for people who chose a career with cancer patients.

She led Owen to an exam room. After opening the door, she said, "The doctor will be in with you shortly."

Alone in the exam room, Owen couldn't deny that he was nervous. It seemed a somewhat odd emotion for him to experience in the moment. He often was anxious before he played in front of an audience, but nerves made sense in that situation because he was about to do something at which he could succeed or fail. But in this instance, everything was already set. All that awaited was discovery. There was no reason for him to be nervous, because the die had already been cast.

Easier said than done, he thought. What was discovered in the next few hours would determine whether he had a future.

Jessica sat in the waiting area, trying to keep her emotions in check. The doctors had previously told her that today's appointment would not take more than a few minutes. They only needed to confirm a few things, and then they'd be able to determine whether he was a viable transplant candidate.

After thirty minutes of waiting, Jessica told herself that she wouldn't be one of those moms—demanding answers from an intake nurse who didn't have any to give. Instead, she'd quietly bide her time. Maybe at the one-hour mark she'd make an inquiry, as politely as possible, of course.

While she was mentally composing her request, she felt her phone vibrate. The room had at least four signs that said **ABSOLUTELY NO CELL PHONE USAGE**. That couldn't apply to *checking* your phone, she reasoned.

The caller ID said *Reid Warwick*.

Sorry, everyone. Gotta answer it.

"Hello?" she whispered.

"Have you spoken to James today?"

She remembered her husband saying that Reid would kill him if he wasn't back in New York first thing this morning. Still, it was barely nine. Even if James had taken an early Acela, he wouldn't be back in Manhattan for another hour, at least, so it seemed early for Reid to get antsy about not getting his money.

"Um, no. Not since yesterday."

"What time yesterday?"

The nurse said, "Ma'am, you can't talk on the phone in here. Please go outside."

"I'm sure he's on his way," she said, still whispering.

Reid didn't reply. At least not at first. Then he said, "I'm at James's office. There are police everywhere. James wasn't answering my calls, so I decided to see if he was back already. But when I told the cops that I was going to apartment 7E, they said that they couldn't let me up because it's a crime scene."

———

Wayne knew Owen's appointment was at 8:30 a.m. He had hoped to receive a text from Jessica during his second-period class. But it passed without word from either of them. He was well aware that bad news did not take longer to disseminate than the good kind. He assuaged himself with the thought that there must be some delay at the hospital and that Jessica would call or text as soon as she had any news.

By the time his third period began, Wayne could no longer help himself. He had fifty minutes without students, a break he wouldn't get again until lunchtime.

He left the school building, and almost the moment he stepped outside, the snow began to come down in earnest. As soon as he positioned himself under some scaffolding across the street, he called Jessica. It rang twice, then went to her voice mail.

He assumed that had happened because she'd declined the call, but he wasn't the most tech-savvy person, so he wasn't entirely sure. He tried again. This time it went directly to voice mail. That confirmed his initial suspicion that Jessica had turned off her phone after screening him the first time. Again, though, he couldn't be sure.

After the beep, he said, "Hi, Jessica. It's Wayne." He hated identifying himself when he called, but for some reason he felt that was now required, as if their divorce decree also erased Jessica's ability to recognize the sound of his voice. "I'm just calling to find out how Owen's appointment went. I figured that you'd call if there was any news, so that means that the doctor doesn't know anything yet, but if you could call me as soon as you're done, or even if you're not done, and just tell me whatever he said, even if he didn't say anything, I would really appreciate it."

It was a stupid message. He should have sent a text. At least then he could have reviewed it. Ironically, he took some solace in the fact that he was near certain that Jessica never listened to his voice mails. She likely would see that he'd called and either call him back or not, but he couldn't imagine she'd spend time listening to the message he'd left. After all, she knew why he was calling.

Trying to reach Owen directly would be a fool's errand. He was probably still in with the doctor. *Still . . .*

Sure enough, his call to Owen followed the same pattern: rang twice, then went to voice mail. His second try ended the same way.

He sent Owen a text instead:

Can't reach ur mom. If ur out of dr, please call asap.

———

It was Gabriel's job to get up with their newborn daughter. Ella handled Annie's 3:00 a.m. feedings solo, but after that, she was off the clock until he left for work.

Gabriel Velasquez enjoyed these predawn hours as much as he could recall enjoying anything in his life. Time spent on his knees beside Annie, making funny, soothing noises and waiting until she rewarded his efforts with a smile, even though he knew her reaction resulted from gas rather than amusement.

He often wondered what the other cops would think if they saw him in these moments. They'd give him shit for it—that he knew. Gabriel had spent years cultivating something of a tough-guy, no-nonsense reputation among his fellow officers. At the same time, he assumed that everyone made animal noises and rolled on the floor with their newborns. If they didn't, they definitely should.

His phone rang before seven. He grabbed it quickly so it wouldn't rouse Ella from the few hours of sleep she enjoyed each day.

Only his captain would be calling at this ungodly hour. And he'd be doing so only if he wanted Gabriel to run point on an important new case.

That was the last thing Gabriel wanted today. Six months ago, he would have crawled through broken glass to be put in charge of a big case. But now, with a new baby and a sleep-deprived wife, he'd gladly let someone else in the unit have the honor.

"Absolutely," was what he said instead in response to Captain Tomlinson's request. You did not get promoted by turning down high-profile cases, after all.

Gabriel had made lieutenant five years earlier. All indications were that he was on the fast track to captain and a precinct of his own to run. After that, who knew how high he could climb? The Commissioner Velasquez jokes that had been made since he was a rookie didn't sound so silly now.

"Excellent," Tomlinson said. "Asra can back you up. Show her how to run a first-rate investigation. That way, when you're sitting in my chair and you need to assign someone to get the Chief off your ass, you'll have someone as good as I do."

Gabriel smiled at the compliment. "Thanks, skip."

Tomlinson was a navy man, having served a tour of duty in the first Gulf War. He preferred to be called skip or skipper, even though, as Gabriel understood it, Tomlinson had been only an ensign in his navy days.

"I don't have to tell you that the press is all over it."

Tomlinson was right. He didn't have to tell Gabriel that.

Despite the many crime dramas set in New York, Manhattan had one of the lowest crime rates for a major US city. Barely enough murders to fill a full season on network television. Fewer than thirty murders for all of last year. Those would hardly be compelling viewing, and certainly not whodunits. Ten had been gang-related, and half that many involved a drug deal. The rest were either the result of some other type of criminal activity or domestic violence cases.

All of which meant that Gabriel would likely be arresting a spouse.

Two hours after Captain Tomlinson had given him the assignment, Gabriel was behind the wheel of his NYPD-issued unmarked Ford Fusion with Asra Jamali riding shotgun. The traffic was stop-and-go, partly due to the falling snow but mainly because that's the way traffic always moved in Midtown Manhattan.

Gabriel knew next to nothing about his new partner other than the fact that she had earned her gold shield about three years ago and was Muslim. Although the ranks of Arab American cops had been growing steadily since 9/11—enough that the department had amended its no-beard policy to allow for religiously observant Muslims to serve—Muslims were still something of an anomaly in the NYPD, and female Muslim officers were rarer still. That Asra had also made rank meant that she was likely in a class by herself.

The other thing he knew about her was that some of the cops referred to her as Jasmine, the name of some Disney princess. They claimed it wasn't racist because it was a compliment. Gabriel knew better. He'd endured being called Ricky Martin and hearing chants of "Livin' La Vida Loca" for a good part of his early career.

He suspected that he was as much a mystery to Asra as she was to him. Likely all she knew about him was that he had run the investigation into the murder of Charlotte Broden a few years back, and once it was solved, he'd started dating the victim's sister. At least the relationship was no longer considered scandalous now that he and Ella were married and had a baby.

They rode up Park Avenue, barely saying anything to each other. At around Grand Central, the silence was broken by the ring of Gabriel's phone.

"My wife," he said. "I need to answer. We just had a baby."

Asra smiled as if to say that he didn't need to explain.

"Hi, sweetheart," he said into the phone.

"Annie misses her dada," Ella said. "I thought I'd put the phone up to her ear so she could hear your voice."

Gabriel knew it was Ella who missed him. She'd been half-asleep when he brought Annie into bed and said he had to go to work. He understood how isolating it was for a new mother to be alone with a baby. He sometimes said that he envied all the time Ella spent with Annie, but the truth was that he'd been happy to return to the job, much as he knew that Ella was champing at the bit to return to the DA's office as soon as her three-month maternity leave ended.

"I'm in the car on my way to a crime scene," Gabriel said. "But a quick call with Annie would be great."

He heard Ella's voice, now sounding far away. "She's on."

"Hi, sweetie," he said, his voice a few octaves higher than usual and feeling self-conscious about being "Dada" inches away from Asra. "Are you and Mommy having fun? Daddy loves you so much."

He heard nothing from the other end. Then Annie started to cry.

Ella's voice got louder as she resumed speaking directly into the phone. "She's been fussy this morning."

"I'm sorry if I revved her up before leaving."

"No, I'm sure that's not it. I think she really likes her daddy time. I know I do."

"What's on your agenda today?" he asked.

"I wanted to go to this exhibit at the Met on Roman architecture that closes this week, but it just started snowing."

"Go, Ella. Annie won't freeze. Besides, it's high time that baby got some culture."

He heard Ella laugh. "Okay. Maybe. I love you."

"Love you too."

After the call ended, Gabriel put the phone into the cup holder. He was now close enough to their destination that he was checking which side of Madison Avenue had the even-numbered buildings so he'd know where to park.

"Congratulations on your new baby," Asra said.

"Thanks."

"What's your little girl's name again?"

"Annie. Anne, actually."

"Old school. I like it."

"She's named after my wife's mother."

Asra smiled. "Me too. I mean, I'm named after my mother's mother. I like the idea of family names. It ties the past and the future."

Gabriel nodded. He liked that too.

The press vans were lined up one after another. They were all there: ABC, CBS, NBC, CNN, FOX. Even NY1, the city's local news station, had sent a camera crew. Gabriel pulled their vehicle beside a black-and-white cruiser parked in front of a fire hydrant.

"We just walk past the reporters," he said. "Nothing for us to tell them yet."

11

For once, Haley arrived on time for an appointment with Dr. Rubenstein. She took off her shoes, assumed the position on the couch, and immediately launched into the very serious problem on her mind.

Dr. Rubenstein didn't let her get ten words out before stopping her.

"I'm sorry, Haley," he said, not sounding the least bit contrite. "We can't discuss this."

She sat up so they were facing each other. One of the things that was so strange about the relationship Haley had with Dr. Rubenstein was that even though she saw him every week, and even though they had the most intimate relationship in her life at the moment, sometimes she doubted whether she could have picked the man out of a lineup. She saw his face only briefly, at the start and end of their sessions. Staring at him now, she was surprised to find that he was rather handsome. Strong-chinned with large dark eyes and a full head of chestnut curls.

Haley told him she didn't understand. Not even a little bit. She was in extremis, and Dr. Rubenstein was her therapist.

"There are certain ethical rules that therapists need to follow," he explained matter-of-factly without breaking eye contact. "Even regarding past acts, which this is, I prefer to err on the side of caution with my patients."

She knew what he was saying. And why. But he had never before told her to stop talking about a subject.

"I don't think that's right. I mean as a legal matter, Dr. Rubenstein. I'm not talking about committing some crime in the future. This has already happened."

She had googled this on her phone before today's session and was confident that she was correct. After all, criminals always tell their lawyers about their guilt. Wasn't that the whole point of attorney-client privilege? And she knew for a fact (or at least from TV) that murderers on death row were allowed to make confessions to clergy. Didn't therapists operate under the same principles?

"I really don't want to debate this with you, Haley," he said, a trace of anger in his voice that contrasted sharply with the soothing way he normally addressed the issues in her life. "There are lines in the doctor-patient relationship that I will not cross. I'm sorry, but this is my call to make, based on my interpretation of my ethical obligations. I'm not going to be talked out of it by you. If you would like, I can refer you to another therapist, and perhaps he or she will have a different interpretation than I do."

The last thing Haley wanted was a new therapist. It had taken so long for her to get to this point with Dr. Rubenstein. He knew her backstory and her secrets, at least most of them. The idea of reestablishing that intimacy with another person seemed impossible.

On the other hand, she knew that when a relationship was over, there was no point in pretending otherwise. At least the good doctor had been helpful in that regard.

"That's what I'm going to do, then," she said. "And I don't expect to be billed for this session either."

———

From Gabriel's vantage point on the street, the eighteen stories of pre-war limestone and brick before him looked like just another Upper East Side apartment building. The one difference was the lack of a doorman.

A keyed door, which could be opened remotely by tenants to allow guests entry, was the only security.

The directory revealed that many of the residents used their units for business purposes. The apartment they were going to—7E—was listed under the name Prestige Art LLC.

Gabriel and Asra arrived to a flutter of activity. The crime scene unit techs in their windbreakers doing their thing, and half a dozen uniformed police officers milling around. A photographer was on his knees, memorializing it all.

The living room was set up like an office. A desk sat under the window on the opposite side from the front door but faced into the room, two guest chairs on the other side of it. A second seating area was in the corner, comprised of four leather club chairs surrounding a large square coffee table, which had seen better days. Its glass surface was completely shattered, and its many shards were stained with blood, as was the expensive Persian rug beneath it.

The walls were stark white, the furniture all dark. The room's only splashes of color were provided by framed works of art on the walls. Gabriel was hardly a connoisseur, but he didn't recognize any of the pieces. Ironically, that almost surely meant that they were valuable.

The main point of interest, of course, was the dead body lying facedown on the floor between the seating area and the desk. The male figure was clad in a white terry-cloth robe. Even from across the room, the pool of dark crimson blood around the man's head was jolting.

A CSU tech was dusting for prints. The medical examiner, a woman named Erica Thompson, crouched by the body. She looked up and nodded toward Gabriel, and he returned the gesture.

"Why don't you look at the body and talk to the medical examiner to find out what she knows so far," Gabriel said to Asra. "I'm going to look around the place a little."

Gabriel began his investigation in the kitchen. Despite its small size, it was obviously high end. The cabinetry looked custom-made, the appliances were Sub-Zero stainless steel, and the countertop was granite.

The counter was barren, aside from an older-model microwave and a state-of-the-art coffee/cappuccino machine like Gabriel had seen in high-end restaurants. He opened the fridge. It was mostly empty. Four bottles of champagne and a bottle of white wine were lying on their sides, with a few cans of Diet Dr. Pepper beside them. No perishables other than a container of half-and-half. The butter compartment and the crispers were empty. The only item that appeared to have been put there in the last few days was a container of Chinese food. General Tso's chicken, if Gabriel had to guess from the orangey color.

The silverware drawer likewise revealed that the apartment's occupant didn't have people over for meals. There was a hodgepodge of utensils made out of cheap metal. The kind of spoons that would bend if you stuck them in frozen ice cream. That thought prompted Gabriel to open the freezer, which was even more barren than the refrigerator. A pint of Häagen-Dazs vanilla, a bottle of vodka, and nothing else but ice cubes.

On his way to the second room, Gabriel stopped in front of a credenza against the wall. It was wood but sleek, undoubtedly purchased more for aesthetics than security. He pulled on the door. Locked. It would have been the first place a burglar would have tried, and the lock was flimsy enough that anyone who was there to steal would have been able to pry off the door easily.

That meant that whoever did this wasn't trying to get rich. Their one and only objective had seemingly been accomplished when the dead man hit the floor.

Despite the fact that the living space was set up like an office, the second room had a king bed against the main wall. Apart from that, however, it was empty, giving off the vibe of a hotel room.

Gabriel's first thought was that their vic was a bachelor. A man who literally lived at his office.

The bed was disheveled. Gabriel leaned over to examine the sheets. You didn't have to have a degree in forensics to know that a woman had been in them since they'd last been laundered. A high-end man's timepiece sat on the night table.

The bathroom reminded Gabriel of the kitchen—small but with high-end finishes. The medicine cabinet housed the essentials: tooth-brush, toothpaste, deodorant, a bottle of aspirin, and dental floss. A single white towel hung on one of the two hooks. The white robe on their vic had most likely resided on the other.

One dark suit hung in the closet. Gabriel checked the label. Tom Ford. Gabriel wasn't much of a fashionista, but he knew that Daniel Craig had worn Tom Ford in the last few Bond films, which meant this suit didn't come cheap. A tie and a white shirt were on a separate hanger, and a pair of black high-shine oxfords and dark socks were on the floor beneath them. Apart from that, the only other garment was a pair of boxer shorts that were on the floor beside the bed.

The lack of clothing caused Gabriel to rethink his initial bachelor-pad assumption. No one lived here full time. The term *love nest* came to mind, though the space could have been used for anything from an Airbnb rental to a commuter's pied-à-terre.

Whatever the apartment's purpose, the dead man had apparently come from a business meeting. Maybe he was on his way home before fate—or, more accurately, an attacker—intervened. On the other hand, perhaps he was planning to stay the night and wear the same suit, shirt, tie, and socks the next day.

When Gabriel reentered the main room, Asra and the medical examiner were crouching beside the body. Asra stood as Gabriel approached, but the ME continued her closer examination of the corpse.

"It looks as if the murder weapon is likely going to be the corner of the table here," Asra said.

Gabriel nodded, looking at the relative positions of the body and table. "You said murder weapon. So not an accident?"

"He wasn't alone. See here?" Asra was pointing at the streaked blood. "Someone moved him a bit. I'm hard-pressed to think of a scenario where he accidentally falls and there's this kind of blood, and whoever is with him moves the body but doesn't call the police."

"You have a preliminary TOD?" Gabriel asked.

Asra looked to the crouching ME. This was her bailiwick, after all.

"Right now, my best guess is sometime between three p.m. to maybe eight p.m. yesterday," Erica said while coming to her feet.

Gabriel considered the fact that the sheets had been used in the middle of the day. That said affair. Married people wait until bedtime, at least in his experience.

"The bed was used recently. For sex, not just sleeping," Gabriel said. "Maybe that's our vic's less-than-helpful friend."

"We'll do a full workup of the sheets," Erica said.

"Which likely means it's a *she* we're looking for," Gabriel said.

"Not very PC of you," Asra said, teasing him.

Gabriel considered the point. She was right. No reason the vic's lover had to be a woman.

"You have anything we can work with, Erica?" Gabriel said with a smile, the one that usually got him what he wanted.

"Well, since you're asking nice . . . I don't think someone deliberately smashed the man's head against his table. Might have happened that way, but not likely. What probably occurred was that someone took a swing at the vic, and he toppled over, causing him to hit his head, and that's all she wrote."

"What makes you say that?" Gabriel asked.

"The chin is scratched a bit, consistent with what you'd see from a blow to the jaw from a punch. Hard to tell definitively right now, though. Maybe he got the scratch when he hit the floor."

"Who is he?"

"There was a wallet in his coat pocket," Asra said. "James Sommers. His driver's license has a SoHo home address."

Gabriel took out his phone. "Summers like the season?"

"No. With an *o*."

He typed the dead man's name into Google. The search engine asked if he meant Jaime Sommers—the Bionic Woman. Gabriel smiled, recalling reruns of the show from when he was a kid.

"James Sommers" came up with a lot of hits. Gabriel refined the search to include "Prestige Art."

That did the trick. Staring up from his phone was information for James Sommers, president of Prestige Art. The address listed matched this apartment. A click later, Gabriel was looking at a picture of the dead man, whose actual face he still had not yet seen.

———

Reid felt less than comfortable standing around outside James's office building. He should have never even come here in the first place. Once he had and had seen all the commotion, he should have left at once. What kind of an idiot returns to the scene of the crime?

He assumed it would take Jessica close to an hour to get there from the loft, but less than ten minutes after he called, he saw her get out of a cab and run toward the front door, only to be intercepted by a uniformed policeman.

Reid watched her frantically gesturing to the cop. From her arm movements he deduced that she was asking to go inside. And from the shaking of the cop's head, it was clear he was having none of it.

"Officer," Reid said, walking toward them. "This is the owner of apartment 7E, Jessica Sommers."

"Who are you?" the cop—a boy in a uniform, actually—asked.

"I'm a friend of Mrs. Sommers. I just thought it might help if I vouched for her."

"Thank you," the boy-cop said, seemingly not thankful at all. "I'm sorry . . . Ms. Sommers, is it?" Jessica nodded. "Let me see if a detective or someone can talk with you. But until then, you have to stay here, behind the yellow tape. No one's allowed upstairs at this time."

"Officer, please, I just left my teenage son in the cancer ward at Sloan Kettering. Now I'm being told that there's some type of criminal activity in my husband's office. I didn't even know he was here. He told me he was in Washington, DC, last night. So, please, just tell me what's going on. I'm begging you."

"I don't know any of the details. But I'll make sure that a detective comes downstairs to talk to you as soon as they have any information."

Reid didn't think Jessica would remain upright when the police officer walked away. He put his arm around her, feeling her weight pull on him.

"It's going to be okay," he said.

She didn't even look at him. It was as if she already knew it wasn't going to be okay. Reid could hardly blame her, of course. He knew it too.

———

Neither Jessica nor Owen had replied by the time Wayne was back in his classroom, awaiting the arrival of his fourth-period class—AP bio. The kids swarmed in en masse, the normal rowdiness of seniors who had already submitted their college applications and no longer cared about anything that occurred during the school day.

Wayne had always felt a bit of resentment toward his students. To a one, they had no idea how privileged they were. The worst of the bunch actually thought he worked for them because the tiniest fraction of the ungodly tuition their parents paid went toward his salary. When Owen had fallen sick, however, Wayne's anger toward his students intensified.

Now they were not only rich but healthy, and each and every one of them took both for granted.

Normally he kept his anger toward his students in check and thought he did a pretty good job of educating them. But today, Wayne felt like he was about to burst.

"Settle down, everyone. We've got a lot to cover, so please, just settle down."

"Relax, Mr. Fiske," said Taylor Ferguson, one of God's favorites, born rich, handsome, and smart, though not as smart as he thought. "It's all good. No need to stress."

Wayne shut his eyes and took a deep, cleansing breath. Now was not the time to lose control. He needed to continue as if everything were fine.

———

To Owen's surprise, it had begun snowing while he was in the doctor's office. He doubted it would stick because nothing short of a nor'easter provided snow cover in Manhattan. But for the moment, at least, the snow gave the city a magical feel.

After the doctor, Owen would usually go back to school. But he had already missed orchestra practice and music theory, which were the classes he cared most about anyway. The rest of the day held the usual math and science crap, which bored him to tears. So he cinched his winter coat and began walking toward James's office, which was only about fifteen blocks away.

The falling snow had collected in his hair to the point that when he caught his reflection in one of the shop windows, he looked like he was wearing a powdered wig from the Revolutionary War. When he passed the diner that he and his father had gone to the other day, he caught the eyes of two girls wearing the green tartan skirts of some nearby private school—they must have been cutting class. They giggled in his general direction in a way he thought was complimentary, so he smiled back in their general direction.

A few blocks later he saw a line of police cars and an ambulance parked in front of the building where James worked. When he reached the corner, he became part of a small throng of people standing there.

Even through the crowd, Owen immediately spotted his mother. She was standing next to the long-haired guy he remembered who had taken up her attention at the party.

"Mom?" he called.

"Owen?" she answered, seeming surprised to see him.

"You told me that you'd be here, remember? That there was some problem at James's office."

His mother grimaced, her tell that she was about to lie. Maybe not a complete untruth, but Owen knew she wouldn't share everything she knew.

"I'm sure it's all going to be fine." Then, as if she had just remembered where he'd come from, she said, "What did the doctor say?"

"He said I'm in the program. He wants me to start the chemo as soon as possible. Like tomorrow, even."

It was almost like a switch had been flipped in her. His mother pulled him into her embrace. "That's wonderful news."

When she released him, the man beside her extended his gloved hand. "Hey, Owen. I'm Reid Warwick, a friend of . . . of James."

Owen shook Reid's hand with his own gloved one. As he did, he asked his mother, "What did they tell you about James?"

"Nothing yet. They told Reid that there was apparently some type of robbery or something in James's office. Unfortunately, James is not answering his phone, but I know he was in DC last night, and Reid hasn't heard from him either, so I just assume he's still in transit. His phone must be dead, and all this break-in stuff has nothing to do with him. Anyway, a police detective said he'll be down to talk to me soon. Of course, he said that nearly a half hour ago. I'm starting to freeze out here."

A man was approaching. By the swagger in his step, Owen knew he was a cop even before he saw the badge dangling from a chain around his neck.

12

Gabriel found this to be the toughest part of the job. Breaking the news of a loved one's death was always difficult, but in a murder, it was also the beginning of the interrogation.

Stepping into the cold, he saw that the snowfall was roughly the same intensity as earlier in the day. The cars already had a dusting, as did the shoulders of the people who thought it was important enough to stop whatever they had planned on doing that day in the hope that they might see a man leaving the building in handcuffs. Or more likely, based on the ambulance, laid out on a gurney.

It was always easy to pick out the family members from a crowd. Gawkers had an entirely different facial expression. For cops it was like the joke about the chicken and the pig concerning a bacon and egg breakfast. The chicken is involved, but the pig is committed.

He spotted the victim's spouse at once, aided by the fact that she fit his preconceived notion of the wife of an Upper East Side art dealer—attractive and wearing expensive shoes. Beside her was a man whom Gabriel might have mistaken for her husband had James Sommers not been lying dead upstairs. The man was also attractive and wearing expensive shoes. Between them was a teenage boy who didn't seem like he belonged to either of them, on account of the fact that he just didn't read as rich—he was too skinny, with long, unkempt hair and clothing on the grungy side.

"I'm Lieutenant Velasquez. Are you Ms. Sommers?"

"Yes," the woman, who seemed barely able to speak, said.

"Let's talk privately." He steered the woman away. The boy should not hear what he was going to tell her. At least not from the mouth of a cop.

They walked together until they were out of earshot and a police cruiser blocked them from the boy's view.

"I'm very sorry to tell you that your husband has been killed."

Jessica Sommers reacted to the news that her husband was dead by bringing her gloved hands up to cover her face. It was a typical reaction, as people often sought to conceal their grief. On the other hand, it also allowed suspects to hide their reactions.

Gabriel always waited at this point, letting the spouse ask what had happened. Sometimes they didn't do so immediately because they were in shock. But Gabriel always thought it was odd when that happened, and it usually made him think that the real reason they didn't ask the most obvious question was because they already knew the answer.

Jessica asked a different question when her hands fell away from her face. "Can I see him?"

She wore the unmistakable mask of grief. Everything fallen: her eyes, her mouth, her shoulders. Bereavement didn't look like anything else. Of course, that didn't mean it couldn't be faked.

"Yes. But not right now," Gabriel said. "It's a crime scene upstairs. No one's allowed in."

She nodded, as if she were hearing him in a foreign language and translating the words in her head. Then she asked the question that most people asked right away.

"What happened?"

"We're still investigating. But the preliminary conclusion is that it was a homicide."

She winced at the terminology. Gabriel had used it intentionally because of its vagueness. He wanted to see if the widow would seek more specifics. "How?" would be the most likely first question.

Instead she asked, "Who would want to kill James?"

"I was going to ask you that, Ms. Sommers. The first few hours of an investigation are the most critical, so any information you could give us would be extremely valuable. When did you last see your husband?"

"Yesterday."

"At what time?"

She started to cry. "No. That's not right. I didn't see James yesterday at all. He left for work before I got up, and he went to DC last night. We spoke by phone yesterday. That's when he told me that he needed to go to DC."

"What time did you speak to him yesterday?"

"I don't know, exactly. Five, maybe."

"Can you check? It's important to narrow down his time of death. Maybe you have the exact time on your phone."

She pulled her phone out of her handbag. Gabriel couldn't help but notice her screen saver was a family portrait.

"It was 4:53," she said. "That's when he called me."

That tightened the time of death by ninety minutes. Of course, that was only true if she was telling the truth. It would not have been difficult for her to have killed her husband an hour earlier, then used his phone to call her own to make it seem as if he were alive at 4:53.

Jessica Sommers certainly looked sincere. On the other hand, Gabriel knew from hard experience that was the worst way to assess a witness's veracity—by the way he or she looked. Sometimes he thought the most effective interrogations could be done blindfolded.

As if she could read his mistrust, she said, "Ask Reid."

"Is Reid the man who is here with you now?"

"Yes. Reid Warwick. He's my husband's partner on the deal that caused him to go to Washington."

"And is the boy with you your son?"

"Yes. Owen."

Gabriel knew that as bad as it was breaking the news to this woman that her husband had been murdered, it was nothing compared to what she was about to go through in the next few minutes when she had to tell her son that his father was dead.

"Why don't you break the news to your son, and I'll take a moment to talk to Mr. Warwick. After that, I'd like you to come back with us to the police precinct. You might be able to give us some helpful background information about your husband."

———

As she walked away from the detective and back to Owen and Reid, Jessica prepared herself to share the news with Owen. But when the moment arrived, she was unable to say the words.

"What?" Owen finally said.

She glanced at Reid; from the look in his eyes, he already knew.

"Let me give you some privacy," Reid said.

After he departed, Owen's patience ran out. "Just tell me, Mom."

"He's . . . dead," she said through tears. Then she added, "James," as if that part weren't clear enough.

She threw her arms around her son, burying her face into his shoulder. Owen usually resisted any physical intimacy, but this time he put his arms around her.

When they finally parted, she saw he was crying too. It had been a long time since she'd seen Owen shed a tear.

"How could this have happened?" she asked.

Owen didn't answer. Of course he didn't. How could he? He was seventeen years old, struggling to survive his second bout with leukemia.

She blinked hard. The second time her eyes stayed shut. When she opened them again, she looked past Owen and blinked twice more.

"Oh my God," she breathed.

The bystanders had finally been rewarded for their perseverance. The techs were wheeling her husband's body out of the building.

———

Reid was going to leave. He figured that Jessica would have her hands full with the police, and it wouldn't even register with her that he'd bolted the first chance he got. After all, he'd called her, which was more than his lawyer had said he should do.

"Sir," he heard a voice call to him. The tone was such that it could only be a cop speaking.

Reid acted as if he hadn't heard it, but a step later he felt a hand on his shoulder. When he turned, he saw the boy-cop again.

"Lieutenant Velasquez would like to talk to you for a moment," the boy-cop said.

"I have a business thing I'm already really late to—" Reid stopped his excuse. The detective who'd broken the news to Jessica was approaching.

"Reid Warwick?" he said, extending his hand.

Reid shook it. "Yes."

"I'm Lieutenant Velasquez. I'm sorry for your loss, but I wanted to ask you a few questions. Ms. Sommers told me that you and her husband were business partners, and so I was hoping that you could fill me in a little on what you were working on."

Reid's mind whirled, trying to figure out how to get out of this.

"Mr. Warwick?" Lieutenant Velasquez said, as if he thought that Reid's failure to respond had to do with his being in shock, rather than cold calculation.

"Yes, I'm sorry. It's . . . I just can't believe it. James and I were together just the other day."

"I understand how difficult that this must be for you. I'm not sure if Ms. Sommers told you this, but we have reason to believe that Mr. Sommers was murdered. The first few hours in the investigation are critical, and we need to re-create his whereabouts over the last few days. Who he met with, what he was doing, that kind of thing."

"Unfortunately, I can't right now. I have another appointment, and I have to be there. Give me your card and I'll call you later."

Reid moved to the right and took a step forward.

Velasquez blocked him with an outstretched arm. "Sir, I'm certain that what you have to do is very important. But I'm equally certain it's not as important as finding out who killed your friend and bringing that person to justice. I promise I won't take up too much of your time, but I do need for you to answer some questions now. The first one is for you to explain to me the business transaction you were doing with Mr. Sommers. I understand it required that he go to Washington last night, but it seems as if that didn't happen. Do you know why that is?"

Reid was boxed in, and he knew it. He was regretting not following his lawyer's advice from the get-go.

"Here's the thing, Detective . . . I can't go into any of that because I have pretty hardcore NDAs—nondisclosure agreements—with my clients. So even just telling you what I was working on would be a violation. Obviously, you need to know this stuff, and I'm happy to tell you; I just need to get client permission first. I'm sorry. I know that is making your job harder, but I just can't violate the terms of an agreement with a client and expect to keep the client in the future."

Lieutenant Velasquez didn't give ground but kept looking hard at Reid, as if that would cause him to divulge everything. Needless to say, Reid felt more than up to withstanding a withering stare.

He stepped to the left and walked by the lieutenant.

Wayne called Jessica's phone twice more in rapid succession when he entered the faculty lounge for lunch. Still going straight to voice mail.

"Wayne will know," Sandy Zukis said as Wayne was putting his phone away.

Zukis taught physics. He was a fat man who wore a god-awful hairpiece and had a penchant for loud plaid sports jackets.

"Know what?" Wayne asked.

"We're engaged in a rather high-stakes wager," Lori Tennyson said.

Lori was chairperson of the LOTE—Languages Other Than English—department.

"Lori *claims* that she's a *Star Wars* fan, but she doesn't think my Honda can do the Kessel Run in less than twelve parsecs," said Zukis.

That was the kind of thing Zukis would bet on. Especially to pull something over on someone who enjoyed movies because they were fun and didn't see them as an opportunity to demonstrate how smart you were.

"Um, I'm afraid I'm not in the mood for that today," Wayne said.

"There's twenty bucks on the line," Zukis said. "Not to mention the pride of the science department, which she's mocking by her challenge."

"Just google it," Wayne said.

Zukis was laughing. "A parsec is a unit of distance. Three point two six light-years. So when Han Solo claims the *Millennium Falcon* could do the Kessel Run in twelve parsecs, he's not saying anything that anyone can't do. Hell, I could crawl the Kessel Run in twelve parsecs, because a parsec is a distance of measure, not time. It has nothing to do with speed." He was laughing again. "But I won't have to crawl, because I can take a cab with the twenty bucks I just earned from Lori."

Lori was smiling, but it was the smile of someone who knew she was being laughed *at*, not *with*. As she reached into her purse to satisfy the bet, Wayne decided to be her knight in shining armor.

"What were the actual terms of the wager?" he said.

"That, given enough time, my Honda could do the Kessel Run in less than twelve parsecs," Zukis said. "It might take my Honda forever, but it would eventually cover the twelve parsecs."

"Well, I'm not an expert, but because George Lucas isn't here, and since you've empowered me with this decision, I call it a push. The Kessel Run might not be a race, after all. It could be a route. Maybe he was saying that he found a unique way to make it through that path and was able to reduce the distance to get there. Like saying you made it to the airport in fourteen miles by taking side streets. And since it's in space, I'm not sure your Honda could navigate that path, Sandy. Even if you had all the time in the world."

"Good enough for me," Lori said with a victory smile that a Super Bowl champion would envy. She put the twenty dollars back in her purse. "Wayne, I owe you a drink. The Smith? After work."

"Thanks, but I'm gonna need to take a rain check on that. Today's not a good day for me."

———

Owen's mother told him to go to his father's home.

That was the first significant thing Owen had learned about his parents' divorce. He had no home of his own. Before, they'd told him to "go home." Or they'd meet him "at home." No qualifier needed. It was as much his as anyone else's. But after, he was going to *his mother's* apartment, or *his father's* house. Neither belonged to him. He was, essentially, homeless, despite the fact that he had two bedrooms filled with his stuff.

"You sure?" he said. "I mean, I don't want you to be alone tonight."

She smiled through her tears. "That's so sweet. But, yeah, I'm sure. I'm going to be at the police station for a while, and then I have some phone calls to make. It will take one thing off my plate if I know you're being fed and getting to school in the morning. I'll call your doctor too and set up the chemo."

"Are you sure about the treatment?"

This question seemed to strike his mother as odd.

"Of course. Why would you say that?"

"I don't know. I just thought . . . I mean, I know that James was paying for my treatment. I just didn't know if . . . I guess I just don't know."

"I'm so sorry you need to worry about these things, Owen. But don't. I know that this is a shock to all of us. But your treatment, that's the most important thing in my life. Believe me about that. And we can pay for it, so at least that is going to be fine."

13

The last time Jessica was in a police station had been when she was sixteen. She had made the mistake of accepting an offer from Ricky Solowosky to drive her home from a party at Andrea Levy's house. They hit a DUI roadblock as soon as they reached Ryder's Lane, and although Ricky was under the legal limit, the fact that he was seventeen and had been drinking was enough for the cops to scare the bejesus out of him.

She didn't remember anything about the police station from that first time except that she was scared to death. She wasn't scared this time, however. She felt nothing. As if she were dead herself.

The room she was placed in could scarcely have been made more unpleasant if that had been the police department's intent. It was almost as cold as it was outside, forcing her to keep on her gloves and coat. There were zero windows, battleship-gray walls, a single metal table, and four metal chairs. At least it didn't have the one-way mirror, although Jessica figured that meant only that they were filming her from somewhere else.

The young woman with an Arabic-sounding name said that she and her partner, the handsome man who'd broken the news of James's death, would return shortly. She asked if Jessica wanted anything to eat or drink, even offering to go out to get her something. Jessica declined. She was already sick to her stomach, and the thought of food, or even coffee, made her want to throw up.

Jessica had watched enough TV to know that the spouse was always the first suspect. Another thing she knew from television was that many a suspect made the mistake that ended up getting them convicted in this exact setting. On the other hand, she also knew that cops found it suspicious if the victim's spouse was uncooperative. Which meant that, no matter what she did, she was about to make a grave mistake.

The handsome lieutenant entered the room, the female officer who had offered to get her food a step behind him.

"I introduced myself earlier, but I know that with everything that has happened, remembering names is difficult. I'm Lieutenant Velasquez. This is my partner, Detective Jamali. We're both very sorry for your loss, Ms. Sommers."

Her inquisitors made a handsome couple, and Jessica wondered if they were, in fact, a couple. He might be a tad old for her, probably Jessica's age, if she had to guess. The female detective looked no more than thirty.

"As I told you before, the first few hours in an investigation are the most critical," he continued. "We know that this is an extremely difficult time for you, but we have to ask you some questions that will hopefully help us catch whoever did this to your husband."

Jessica felt the need to hear her own voice. "Yes. Anything I can do."

"Thank you. How long had you and James been married?"

Jessica wondered if the lieutenant consciously used the past tense to bring home that James was truly gone or if it was what he always said in these situations.

"One year. We actually had this big party for our first anniversary on Saturday night."

"This past Saturday?" Jamali asked.

"Yes."

"Your husband called you at"—Velasquez looked at his notes—"4:53 yesterday, and at that time he said that he was going to Washington and spending the night there. Is that right?"

"Yes."

"Did he say why he was going?"

"Yes. He had a business meeting. James is . . . was an art dealer. He took the Acela to DC last night to meet a buyer and promised me he was going to take the first train back in the morning."

The man's face twitched. It was almost imperceptible, but it suggested something was amiss.

"Was he traveling with Mr. Warwick?"

"No. He was with a woman named Allison. But Mr. Warwick was working on the deal too."

"What is Allison's last name?"

"I'm sorry, I don't know her last name. But ask Reid. He should know it."

"Any tension between your husband and Mr. Warwick?"

The question struck Jessica as odd. Were they thinking Reid killed James?

"No. Not as far as I knew. Reid came to our anniversary party last week. And like I said, they were doing this art deal together."

She thought for a moment about whether it looked good or bad for her to be interested in the police's suspect list. Of course she would be, she concluded quickly.

"Do you think maybe Reid . . . ?"

"We don't think anything at this point. But I will tell you that Reid refused to cooperate with us."

"He did?"

"Yes. And that's never a good look for an innocent person."

Jessica was still wrapping her mind around the fact that Reid had refused to cooperate with the police when Detective Jamali asked, "Can you think of anyone else who would want to harm your husband?"

It was the *else* that struck her. Apparently, Reid had joined the category of potential murderers merely by his refusal to cooperate.

She took a deep breath and then said aloud what she hadn't said to anyone, other than Wayne. "James and I were both married before, and we had an affair and then left our exes." She could see the look in her inquisitors' eyes, judging her. She might as well be wearing a scarlet letter. "My ex and I get along well, probably because we share custody of our son. But James's ex, Haley . . . she's crazy. He had to take out a restraining order against her. She showed up at our house on the night of our anniversary party. We hadn't invited her, of course. But she was there and made a scene."

"What is Haley's last name?" the lieutenant asked.

"I think she still goes by Sommers. I'm not a hundred percent sure, though."

"What type of scene did she cause at the party?" Jamali asked.

"During the toasts, she started cursing at James. Me too. Then, just the other day, I got this strange phone call. It was from a man, but I knew that Haley was behind it."

"What did the caller say?" Velasquez this time.

"He said I should ask James about the short-haired woman he was . . . allegedly . . . having sex with. Of course, he didn't phrase it like that."

"What short-haired woman?" Jamali now, continuing the tag team.

"She meant Allison. The woman James was working with on the deal. James said that Haley must have seen the two of them together at dinner and decided to try to make me jealous. Or maybe she was hoping it'd cause a fight with James. Who knows what goes through her mind?"

The two police officers looked at each other. Now Haley was a suspect too.

Good, Jessica thought. It couldn't happen to a nicer person.

At 3:45 p.m., school was finally over, and Wayne left the Sheffield Academy for the day. He had seen from the window that it had been snowing all day, but once he was outside, he realized that it was heavier than he had thought. Unfortunately he was wearing his loafers with the soft soles, which meant that he'd be sliding on the slick streets with each step.

It was only a few blocks to the subway. If he stayed under the scaffolding for the next block, he'd make it there without becoming fully soaked.

A few steps into the walk, he reached for his cell to call Owen again. At last, he saw that he had a text.

But when he clicked on it, it was not from Owen. Instead it was from PayPal, telling him that a thirty-seven-dollar Uber had been charged to his account. That was the fare to go from Manhattan to Queens, which meant that his son was now at his house.

This wasn't one of his normal nights with Owen, though. Yesterday had been. Moreover, the timing wasn't right. Owen had gone straight from the doctor, apparently, which meant he had missed the rest of the school day. And although Owen taking an Uber to Queens wasn't unprecedented, he knew better than to blow that kind of money during daylight hours when the subway provided perfectly suitable transportation.

He called Owen again, hoping he'd pick up. No such luck. Straight to voice mail. Same thing happened when he tried Jessica.

It took Wayne more than an hour to get home by train. (A thirty-seven-dollar Uber was outside his commuting budget.) Owen was on the living room sofa when Wayne walked in. He was playing the violin. *A new piece,* Wayne thought, given that he didn't recognize it.

There were few things that Wayne enjoyed more than his son's playing, which always made it seem that everything was right in the world. Like that old saying about music having charms to soothe the savage breast . . . Hearing Owen made Wayne's dread disappear.

"Hey, O. You know how much I love to see you, but I still need to ask—what are you doing here?"

"Mom told me to come here. James was killed."

Leave it to Owen to impart this news with the emotional detachment of an anchorman reporting on a natural disaster. But that's what life as a teenager was like, Wayne knew. Or maybe only for *his* teenager.

Wayne didn't verbally respond, though his mind was going a mile a minute while his son continued in the same flat inflection. "Someone broke into his office and killed him. Mom left me at the doctor because she got a call from the police or something. After I was done, I met her at James's building. There were cops all around, and they weren't letting anyone inside. Mom went to the police station to . . . answer questions, I guess. She told me to come here."

"That's terrible. I'm . . . sorry."

"Yeah. It's . . . I mean, who would want to kill James, you know?"

Wayne didn't respond. He assumed that Owen knew perfectly well that Wayne would be at the top of the list of people who wanted James dead.

———

"First impressions?"

The question was aimed at assessing Asra's detective skills, as Gabriel had already formed his own first impressions about the case. From the look on her face, Asra intuited as much, which meant that she had actually passed this test before even answering his question.

"Whether it's murder or not, I don't know, but someone was definitely with him when it happened, and that's not a good look for them not being guilty of something."

Gabriel nodded for Asra to continue.

"If you're asking me to speculate on who might be the person who was with Mr. Sommers at the time of his demise, certainly the business partner looks good for that. He's big, so I could see him landing a punch like the one that took Sommers down. I also got the impression that Reid's the kind of guy who's not opposed to starting a fight. And given his refusal to cooperate, he might as well have put a target on his forehead."

"What do you think about the wife?"

"Seems legitimately distressed to me. And I don't see her going to his place of business to kill him."

"Maybe she showed up at the office and saw this Allison person and her husband going at it. There's a scuffle and he winds up dead."

"How does Allison make it out alive?"

"Maybe she ran the moment Jessica arrived, and that's when the marital discord turned deadly. Then again, this might be a classic Occam's razor situation."

"How so?" Asra asked.

"We've got someone who's made a death threat against the vic. His ex-wife. Hard not to conclude that Haley Sommers is our murderer when the guy ends up dead less than a week later."

They'd used James Sommers's face to unlock his phone. Nothing was suspicious about his phone activity, no obvious mistress or dispute with anyone. They called the number listed under the contact *Allison* a few times, but no one answered. Gabriel was certain that when they checked the number, they'd find it was a burner.

The one outlier in this perfectly normal, enemy-free life was a voice mail James Sommers had received from his ex-wife on the day of his wedding anniversary to Jessica:

"James, you miserable fuck. I hope you and that skank bitch of a wife of yours both die. But don't worry, after you're dead, I'll be sure to dance on your graves."

Reid knew that Allison would call. It was only a matter of time.

It came at 10:00 p.m. that night.

"Why the fuck didn't James meet me at the train?" she said. "And why won't he return my calls and texts?"

"I wouldn't take it personally, sweetheart."

"Where the hell is he?"

"Six feet under."

"What?"

"You heard me. James is dead. He was murdered."

"Did you kill him?" she asked.

He laughed. "Yeah. I killed him. Had to. I was really upset about the shitload of money he was going to make me. The better question, Allison, is why *you* killed him."

"Don't be an idiot. Why would I kill him?"

"Let me see if I can think of a reason. Off the top of my head, I've got two-point-seven million of them. Where the fuck is the money, Allison?"

"James never met me at the Acela. So I never got the Pollocks, which means I never went to DC, so I never sold them to my client, and that means that I never got the money. So let me ask you, Reid: Where the *fuck* are the Pollocks?"

14

Jessica had no interest in going back into James's office. The police had told her that she could, but that wasn't the issue. She knew someday she'd have to return, if for no other reason than to empty it out when the lease expired, whenever that was. But she wanted to put that off for as long as possible.

Reid clearly had a different timetable. He hadn't raised the issue the day they learned James was dead, but a one-day moratorium was apparently all he could abide.

"I know this is terrible for me to ask, Jessica," he'd said over the phone earlier that morning, "but I figured you'd understand that it's the nature of the work James and I do that we need to sell pieces when we have a willing buyer because they just don't come along every day. So I need the keys to both his office and the credenza inside it so I can get access to the Pollocks. And don't worry, I'm still going to honor my deal with James. You'll get your fifty thousand dollars for each one I can sell through Allison because she's James's connection."

James had earned $90,000 on the first sale, but Jessica decided not to raise the issue. Reid wouldn't be Reid if he wasn't trying to screw her over.

"If you come down here, I'll give you the keys," she'd told him.

———

Reid wasted no time in showing up at Jessica's home.

"Thank you," he told her. "I'm really sorry to ask you for this before the funeral, but like I said, I have this buyer and I'm afraid he'll go on to something else."

"I understand. The world moves on."

She excused herself to go to the bedroom to retrieve James's keys. As he waited for her, Reid decided to get out in front of things. So when she returned, he said, "I need to tell you something, Jessica."

She looked at him with fear in her eyes. He wondered what she thought he was going to say that would make her that afraid.

"You probably heard that I didn't talk to the police about the work James and I were doing. You need to do that too, Jessica. Not cooperate with them, I mean. I know that's hard for you, and it'll make the cops suspicious if you shut them down, but the sale of these Pollocks . . . they're not, strictly speaking, legal. I need this deal badly, to get out of a very deep hole I've dug for myself, and I know that James needed the deal to pay for Owen's treatment, or he wouldn't have done it. The thing is, we can't sell them if the police are in our business. That's why I didn't tell them anything about Allison, and I suggest you don't either. I'm sorry to put it this way, but it's the truth: Would you rather help the police contact Allison or get the money to pay for Owen's treatment?"

She looked as if she didn't understand. "What are you saying, Reid?"

"I'm saying that we both want whoever did this to James to be caught, but I also know that we both really need the money that's going to come out of these sales. And I'm saying that those two things are in direct conflict right now."

"I don't need the money that badly," she said.

That wasn't what James had told him. But there was no reason for James to lie about his need to raise funds. More likely, Jessica was lying about being flush now. Or maybe she just didn't know how precarious their financial position was.

"That's not what James said to me," Reid countered. "But, look, even if that's true, *I* need the money that badly. And to make this deal happen, I need to keep the cops away from Allison. She has a buyer on the hook for all three pieces. Once she knows I've told the police where to find her, she's gone."

Jessica looked at Reid hard. He didn't have the faintest idea what she was going to do next, but she handed him James's keys.

"I don't know anything about Allison," she said. "But there's no way I would ever put money above finding who killed James."

"Understood," Reid said.

He saw no need to posture any longer. He'd come for the key, and now he had it. He didn't care what Jessica thought so long as he could sell the Pollocks.

Which was why immediately after leaving Jessica, Reid headed uptown and let himself into James's office. To his surprise, the blood was still on the floor. He'd thought the police would have cleaned it, but of course they hadn't.

He stepped around the red stain that had soaked into the rug and went over to the credenza. He fumbled a little before finding the key that fit the lock. When he opened the credenza, all three Pollocks were still there.

He pulled out his phone and dialed. Allison answered right away.

"I've got the Pollocks," he said. "When can we meet?"

———

Haley's doorman alerted her to the visitors. "Two police officers are coming up," he said.

That was fast, she thought. It had been less than twenty-four hours since James's death, and they were already onto her.

Jessica no doubt had pointed the finger in her direction. Of course, she had done a pretty good job of incriminating herself too, what with her one-woman show at the anniversary party and her text messages that the police must have considered akin to a confession.

Haley had done some acting in high school. She remembered the nerves she'd felt before going onstage. This felt like that, only the penalty for failure was not being ridiculed by your friends in homeroom the next day, but rather lifetime imprisonment.

Haley opened the door before they arrived. She thought that would make her seem more open to them.

There were two of them. A man and a woman.

"Good morning, Ms. Sommers. My name is Lieutenant Velasquez. This is Detective Jamali. May we come in?"

Haley wondered if the NYPD sold a beefcake calendar at Christmas for fundraising, and if so, whether Lieutenant Velasquez was Mr. December. She wished he weren't so good-looking. She found it much easier to manipulate men who were appreciative that she was giving them the time of day.

"What's this about?" she said, hoping it came off as if she really didn't know.

"I'm sorry to have to tell you this, Ms. Sommers, but your ex-husband, James Sommers, was killed."

"Oh my God," she exclaimed and brought her hands up over her face, the way someone who had found out for the first time that their ex-husband was dead might do. She tried to force out a tear, but it was beyond her skill set.

"You didn't know?" Lieutenant Velasquez said.

She shook her head, as if it were less of a lie if she didn't speak it. "No. We don't have any friends in common any longer."

"May we come in?" he asked.

"Yes. Of course. I'm sorry."

She led them to the living room, with its panoramic view of the Hudson River. She had purchased this place before marrying James. The thing she liked best about it now was that it didn't have a single piece of art on the walls.

Once they were seated, the cops in the armchairs and Haley on her sofa, the interrogation resumed.

"We know there's been some animosity between you and your ex-husband," Lieutenant Velasquez said. "Obviously, that makes you a suspect in all of this."

He stopped there. No question. Just stating as an indisputable fact that Haley hated James, and they thought she might have killed him as a result.

There was no point in denying her animosity toward James, of course. Every guest at the party would testify that it was true. Not to mention her emails and text messages and voice mails and various violations of the restraining order.

"Yes. James left me for Jessica, and that kind of betrayal is hard to forgive. At times, I have acted . . . let's just say inappropriately. I'm sure you heard about my outburst at his anniversary party. Not my finest hour, by any means. But I did not kill him. I swear that I didn't. It wasn't that way between us."

"What way was it?" Detective Jamali asked.

"It's hard to explain. I loved James and I hated James. I wanted him to know both those things. That's why I acted out from time to time. But killing him? No, I'd never do that. It would end things. Forever. And I didn't *want* them to end. That was my problem: I wanted a relationship with James, albeit a destructive, one-sided, and completely dysfunctional one. But still . . . Now that he's gone, that's over for me. And, believe it or not, it makes me incredibly sad."

She didn't expect them to believe it. Still, she thought it was a good speech.

"We need to know your whereabouts the day he died," Lieutenant Velasquez said. "Start with when you woke up."

"Did it happen yesterday?" she asked, proud of herself that she did. If the police were going to trick her into revealing that she knew more than she let on, they'd have to work harder.

"Actually the day before yesterday. Two days ago."

Haley considered this, the way she imagined she would if she didn't know exactly when James had died. "Okay. So two days ago. Well, I'm unemployed, which while unfortunate in many ways, does have the one upside that my time is my own. So two days ago, let's see . . . After I got up, I went to the gym. I'm sure there will be a swipe record of me being there from maybe eleven to noon. Then I came back home and showered. And I just puttered around here alone for a while."

She thought about whether to mention anything about her time in Sant Ambroeus. If they asked around, someone was bound to remember her being there. But maybe it would never come to that. She decided to go straight for the alibi. If the police later learned that she'd been at Sant Ambroeus, lying to them would be the least of her worries.

"After that, I went to a friend's apartment in the Bronx. I got there at around five. I was with him until the morning, at which time I went home to my place."

"Write down the name, address, and phone number for this friend of yours, please," Detective Jamali said.

———

Wayne knew he should do this face-to-face. At least that's what people always said about breakups. He actually had never done it before. The few girlfriends he'd had prior to Jessica had dumped him. Some not even face-to-face.

He wondered if the in-person rule still applied in the smartphone era. Wouldn't Stephanie prefer to hear the news by text rather than have to endure it in person?

Nonetheless, he suggested that they meet for a drink. That should have been a tip-off to Stephanie. Not dinner, as was their usual Friday-night activity. On the other hand, he said that he was tight for time because he had to see Owen right after. If she accepted that at face value, she'd be blindsided by what he was about to reveal.

He half expected (or maybe hoped) that Stephanie would decline. They hadn't seen each other all week, and he held out some hope that was another sign she'd read. But she said she'd come straight from work, and they agreed to meet at six. Perhaps she thought he wanted to talk about James's death, which he'd told her about over the phone when making their date.

Wayne arrived at 5:30 p.m. He selected a table that would allow him to see Stephanie enter—and provide quick egress when the deed was done.

When she walked in, the look on Stephanie's face suggested that she was dreading this as much as he was. No smile of recognition when he waved, and she didn't take off her coat when the coat-check girl asked for it. She clearly wasn't expecting to stay too long.

He stood when she approached and gave her a peck on the lips to keep up appearances. As soon as he did, he realized how stupid that was. He wasn't trying to maintain suspense here. The purpose of this get-together was so that they wouldn't have any more dates.

As soon as Stephanie sat, the waitress arrived. While waiting, Wayne hadn't ordered anything to drink, in case Stephanie didn't show up. A half hour of him nursing an ice water had made the waitress particularly attentive.

"Give us a minute," Stephanie said.

The moment the waitress left them, Stephanie said, "Let's get this over fast, shall we?"

Well, at least she wouldn't be blindsided.

"I'm sorry, Steph. It's just that . . . I've got so much going on now, it's not fair to you, really."

She chuckled. "So this is really you thinking of me, then. Thank you for that, Wayne. As always, so considerate."

He didn't react to her sarcasm other than to say, "I'm sorry, Stephanie."

"Yeah, me too. Not that it's over. I think that's for the best too. I'm sorry that . . . you know . . . that it never really started, in a way. I thought that enough time had passed for you to be over Jessica. That maybe you were ready to start your life again. You certainly talked a good game about it. But I think we both know that just wasn't true."

She waited for him to respond. Probably thought he was going to deny it. The only thing that occurred to him to say, however, was to repeat that he was sorry, and that would only escalate the situation.

"I . . . tried," he said instead.

"I guess you did. At least as much as you could. In a weird way, as soon as you told me that Jessica's husband was killed, I knew that our relationship was dead too. I know that sounds terrible. The man died and all. But I knew you would see it as some type of opportunity for you rather than as a tragedy for your ex-wife."

She was right, but he wasn't about to admit that. Then it occurred to him that her statement sounded like an accusation.

Could she be wearing a wire? Was *that* why she'd decided to come? To help the police?

"I . . . don't think that's true."

He meant to issue a more forceful denial, intended for the police who were listening rather than for Stephanie, who was spot-on in her appraisal.

"Okay, then," she said. "I guess we've come full circle." She stood. "No reason to prolong this. Let me just say goodbye, tell you that I enjoyed . . . at least some of our time together, and wish you the very best."

He stood too but didn't move any closer to her. If she wanted to embrace, she'd have to make that move.

She didn't. Instead, she turned on her heel and left the bar.

———

"I'm going to do it now, I think," Owen told his mother that morning.

He'd come straight from Wayne's house to the loft that morning and asked his mother for permission to stay home from school. "I'm not going to be able to concentrate on anything," he'd explained.

At first Jessica said that he'd be missing so much school after the transplant that he shouldn't be missing even more. Plus, James's funeral was Friday, and he'd miss school that day too.

"Another day isn't going to matter, Mom. Not in the big scheme of things."

That argument had won the day, though Owen figured his mom had her own reasons for letting him stay home: she didn't want to be alone.

"Are you sure you want to do it?" she asked, the beginnings of tears in her eyes.

"Yeah . . . I think maybe it's better if I take some control over it, you know? And tomorrow I start chemo again, so I've got to do it today if I want to do it myself rather than have it happen to me."

"Okay. I mean, if that's what you want. Is there anything I can do to help?"

"Nah. I think it's a one-man job."

"I'm so sorry, Owen. I know I say that a lot. It's just that I don't know what else to say, you know?"

He did. "I know."

"One of the things that is so unfair about all of this . . . one of the ten billion things, I should say, is that I'm supposed to have experienced everything you're going through. That's why the universe created parents. I've done long division and not made the team and all the rest. But I have no idea what *this* is like for you. And for that, I'm so sorry, because I feel like I'm . . . useless."

They'd had this discussion before. Many times, actually. It always seemed to him a silly thing for her to focus on. First, because he doubted very much that even if his mother had suffered from leukemia as a teenager she would really know what he was going through . . . or that he would have cared. He remembered being stressed out about a million different things before he got sick, and it never made him feel any better when his mother claimed to understand.

But the other reason was that he didn't spend a lot of time thinking about fairness. If having leukemia had taught him anything, it was that life was unfair. Not just having leukemia, truth be told. His parents had taught him that too when they had divorced. James's death had only reinforced the point.

Without any further discussion on the topic, Owen went into the bathroom and shut the door. It was like déjà vu, except that the last time he'd done this, his hair hadn't been very long and the bathroom had been his father's in Queens.

He found a pair of scissors that he assumed were a relic from his art projects in middle school. Still, they were sharp enough to do the job. He couldn't remember if he had used the same ones the last time. Maybe.

Owen stepped into the bathtub, grabbed a fistful of hair, and began cutting. He didn't look down until he had reached the end, and ringlets and stray hairs covered the tub.

He took a break, looking at himself in the mirror. His hair was now the length it might have been if he had never had cancer. Like a regular seventeen-year-old's.

That wasn't who he was, of course. Cancer made sure that he would never be a regular kid. He might as well look the part.

He brought the scissors up to his scalp and resumed snipping. He'd need to switch to a razor at some point, but he wouldn't stop until he was completely bald again.

15

Wayne went directly to Jessica's loft after the school day ended. He had called ahead to ask her permission and told her he wanted to visit to check on Owen, because phrased that way, he knew his request would not be denied. In fact, he was there first and foremost for her.

Wayne had seen Jessica at her lowest. He recalled only too vividly the days after Owen was first diagnosed. Jessica had been inconsolable, and nothing Wayne attempted to lift her spirits had made the least bit of difference.

Yet when he entered her apartment, it was worse than anything he could have previously imagined. She looked practically dead herself. As if her inner light had been snuffed out with James's passing.

"Owen is in his room," she said.

From her attire—sweatpants and a T-shirt, no shoes or socks—Wayne assumed that Jessica had not breathed any fresh air that day. "Before I see him, is there anything I can do for you?"

"That's sweet of you, Wayne, but no."

"How about if I go out and get some dinner? Then we can all eat together."

The concept of food seemed foreign to her. Wayne wondered if she'd eaten anything in the last twenty-four hours. Then she eked out a smile.

"I suppose we do have to eat. Although I don't think either of us have much of an appetite."

Wayne went to the Morton Williams a few blocks away. He got ingredients to cook penne alla vodka, which he hoped Jessica still liked. Or at least liked as much as she'd claimed when they were married. From there he stopped at the liquor store and bought a twenty-dollar bottle of Chianti, which was twice as much as he'd otherwise spend on wine.

Jessica's kitchen was certainly an upgrade from his in Forest Hills. A six-burner Viking range and All-Clad pots. In the end, however, the penne alla vodka came out the same as it had when he made it with inferior appliances and cookware.

He left the pasta to sit for a little, his trick to get the noodles to soak up the sauce. While he did, he checked in on Owen. Much like at his house, Owen's room here was arranged so he sat with his back to the door, staring at his computer.

One thing Wayne had not expected, however, was that his son would be hairless. Jessica hadn't told him that. How could she *not* have shared this? Well, now was not the time to raise that issue, but the sight of his bald son did cause a lump to form in his throat. A *not again* feeling seized his heart.

"Nice 'do, O."

Owen started and turned around in his chair. "What are you doing here?"

"I decided to come here after school to check up on you and your mom. See if I can be of any help. I've already been here for about an hour. I made some penne alla vodka for dinner. It'll be ready in about ten minutes."

If Owen found this odd—his father at his mother's house, calling him for a dinner that he had prepared—he didn't show it. He only gave a small nod of his bald head.

Wayne couldn't remember the last time they had all sat around a table together for a meal. Jessica commented that the penne was great, and when Wayne asked if it was too spicy, she assured him it was perfect. Even Owen said it was good, although when dinner was over, his plate remained nearly full.

The dinner conversation was stilted. Owen gave his typical close-mouthed account of how the first day of chemo had gone. Jessica was largely mute, undoubtedly thinking about the funeral to come, as well as the rest of her life without James.

And there Wayne was, sitting between them, wanting so desperately to solve their problems by giving of himself. And it broke his heart that neither wanted his help.

———

Malik was busy pounding away. He had reached out to Haley earlier that day to report on how well he'd done with the police interview. So well that he thought he should be rewarded with another throw.

She was tempted to tell him that she was too tired. Or that she shouldn't have to reward him with sex because he'd told the police that they were having sex the other night. But the very fact that he was expecting it told her that he knew the truth. That she hadn't actually arrived at his place at five. Which meant that if he was telling the police that she had, he was lying to protect her. And given that, the least she could do was fuck him.

Besides, it wasn't as if having sex with Malik was digging ditches. She could get into it too.

When it was over and he had left, Haley considered her circumstances. They were, to put it mildly, less than optimal. The man she was on record threatening to murder had just been murdered, she had lied to the police about her whereabouts at the time of the crime, and now her alibi witness was demanding sex in exchange for maintaining that lie.

———

After Wayne left, Jessica contacted the life insurance company and asked how she could collect the proceeds of the policy on James's life. She explained that her son was undergoing an operation, and she needed the money quickly. The claims adjuster expressed her condolences and explained that the process was fairly straightforward: fill out a form and attach the death certificate.

Jessica wondered if there'd be a delay in processing the payment because James's death was being treated as a homicide. She knew from the movies that there was some rule against rewarding murderers with benefits of their crime, like collecting on life insurance. That meant the payment might not be issued right away.

The irony of the situation was not lost on her. The fact that she desperately needed that money only made it more likely that the police would use the existence of the policy as evidence against her, which would in turn delay her receipt of the funds.

Worse than that, the moment the police discovered James was worth more dead than alive, they'd assume she'd killed him to save her son.

—

Gabriel was disappointed to hear that Annie had already been put down for the night. He had come home early just to see her.

"Don't worry, you'll get to see her at five a.m.," Ella said with a laugh. "Earlier if you want to wake up for the middle-of-the-night feeding."

"That's okay. Besides, a quiet evening alone with my beautiful wife sounds pretty great."

"You want a beer? You look like you could use one."

He laughed. "No. I'm still in complete solidarity."

"Well, partial solidarity, at least."

When Ella became pregnant and had to swear off alcohol, as well as caffeine and sushi, Gabriel agreed to do likewise. He'd been able to keep that promise for the most part, but he'd confessed to her that he couldn't function at work without coffee. And because he never really liked sushi anyway, her dig was on point.

"Touché. How was your day?"

"Same. Annie was perfect, but she's not the best conversationalist. Tell me about the case."

While Ella had been on maternity leave, her only connection to the justice world had been through Gabriel. In their pre-Annie existence, they would share their respective cop and prosecutor war stories over dinner each night. In the post-Annie world, it was a one-way street, but Ella always seemed excited to hear about Gabriel's work.

"We seem to be looking for a skinny, short-haired woman in a haystack," he said. "Asra contacted more than fifty galleries and auction houses, none of which had a short-haired, thin Allison on staff. Well, that isn't entirely true. This glorified poster shop in SoHo claimed to have one, but when we hiked down there, it turned out the woman in question was actually named Alicia, and her hair wasn't that short. She *was* pretty skinny, though, so one out of three. Needless to say, she had no idea who James Sommers was, so it turned out to be a dead end."

"Maybe your mystery girl doesn't exist," Ella said.

"Why would Jessica Sommers make her up?"

"Maybe because her husband made her up, or at least gave her a false name and vocation."

"Come again?"

"Maybe he was sleeping with this Allison, like you think. But he didn't want his wife to know that, obviously. So, when she confronts him, he just makes up a name. And says, 'Oh, she's working with me on a deal, so it's all legit.' Without the real name, the wife can't google her and cause a scene, and the fake job gives him a reason to be seen with her in public. Kinda brilliant if you ask me, in a lying-cheating-sack kind of way, of course."

Even while on maternity leave, Ella was still a step ahead. Seeing things that he should have noticed.

"So you're suggesting that James Sommers has a piece on the side, the ex-wife sees her or something and tells the current wife, then the wife confronts Sommers, and he says, 'Oh, that's my business partner, Allison.' And Allison is a name he just made up to throw suspicion away from the actual short-haired, skinny woman he was with?"

"Yeah. Why not?"

Gabriel considered the possibility. That it might be right only highlighted how little evidence they had at the moment.

"So that means we need to add to our suspect list a skinny, short-haired woman *not* named Allison?"

Ella laughed. "I would."

"Thanks for making more work for me."

"Anything to help."

They ordered in pizza, but Ella lit candles for the table, commenting that she wanted to take full advantage to make it a date night. Still, 95 percent of the conversation concerned Annie, so it wasn't quite like a date.

Watching his wife through the candles' glow, Gabriel realized just how lucky a man he was. His days were usually spent among people whose lives were in ruins, more often than not as a result of their own bad choices. Jessica Sommers was a case in point. Either she had lost her husband in the worst way imaginable, or she had killed him, which meant that she'd end up living out her days in the penitentiary. Either way, she was staring at years of darkness ahead. By contrast, Gabriel saw nothing but light in his future. With Ella, he had filled that space he hadn't even fully realized was empty, and with Annie's arrival, his cup truly runneth over with joy.

"What?" Ella said, although her tone suggested she knew what he was thinking.

"I love you, Ella," he said.

"Yeah, yeah," she said back. "Prove it."

"Give me fifty years, and I will."

She smiled the same full-on smile that Gabriel had first fallen in love with. "Deal."

———

Owen couldn't sleep. He kept touching his scalp, feeling the soft skin that had been hidden for the last few years.

Of course, that wasn't the reason he was still awake in the middle of the night. To say that he had a lot going on at the moment would be the understatement of all time. Tomorrow was James's funeral. In a week's time, he would undergo an operation that would determine whether his own funeral would follow shortly.

Before they said their good-nights, his mother let him know that she hoped he'd say a few words at the funeral.

Owen would have preferred not. Truth be told, if given the choice, he would have spent tomorrow in bed. The chemo already had him feeling sick to his stomach. So much so that he was worried he might puke if he had to give a eulogy.

He'd asked if he could perform a violin piece instead. He always thought he was more eloquent when playing someone else's composition than when trying to express his feelings verbally. His mother said that he could do both, but she still thought someone from their family should speak, and she didn't think she could summon the strength.

"You don't have to talk long," she'd said. "Five minutes would be more than enough. But I think, in light of the fact that James was paying for your treatment, it would be appropriate for you to tell everyone that he lives on in you."

He nodded. His mother was right. James would live in him for the rest of his life. The least he could do was offer up some platitudes about his stepfather at his funeral.

16

James Sommers was laid to rest three days after his murder.

There had been some last-minute procedural snafus that threatened to delay the funeral—the medical examiner's office hedged on whether they could release the body on time, and the funeral home thought it had double-booked. But in the end, James's body was released and a vacant chapel was procured.

Jessica and Owen arrived early to the chapel. Owen was wearing the same outfit he had put on for the party, but without Jessica asking, he had worn a pair of James's work shoes to replace his Nikes.

She held her son's hand, which she could not recall having done in years. Not since the start of the chemo the first time. Even then, her recollection was that at some point during the treatment, he had stopped. That had been her son's rite of passage into adulthood—chemotherapy. He began it as a boy and finished it a man (albeit one who was still in ninth grade).

The minister did a slight double take at the sight of a bald teenager but didn't otherwise comment. He didn't look the part either. Short, stout, and also bald.

"Would you like to see your husband?" he asked.

For a moment, Jessica thought he meant that James was alive. Then it clicked that he was asking whether she wanted to see his corpse in the casket before the ceremony began.

"Some loved ones find it comforting to say goodbye one last time," the minister said. "Others, however, prefer to remember how they looked in life. It's entirely up to you."

"Yes. I think so. Owen, do you want to?"

"No," he said. "Is that okay?"

"Of course," she said. "It's totally up to you. There's no right way to do this."

She followed the minister through a door that led into a small room that contained only the casket. Her first thought was that the coffin was too small for James.

"I'm going to lift up the lid, and then I'll leave you to be alone with your thoughts," the minister said.

Without waiting for a response, he did exactly that, lifting the lid, then leaving Jessica alone in the room. She couldn't see into the casket until she was standing right beside it, peering down. When she did, James looked less like her husband than a wax figure of him.

It was his expression that made the most indelible impression. It looked as if the undertaker had tried to give him a peaceful smile, but the end result made it appear as if James had been on the verge of saying something right before he was killed.

What would he say now? she wondered.

Would she be able to bear it?

"I love you so much, James. And I always will. I'm so sorry that our time together was so short. Please believe that I love you. More than you can even know."

She waited a beat, even though she knew that he wasn't going to answer. She'd never hear his voice again.

———

Wayne took a seat in the back of the chapel. He had considered sitting up front, to be closer to Jessica and Owen, but he worried it might look like he was pushing too hard.

He spotted Jessica at the front. She'd always looked her best in basic black.

Owen sat beside her. Seeing the two of them together, Wayne felt as if he were looking at identical profiles.

There is an old wives' tale, although some claim it as scientific fact, that newborn babies look like their fathers as a way of ensuring their survival, given that maternity is provable but paternity can be in doubt. Wayne had done some reading on this topic after Owen was born, purely as an intellectual pursuit. What he found was that the science was uncertain as to whether babies actually looked like their fathers, but the research was more definitive that fathers who *believed* their babies resembled them were more present in their children's lives.

Wayne, however, had never thought Owen looked even remotely like him. When his son was an infant, Wayne joked that the male figure Owen most resembled was Elmer Fudd. As Owen grew, his maternal resemblance became pronounced. He and Jessica shared the same square jaw, straight nose, and large smile, as well as some other recessive traits, such as blue eyes and left-handedness. Whenever Jessica posted Owen's picture on social media, the comments poured in. "He's a little you!" they'd say. In fact, other than Owen and Wayne both having detached earlobes, Wayne was hard-pressed to note a single physical characteristic he shared with his son.

After Jessica's infidelity was revealed, Wayne couldn't completely banish the thought that, despite her insistence to the contrary, James had not been her first indiscretion. An unwanted pregnancy from another man might have explained why she had accepted his marriage proposal, an enduring mystery that Wayne hadn't been able to wrap his mind around to this day.

Wayne had felt a modicum of relief when he'd been selected as Owen's bone marrow donor. He viewed it as being akin to a paternity test. Of course, he knew that being a partial donor match for the stem cell transplant wasn't that at all. Indeed, if he hadn't been selected, an anonymous donor would have been found. Still, the fact that he had been selected was enough for him to once again push away his deepest fear about his connection to his son. There are things you *know* about your child, and one of those things was that Owen was Wayne's flesh and blood.

The process, it turned out, was not all that dramatic. All Wayne would have to do was go under general anesthesia while the doctors harvested his bone marrow through a syringe. The doctor said the only side effect he'd anticipate was general soreness. Wayne wouldn't even have to stay overnight in the hospital. The procedure was scheduled to occur next week, the day before Owen's transplant.

Wayne doubted Owen cared that he'd be the one contributing the stem cells as opposed to some anonymous donor. But he still hoped that somewhere, deep down, it would provide some tangible evidence to Owen that there was nothing he wasn't willing to do for him, even to the point of putting his own life at risk.

———

Haley listened to the minister tick off the virtues of a man she had once loved, then hated. The biography being recounted was one she knew well. How James had been raised in a hardscrabble town, put himself through college, and developed a love for art. How his apprenticeship in some of the city's finest galleries had led him to branch out on his own.

None of that sounded like James to Haley. He was not his work, at least not to her. When Haley shut her eyes to conjure James, he lay on the sand beside her on their honeymoon, looking out at an anchored yacht.

171

"You think you can swim that far out?" he asked her.

"Yes," she said with a laugh. "The coming back might give me some trouble, though."

"You won't have to do it all at once. After we swim all the way out there, they'll have no choice but to let us come aboard so we can gather our strength before swimming back."

At first, she thought James was joking. But if he was, he wanted to maintain the illusion he was serious, because he stared at her without even the hint of a smile. The last thing Haley was going to do was show James that he had married someone who lacked adventure.

"Okay, then," she said, and raced to the ocean.

The yacht was actually much farther away than she had imagined, perhaps because it was twice as large as she'd estimated from the beach. It took nearly a half hour for them to reach it. When they did, she wondered if her joke about being able to swim there but not back might have been too on the nose.

"Ahoy, ahoy," James called out from beside the hull.

A man stuck his head over the rail and squinted down at them.

"We were wondering if you might like some company," James shouted up.

Just like James had predicted, the man lowered the ladder, and they climbed aboard. It was a scene from a James Bond movie: James and Haley, dripping wet, walking on the finely polished wood floor of a hundred-foot-plus yacht. Also on deck were three women sunning on lounge chairs, each in her twenties and wearing a string bikini, sans top.

"Apologies for not bringing a gift," James said with a grin, the way 007 might have if this were actually a James Bond movie.

"You know, we've docked in many places over the years, and this is the first time anyone has ever swum up to us and asked to come aboard," their host said.

He was James's age and dressed as if he was expecting guests, in white linen from head to toe. His accent was American.

"Is this your boat?" Haley asked.

"I wish, but I'm a guest aboard her." He extended his hand. "Reid Warwick, at your service."

As soon as the image of Reid on that Caribbean day left her head, she spotted the real thing sitting a few rows behind her at the funeral. Except for the fact that he was wearing black, he hadn't changed a bit since their first meeting.

He smiled at her, that wolfish grin that was quintessential Reid. Like he saw you as prey, almost.

———

When Reid caught Haley's eye, it seemed to him that she might truly be in mourning. The thought struck Reid as odd, especially after she'd shared with him some of her revenge fantasies, twisted tales of torturing James usually involving some harm to his manhood. He considered the things he could tell the cops about Haley, if he was so inclined, and what Haley might offer him to not be so inclined.

His mind turned from sex to money—his two most common thoughts, after all. In this case, from one beautiful woman (Haley) to another (Allison).

He had told Allison not to come today. "It'll just raise a bunch of questions about who you are and what connection you have to James," he'd said. "Send flowers or make a donation in his name with some charity. Better still, if you really want to pay your respects, let's close this deal with the three remaining Pollocks so I can get some money to his family."

Reid desperately needed Allison to make this deal happen. Without it, his cash flow difficulties would become far more serious in a hurry. In fact, even in the church, he couldn't stop surveying the crowd to make sure that no one was here for *him*, rather than James.

All that looking over his shoulder would stop the moment he sold the last three Pollocks. Despite what he'd told Jessica about how the money was being split, the truth of the matter was that, with James now out of the picture, Reid's take would be nearly a million dollars. Enough to keep the sharks at bay for a while.

He spied Owen in the front row, beside his mother. Poor kid. Despite what Reid had said to Jessica and to Allison, there was no way that he was going to share a nickel of his take with anyone.

———

Midway through the service, it occurred to Owen that, for all his preoccupation with his own death, this was the first funeral he had ever attended.

He couldn't help but wonder what his own would look like in comparison. How many kids from school would show up? Would Mr. Taubenslag have the orchestra perform something? A requiem, perhaps? Would any of the girls cry?

His daydreaming ended when the minister called his name. "On behalf of the Sommers family, James's stepson, Owen Fiske, would like to say a few words."

His mother kissed him on the cheek, and he made his way to the podium. Once there, he looked out on the crowd and swallowed hard.

"Thank you all for coming here today," he said, his voice sounding squeaky even to him. "I don't like public speaking, so I'm not going to be up here very long, which I hope is okay." The sea of faces before him seemed to be trying hard to smile. "I just wanted to say that James was my stepfather. And I don't think I'm saying anything too controversial when I say that it's tough being the stepfather of a sixteen-year-old, which was how old I was when I met James. I think my dad would say it's tough being a father to a sixteen-year-old, period. But a stepfather? That's got to be even harder because James didn't know me at all. The only thing we had in common, really, is that we both loved my mom. And I kind of thought that James would leave me alone, and I wouldn't talk to him much, and that would be our relationship. But it wasn't that way. He actually wanted to get to know me. To be a part of my life. And I thought that was cool."

Owen lifted his eyes from the paper containing his remarks. His mother was smiling at him. He looked back to his prepared speech.

"Some of you may know that I have a type of leukemia. I got it before my mom met James. The doctors thought I was cured, but I wasn't. It came back, which is why I stand before you today bald once again. I'm going to have this transplant thing, and hopefully that will cure me."

The smiles he had seen only moments ago were now all gone. Only a kid with cancer could make a funeral sadder.

"I'm not telling you this so you'll feel sorry for me, though. I'm telling you because James was there for me. One hundred percent. I'm not going to bore you with a rant about how expensive medical care is, or that treatments like mine aren't covered by insurance. But James . . . he saved my life. There's no other way to put it. He saved my life. So I guess that's another thing we had in common. Not just our love for Mom. But . . . my whole life."

———

After the service ended and James had been interred in his final resting place, Jessica saw Haley walking toward her. She'd noticed Haley in the church and wondered about the etiquette of her attending. Then again, Jessica would attend Wayne's funeral, so maybe it wasn't so odd after all.

At the graveside ceremony, Haley had stood next to Reid. A little too closely, Jessica thought, but then again, perhaps those two deserved each other.

"Jessica!" Haley called out.

Jessica stiffened. "Hello, Haley."

Haley stopped a foot before her, the distance from which someone else might have leaned in for a hug, or at least extended their hand. Neither woman did either.

"I know that this isn't the time or place," Haley said, "but I don't know when I'm going to see you again."

Jessica had intended to be friendly, but already she couldn't spend another second looking at this woman. "I'm sorry. I can't do this, Haley."

Jessica turned away but made it only a single step before Haley's hand on her elbow pulled her back.

"Make time for it, Jessica. I know who killed James."

PART FOUR

17

So much for the procedure being akin to giving blood, with the doctors doing all the hard work. After the transplant, Owen felt like death warmed over. Not even that warm, in fact.

Eight days had passed since James had been laid to rest. During that time everything had followed just the way Dr. Cammerman had said: myeloablation was completed, Owen rested for two days, and then the transplant. As each day passed, Owen could feel his mother's shift from the all-consuming grief she'd experienced at the loss of her husband to an equally overwhelming fear of losing her son. The look in her eye before the surgery told Owen that his mother simply would not survive losing him too.

He must have been wheeled from surgery to a hospital room, because when he woke up, that's where he was. His room had a single window, and from the bed he could see a patch of sky. It looked to be a clear winter day. The kind he usually liked.

Dr. Cammerman was still wearing hospital scrubs when he entered. He looked first at Owen's chart, then at him.

"How are you feeling, Owen?"

"I've been better."

"The procedure went very well," the doctor answered as if he hadn't heard Owen's response to his first question. "Now we're at the stage where we monitor you. You're going to feel weak for a few days. That's to be expected. My advice to you is that you try not to overdo it. Staying in bed is just fine. If you want to get up, don't walk very far."

"I feel kind of like I'm going to throw up."

"Some nausea is also to be expected. That doesn't concern me."

Owen was pleased that Dr. Cammerman was copacetic with him throwing up all over himself. "I also feel a little dizzy."

"Again, that's perfectly normal. Do you have any questions?"

"No."

"In that case, I'll see you tomorrow, Owen."

Before the surgery, Dr. Cammerman told him that some people feel a sense of rebirth after a stem cell transplant. "It's like you're a brand-new person," he'd said.

Owen had desperately wanted to believe that after the surgery, something fundamental in him would change. But now, having emerged from the operation, he felt no different.

———

Jessica sat in the family and friends area at Memorial Sloan Kettering, hanging by a string. A thin, fraying one at that.

Her mantra was *baby steps*. First, she had to get through James's funeral. She had barely done that when Haley dropped her bombshell, knocking Jessica for a second loop. She'd had little choice but to cast aside Haley's claim, however. She needed to be there for her son.

Wayne sat beside her now. Yesterday, he had undergone the donor procedure, and now he sported an ice pack on his pelvis.

"Are you in much pain?" she asked.

"Not too bad," he said.

The last time they'd been together in a hospital waiting room was for Owen's first chemo session, four years earlier. Jessica still remembered that day too vividly for her liking. The way she'd gripped Wayne's hand, using every bit of her energy to not shed a tear in front of her thirteen-year-old son.

When Jessica was pregnant, she and Wayne often talked about the future their baby would enjoy. How the world would change in his lifetime and the kinds of opportunities that would be available to him. The one thing they never discussed, never even considered, was that he'd be sick. Or that before he even graduated from high school, they'd wish for nothing more than survival for their child.

"This is the worst part," Wayne said.

Jessica smiled at his effort to be positive. "They're all the worst parts."

Doctor Cammerman came out at a little past three. At first, he was stone-faced, but as he got closer to them, a small smile crept to his lips. It was enough for Jessica to exhale deeply for the first time that day.

"The transplant is complete, and Owen is doing great," he said. "He's going to rest for another hour. Then you can visit him. Remember, the protocol has to be strictly followed, for Owen's safety. Masks and gloves."

It was nearly two hours before a nurse finally entered the waiting room. She told Jessica and Wayne that they were able to see their son.

The nurse didn't take them through the door where Owen and Dr. Cammerman had exited the waiting room but instead led them to the elevator and then down several floors. Once they were on the third floor, they followed her through a maze of hallways until she pushed open a door with a sign that read **RECOVERY**.

If only that were true, Jessica thought.

From there they traversed another hallway, this one wider than the others, allowing for gurneys to pass both ways. At the end was another door with another sign. This one read **INTENSIVE CARE**.

Behind that door was a reception area, no different from the countless waiting rooms Jessica had seen. The nurse explained why this one was different.

"In the closet are surgical gowns, caps, gloves, and masks. Please put them on," she said.

Jessica watched Wayne suit up. Once he looked like he was ready to perform surgery, she did likewise.

After they were finished, the nurse said, "Owen is in bed two. The doctor only wants you to stay for a few minutes this time. Owen needs his rest now." She opened the door for them and stepped aside, allowing them entry.

In bed two lay their seventeen-year-old son, asleep. He didn't look any worse for wear, but for the hospital-issued pajamas.

"Maybe we should let him sleep," Jessica said.

Wayne nodded that he agreed.

Owen opened an eye. "Hey," he said with a croaky, low voice.

"Hey, O," Wayne said. "You look good, my man."

"Thanks. Feel great," Owen managed more clearly.

"The doctor said the operation was a total success," Jessica said, trying to sound upbeat.

Owen nodded. "I'm really tired."

"Just sleep," Jessica said. "We'll see you later."

Owen squinted through his one open eye, apparently realizing for the first time that his parents were head to toe in hospital scrubs.

"Did you two plan on wearing the same outfits today?" he said.

If Owen had jumped out of bed and danced a jig, Jessica couldn't have been happier. To her, his lame joke meant that maybe Wayne was right after all. Maybe the worst was over.

And then she remembered what Haley had said.

Allison suggested they meet at the St. Regis. She explained that she worked out of her home and normally brought clients to the dealer's showroom.

Reid hardly cared. He worked from wherever money could be made, and if that was the St. Regis, so be it.

It wasn't lost on him that Allison hadn't selected either the Mark or the Carlyle, the two hotels closest to James's office. That worked fine for him as well. He didn't want to be anywhere near the scene of the crime either.

It had been the typical hurry-up-and-wait process that characterized so many art deals. After she initially told Reid that he needed to secure the Pollock sketches right away, Allison's other commitments delayed the next step. They were supposed to meet last week, and then at the last minute she had canceled. He half expected her not to be there today either.

In the late afternoon, the St. Regis's lobby was nearly empty. Its only occupants were a few businessmen going over spreadsheets, a family who looked as if they were on vacation—probably from Europe, based on their clothing—and one or two women that Reid imagined were prostitutes, but maybe not.

He spotted Allison with her back to the window. In front of her was a small porcelain teapot.

She didn't rise when he approached. Nor did she extend her hand.

Reid took the chair across from her. He flagged down a waiter and asked for whatever tea Allison was having.

"So what are we going to do?" Reid said.

Allison poured her tea. "That's it? No . . . moment of silence for James? Weren't you friends or something?"

"More *something*. We were business partners, at least on this deal. And James would be the first to understand that what matters most to me is closing this deal."

"No offense, Reid, but what matters most to me is not being in business with someone who killed his business partner. I've been thinking about that all week. To be honest, that's why I canceled on you. The more I thought about the situation, I didn't think that we should be in business together."

"And I feel exactly the same about you, Allison. And then I remembered that we can make a boatload of money. So, even though I don't trust you either, here I am."

The waiter came back with a teapot for Reid.

Allison leaned in closer. He could feel the warmth of her breath.

"We seem to have a dilemma, then," she said. "We're both claiming we didn't kill James. Neither one of us really believes the other. But you want to sell the Pollocks and have no buyer; my buyer's still interested, but I don't have any Pollocks."

"Your buyer's still on the hook?"

"Spoke to him this morning."

That was why Allison had set this meeting up. She figured it wasn't worth knocking herself out to *look for* a buyer, but she wasn't going to turn away a bird in the hand.

"He was pissed that I canceled on him the first time, and I think he was giving me the cold shoulder to put me in my place a bit. When I finally reached him, I told him that the seller had gotten cold feet. Then I suggested that if he were to sweeten the deal—say, go to a million per—I could get him to sell. Long story short, he's back in. But he wants to do this as soon as possible. He's afraid the seller will pull out again."

Reid considered the proposal. He liked hearing that the price had gone up.

Still, he was getting the full-on hinky feeling now.

"So are we going to do this thing or what?" Allison asked.

Haley felt stuck in quicksand. She had always been a doer. Proactive. Looking to solve the problem at hand. It had been that impulse that led her to Jessica at the funeral. But now, with that plan in motion, there was nothing left for her to do.

Nothing except wait.

But for what, exactly? She didn't expect to hear from Jessica again. She would either believe Haley or not.

Besides, whether Jessica actually believed her was of secondary importance. Not even secondary—*irrelevant*. The only thing that mattered was whether Jessica decided to keep her powder dry with the police because of what Haley told her. Since the detectives hadn't yet come back to Haley's apartment, she assumed that was the case.

Not being a person of interest in a murder case should have made Haley happy, but she felt little joy at the moment. After wanting James dead for almost as long as she'd been married to him, she was struggling with what to do next with her life. It was a question she had been considering since her sacking at Maeve Grant, but she'd always been able to distract herself from forward progress in her life with her revenge fantasies.

Her fantasy now fulfilled, she kept returning to the same question over and over again. *What now?*

———

At around seven, a nurse came out into the waiting room. "We just gave Owen a sedative to help him sleep tonight," she said. "The doctor said that there will be no more visits today. He'll let you have a longer visit tomorrow, but he wants Owen to sleep through the night. You two should take the opportunity to get some rest yourselves. It's important for you to keep your strength up too. And not just physically. Emotionally too."

Wayne suggested that they get a bite at the diner across the street from the hospital. He would have been more than willing to go someplace more upscale, but he doubted Jessica wanted to do anything beyond utilitarian this evening.

The hostess seated them in a booth toward the back. It could have comfortably sat six.

"Can I interest you in sharing a black-and-white malt?" he asked.

She laughed. "Yes. I think that would be . . . appropriate."

When Owen was born, there had been a diner across the street from that hospital too. Twice a day during Jessica's three-day stay, Wayne had gone downstairs and gotten them both black-and-white malts.

"How's Stephanie?" Jessica asked after they'd ordered.

Wayne had not yet found a way to tell her that he'd ended things with Stephanie. "We're taking a break," he said.

"Oh."

"Well, a breakup is more accurate."

"I'm sorry, Wayne."

"Thanks. It's for the best."

Wayne heard his next sentence in his head and decided it was worth saying aloud. "I think now . . . maybe more than ever, you and I just need each other."

———

In the eleven days since James Sommers's murder, Gabriel hadn't narrowed the suspect list any more than he had in the first eleven minutes. Wife. Ex-wife. Ex-husband of wife. Business partner. Mysterious short-haired woman named Allison.

Allison hadn't showed at the funeral, although Gabriel had known that would be a long shot. Asra suggested that Allison might be dead herself, the victim of a Reid Warwick double cross. For that reason, she had been monitoring the missing persons and Jane Does at the morgue, but no short-haired, thin women in the proper age group had turned up.

Gabriel had a different take. If Allison had been involved, he assumed she was on a beach somewhere, living off the proceeds of the deal she had decided not to split with James Sommers and Reid Warwick. That's why he figured she had killed the former and stiffed the latter.

Then there was Ella's theory: that Allison didn't even exist.

Not that they needed another suspect at the moment anyway. None of the current candidates had an alibi worth a damn. Jessica Sommers claimed to be alone in her apartment all night. No one saw Wayne Fiske between the time he left school at 3:45 p.m. until his son showed up at his house at seven. Reid Warwick's refusal to cooperate suggested that he too lacked an airtight alibi. The crazy ex-wife, who had originally been at the top of the suspect list, had the best alibi of the bunch. Her boy toy confirmed that she'd been with him (or at least on her way to him) during the time frame that James Sommers had been killed. Then again, Gabriel had the sense that her boyfriend would say anything to keep Haley coming back for more.

Unfortunately, closed-circuit TV from the Met Breuer museum didn't capture the entryway to Sommers's building across the street. The building's own security system had been broken for more than a year, the landlord figuring that a visible camera made for a sufficient deterrent by itself.

Jessica Sommers's building did have a working camera. It showed her enter at three and not leave until the following morning. On the other hand, tenants tended to know how to avoid being filmed by their own buildings' security cameras. Which meant that Gabriel couldn't rule out that James Sommers told his wife something on the phone that caused her to go to his office, setting in motion the confrontation that ended with him dead.

Reid Warwick's Fifth Avenue residence had both security cameras and doormen. They all told the same story: Reid came home at a little after one in the morning with zero blood on his clothing. That was hardly airtight, of course. He could have gone to James's office, killed his partner, and then switched clothes before coming home.

A team of cops was assigned the monotonous task of scanning video from the 7 train platform at Grand Central, hoping to see Wayne Fiske. The combination of the grainy footage and the sheer number of people crammed onto the subway platform, even off-peak, made a positive ID impossible. That kept Wayne Fiske very much still in the mix.

One of the odd quirks of law enforcement was that cell records were considered to be more private than financial records. Ever since the Supreme Court's 2018 decision, cops couldn't find out about a suspect's movements through cell tower pings without a search warrant, and that required meeting the probable-cause standard. Gabriel knew that no judge would issue a warrant while they had four equally plausible suspects, so he hadn't even tried to get one.

By contrast, a grand jury subpoena had been enough to obtain the victim's bank records.

The Sommerses' monthly account statements were silent as to whether they had a brokerage account, which was where real wealth would be housed. Usually, among those privileged enough to own securities, bank records showed money being transferred back and forth to the brokerage account. The lack of such transfers meant either that the Sommerses didn't have stocks, or that they had a second source of cash that the police hadn't discovered.

The bank records weren't a total dead end, however. The Sommerses' monthly expenses had outpaced their income by a significant amount over the past twelve months. Which meant that they were not nearly as well off as they appeared to the outside world. Of course, that hardly made them different from many couples these days.

But the real find was the payments to an insurance company. That, in turn, led Gabriel to a half-a-million-dollar policy on James Sommers's life that named Jessica Sommers as the sole beneficiary.

And that was motive.

Jessica Sommers had told them about her son's treatment, and how her husband had stepped up to pay for it. It was an odd thing for her to share if it pointed the finger at her, but people did strange things sometimes. The subconscious at work was often a detective's greatest ally. She had said that her husband's work with the mysterious Allison was going to pay for the treatment, but what if she had decided not to wait for the art sales and to instead cash in the policy for her son's sake?

Or perhaps Wayne Fiske had been the impatient one. Maybe his ex-wife had confided that they didn't have the money for the treatment, and she was *hoping* that her husband could come up with it. And *he* decided to take matters into his own hands to save his son, which had the added benefit of eliminating his romantic rival.

It wasn't just the money that was causing Gabriel to think the cuckolded ex-husband was looking very good for this. CSU had found a plethora of fingerprints at James Sommers's office, but only one match: Wayne Fiske.

Unfortunately for Mr. Fiske, all teachers are fingerprinted due to an NYC Department of Education regulation. As a result, there was hard proof that he'd been in the office of his ex-wife's now-dead husband. The fingerprint evidence couldn't pinpoint the exact day or time he'd been there, however. But fingerprints don't last forever.

Of course, Gabriel was certain that some of their other suspects—Jessica Sommers, Reid Warwick, and Allison—had also left prints. After all, there was no dispute that all three had been in Sommers's office in the forty-eight hours prior to his death. The problem was that their fingerprints weren't housed in any law enforcement databases. And even if they were, their presence in James Sommers's office was not incriminating in and of itself.

Wayne Fiske and Haley Sommers were a different matter, however. They had no good reason to explain their presence inside James Sommers's place of business.

18

That forensic presentation was being made by the Assistant Medical Examiner, Erica Thompson. Gabriel found her something of a breath of fresh air from the sixtysomething grumpy white men who typically filled the medical examiner's office. Not only was she smarter than most of her colleagues, she also explained her findings in a way that didn't require you to be a medical examiner yourself to understand.

"Sorry about the delay in getting you this information," she said. "We've been backed up like you wouldn't believe. Also, I didn't think too much was going to be different from what I saw at the scene. Which turned out to be pretty much the case. Like I said before, cause of death is blunt force trauma. The man's head hit that coffee table at just the right angle and velocity. Or, from his perspective, precisely the wrong one. There were no drugs or alcohol in his system, so nothing that impaired him in any way to make the death blow easier to inflict. Time of death is a little narrower than originally estimated. The revised window is four p.m. to seven p.m."

"If he was the caller to his wife's phone at a few minutes before five, then we can shave an hour off the front end of that," Asra said.

"If you can make that evidentiary assumption, then yes," Erica replied.

"Even so, I was hoping for a time of death that might rule some-body out," Gabriel said. "All of our people of interest are still in play during that window."

"Sorry. I can only tell you what the science tells me," Erica said. "But here's something that might be of some interest to you. Remember I noted the scratch on his chin? Well, it is consistent with his being struck by someone's fist. But he does not have any marks on his own hands."

"Which means?" Asra asked.

"It wasn't much of a fight," Erica said. "The doer inflicted all the damage. And you were right about the sheets. Semen and female fluids galore. The semen is the vic's. No big surprise there. Unfortunately, no matches in the database for his lady friend."

"His wife says it was her," Asra said.

"Easy enough to verify with a DNA sample."

"You're really not helping us, Erica," Gabriel said jokingly. "Isn't there anything that we can actually use to arrest somebody?"

"How about this? There was blood at the scene that did not belong to Mr. Sommers."

"Whose?" Gabriel and Asra asked in unison.

"Don't you think I would have led with that if I knew who left their blood at the scene?" Erica said with a raised eyebrow. "Once again, no database matches."

The NYPD had access to the national criminal database of DNA, which was composed of the DNA of every unfortunate soul who became ensnared in the criminal justice system. It was hardly surprising that none of those folks hobnobbed with the Manhattan art crowd.

"My Spidey sense tells me that if you find the person who left that blood, you've got your killer," Erica went on. "That's because I think it's a strong likelihood that the blood was the result of the killer punching the vic. Even if you're the one that lands the punch, knuckles coming in contact with a chin have a tendency to bleed."

Gabriel turned to Asra. "Do you remember anyone with a cut or scratch on his or her hand?"

"No," she said. "But I do remember that Jessica didn't take off her gloves, even when she was in the interrogation room."

———

The doorman hadn't buzzed up to announce his visitor. That was enough to tell Reid that the police were coming. Building security didn't allow visitors to come upstairs unannounced. No exceptions. Law enforcement were different, however. Especially if the cops said that calling ahead would be construed as obstruction of justice.

The hard rap on his door only confirmed that conclusion.

"Reid Warwick? NYPD."

Reid hadn't yet gotten dressed, though it was nearly eleven. Last night had gone later than usual. Into this morning, truth be told. Luckily for him, he had told his companion that her company was no longer desired somewhere around 4:00 a.m., so at least he was alone now. He felt like hell, though, and looked even worse.

Meeting the police in this state was not ideal. Still, he didn't have too many options. So, against his better judgment, Reid opened the door.

"Good morning, Mr. Warwick. You may recall, my name is Lieutenant Velasquez. This is my partner, Detective Jamali. We're here to ask you to provide us with a sample of your DNA so we might be able to clear you as a suspect."

"I thought I told you before. Anything you have to say, you should say through my lawyer."

"What you said, Mr. Warwick, was that you feared that your cooperation with us might violate certain confidentiality agreements you had with your clients, and you wanted to consult with your attorney about that. We're here just to rule you out as a suspect. Doesn't implicate your clients at all to give us a cheek scrape's worth of DNA. It'll only take a second. Then we'll be on our way." The lieutenant shrugged. "Doesn't even hurt. I promise."

"Let me discuss that with my lawyer," Reid said. "He'll be back to you shortly if there's anything he wants to share. I appreciate you both coming today."

Reid extended his hand to indicate that the meeting was over.

The lieutenant grasped it. But rather than shake hands, he twisted Reid's wrist, turning his palm down.

Reid didn't have the foggiest notion why.

———

Haley's first thought when she saw the two police officers standing at her front door was that Jessica had decided that the best defense was a good offense and had gone all in on pointing the accusatory finger at her. A beat later, she considered that maybe it was Malik who had turned, perhaps reaching the conclusion that even no-limits sex with her wasn't worth prison time. Either way, she was in serious jeopardy.

"My name again is Lieutenant Velasquez. This is Detective Jamali. May we come in?"

She remembered the lieutenant. He was hard to forget. Straight from central casting.

She also recalled his partner from the last time. The one who hadn't spoken very much.

"I'm sorry, but I'd rather you didn't."

The moment the words left her mouth, Haley realized that she should have sent the police away entirely, rather than merely deny them entry. She needed to shut this down before she said anything that could incriminate her—lie or otherwise.

"We'll talk here, then," Lieutenant Velasquez said. "We're here to ask you to provide a DNA sample. It will allow us to clear you as someone who was at the crime scene at the time of the murder. It's a simple swab of your cheek."

He smiled at her. His *C'mon, look how good-looking I am. Don't you trust me?* smile.

Haley knew that trick well; she had often used it herself. More times than she could remember. And nearly every time, she shouldn't have been trusted.

"No, thank you. I would also appreciate it if you didn't visit me again."

"If that's how you want to play it, Ms. Sommers. But I have to tell you that you're making a mistake."

"Won't be the first one of my life," she said.

From the small opening she'd left in the doorway, she saw Lieutenant Velasquez extend his hand. The gesture struck Haley as odd. She couldn't recall having shaken hands with him before.

Fearing if she opened the door any wider, they'd force their way in, she said, "Goodbye" without shaking his hand.

The police officers didn't move.

"Before we go, can we see your hands, Ms. Sommers?" Detective Jamali asked.

"My hands?"

"Yes. Just put your hands out."

The detective demonstrated the pose. Like she was a doctor who had washed her hands before surgery, waiting for someone to put gloves on her.

Haley looked down at her knuckles. Nothing seemed odd about them. She stuck them through the door so the police could confirm that assessment.

Detective Jamali leaned in for a closer look. "You don't have any cuts, Ms. Sommers. Why do you think that you might have left your blood at the scene of your ex-husband's murder?"

Haley didn't understand the accusation. "Blood?"

"That's what we're trying to match with your DNA," she said. "*Exclude* is more accurate. If you're not a match, we know you didn't leave any blood there. That'll exclude you as a suspect. And that's something you really want to happen because we know you were next door to Mr. Sommers's office on the day of the murder. The waiters at Sant Ambroeus told us you're a regular there. Like to sit at the bar and look out the window. Quite the coincidence that the window provided a clear view of your ex-husband arriving and leaving work every day. And, according to the folks at Sant Ambroeus, the timing of your arrival at your friend's place can't be right."

All that time she spent having sex with Malik had apparently been for naught. Not completely for naught, of course, but it hadn't achieved Haley's intended purpose of providing her with an alibi.

"How long do you think your friend is going to keep covering for you after we explain the jail time he's looking at for being an accessory after the fact in a murder?" Lieutenant Velasquez chimed in. "But the good news is that being a stalker is one thing, but it doesn't make you a murderer, right? You were at that restaurant lots of times, and James Sommers never died after any of those visits. But if we can't exclude you because your blood isn't a match for the blood at the scene, what choice do we have but to assume it's yours?"

Haley would have loved to prove that she hadn't left any blood in James's office. But her DNA would go beyond that. It would prove that she *was* in the office, something that they had no evidence of now.

Or at least, none that they were admitting to. They claimed they could only place her next door.

And even though they were telling her that she'd be excluded if she hadn't left blood at the scene, she didn't believe that for a second. It was one thing for her to be stalking James from the safety of a nearby restaurant. Quite another for her to be in violation of a restraining order and breaking and entering into a murdered man's office.

"So what'll it be, Ms. Sommers?" Detective Jamali asked.

Haley's heart was going a mile a minute. She willed herself to remain calm, at least on the outside.

"I'm sorry," she said. "Actually, I'm not even sorry. If you want anything, you need to call my lawyer."

She closed the door on them. It occurred to her when the catch clicked shut that she hadn't even given them a lawyer's name to call.

———

Since James's death, Jessica hated being in the loft. Truth be told, even when her husband was alive, she'd never felt entirely comfortable at home without him. Now, with no hope of James coming through the door ever again, the emptiness of her home frightened her all the more.

There wasn't a single spot within its three thousand square feet where she could breathe. Certainly not her bedroom with its reminders of James, or the living room with art all over the walls. Owen's room made her even more depressed. He should be home now, filling their loft with the sound of his violin, or at the very least, holed up in his room on his computer, *not* lying in a hospital bed at Sloan Kettering.

As a sign of how on edge she was, the knock on her front door made her jump so high she thought she might have hit the ceiling. She checked the peephole before opening the door. She was glad she had. It wasn't a condolence call, which had been her first thought. On the other side of the door were Lieutenant Velasquez and Detective Jamali.

"Sorry to bother you, Ms. Sommers," Lieutenant Velasquez said. "May we come in?"

They all assembled in the living room. Jessica could tell that Detective Jamali was looking hard at her hands. She quickly placed them under her legs, out of view.

"We're here because we're asking everyone for a DNA sample so we can officially exclude them as suspects. That will allow us to focus our efforts on other people, like Reid Warwick and Haley Sommers, both of whom refused to provide us a sample of their DNA."

"Why do you need anyone's DNA?"

"We're trying to see who was in your husband's office at or around the time of the murder," Detective Jamali said.

"I'm in and out of there all the time," Jessica said. "I told you I was there the day before he died."

"We understand that," Detective Jamali said. "Still, it's protocol that we get everyone involved to provide DNA. If for no other reason than to confirm it's your DNA on the sheets in the bedroom."

"Who else's could it be?"

"Forgive me for saying this, Ms. Sommers, but it's possible your husband washed the sheets after you left and then was with another woman. Perhaps this Allison, who we haven't yet been able to find."

Jessica supposed that could be true. But even if it was, she didn't want to know. Not now. Not anymore.

"I don't care," she said. "I just don't want to think about James being unfaithful. It doesn't matter anymore."

Lieutenant Velasquez looked as if he understood. "There's another reason too. We believe that your husband and his killer might have been involved in a physical altercation, which is what led to his death. Perhaps a blow that knocked him down. Or maybe tripped him. We came to that conclusion because there was blood left at the scene that was not your husband's. We believe it will match the killer."

"I didn't hit my husband, if that's what you're insinuating. And he never lifted a finger to hurt me."

"A DNA test will prove that, then," Detective Jamali said.

"I don't need to prove anything to you. I *know*."

"Ms. Sommers, it hasn't escaped our attention that you're keeping your hands out of view," Lieutenant Velasquez said. "Why is that?"

Jessica didn't reply. Not audibly, at least. And certainly not by revealing her hands.

Lieutenant Velasquez sighed loudly. His way of expressing displeasure. "Help us, Jessica," he said.

His use of her first name didn't go unnoticed. She told herself not to get drawn in. They weren't there to help her. Not really.

"I need for you both to leave now," Jessica said.

Rather than get up to leave, Detective Jamali said, "Was your ex-husband in James's office recently?"

"Wayne?"

"Yes."

"I . . . Why are you asking?"

Lieutenant Velasquez jumped in. "It's a simple question. Was he or wasn't he?"

"He was," she said.

"When? And for what purpose?"

"I feel like I'm being interrogated here," she said.

"We're asking about your ex-husband," he said. "His fingerprints were at the crime scene. That struck us as odd. Now you're telling us that he was there, and we're wondering for what purpose he would be visiting your husband."

"Please, you need to leave. Now."

"I don't understand," Lieutenant Velasquez said, looking as if he truly didn't. "Is there something you haven't told us? Something you're hiding? Because that's the only conclusion we're going to draw if you stop cooperating with us."

"If you can't rule me out because I loved my husband and would never hurt him, then I don't want to participate in your investigation any longer," Jessica said. "I've told you everything I know about the night of James's death. There's nothing more for us to discuss. I need to grieve now. In peace. I don't expect to speak to you again."

"We weren't talking about you, Ms. Sommers. I was inquiring about your ex-husband. He's a suspect. Are you protecting him?"

"I'm sorry—you both need to leave now."

Lieutenant Velasquez stood. He still looked completely blindsided. It had to be an act, of course. He understood perfectly well why Jessica had changed her tune. He had said it himself: there *was* something she was hiding.

Jessica moved toward the door, careful to keep her hands out of sight. The police officers followed a step behind. She opened the door in the hopes that it would cause them to vacate sooner. Before he passed out of her home, however, Lieutenant Velasquez said, "You're making a big mistake here, Ms. Sommers."

She shut the door behind them without responding. Then she prayed Lieutenant Velasquez was wrong.

———

Authority figures reminded Wayne of his father, and that was never a good thing. Still, he thought he was ready for the police's arrival.

Jessica had called forty minutes earlier. They went through her interaction with the police in step-by-step detail.

"Don't even let them in the house. I regret doing that," she said. "Just tell them at the door that you do not want to be involved."

"I know what to say," Wayne said, annoyed that she thought he needed to be spoon-fed in this way.

Then, when the time came, he screwed up his first line, allowing the police officers to enter his house.

"Thank you. We won't be long," Lieutenant Velasquez said.

"What can I do for you both today?" Wayne asked, sounding a bit too chipper for the circumstances.

"We're going back to people who knew Mr. Sommers to obtain a DNA sample," Detective Jamali said. "It's just a scrape of your cheek. Takes a second. Doesn't hurt."

She handed him a wooden stick. The kind that reminded Wayne of the spoon that came with Dixie cups when he was a kid.

"Do I have to do it?" he asked.

"I'm sorry, what was your question?" Lieutenant Velasquez asked.

He had an intimidating stare. Wayne remembered how his father would look at him like that.

"I asked you if I can legally say no to your request," he said, trying to keep his voice steady.

"I don't see why you would do that. Unless, of course, you're afraid that providing your DNA might incriminate you."

That answered Wayne's question. Although he already knew as much. He'd googled it. If they didn't have a warrant, which they apparently didn't, he didn't have to do anything.

"I've got nothing to hide, but I do have a deep distrust of the police state," Wayne said. "I don't want my DNA in some database for . . . well, forever, being used in ways that I have no idea." He laughed. "I mean, I'm not even on Facebook."

Neither of the officers thought that was funny. "Mr. Fiske," Lieutenant Velasquez said in a tone used to convey the utmost seriousness of the matter, "up until this moment, we did not think of you as a suspect. But if you refuse to provide your DNA, we have to reconsider whether we're looking at this right. My experience is that people with—as you said—nothing to hide don't refuse to provide their DNA. So, to be very blunt about it, right now I'm asking myself, why would a smart man like Wayne Fiske refuse to provide DNA evidence—"

"Unless he's guilty of murder," Detective Jamali finished the sentence.

"I've got nothing to hide," Wayne said again, wishing he hadn't. He was protesting too much. "But I do know my rights. And unless you have a warrant, I have every legal right to decline your request. So that's what I'm going to do."

"Were you ever in Mr. Sommers's office?" Lieutenant Velasquez asked.

"What?"

"Simple question. Yes or no, were you ever in James Sommers's office?"

"Of course. I pick Owen up there sometimes," he said.

"When did you do that last?"

Wayne decided he had said too much. "I need you to leave now."

In the brief standoff that followed, Wayne could tell that the lieutenant was considering whether to arrest him right then and there.

"Okay. Thank you for your time." Lieutenant Velasquez extended his hand as if to say, *No hard feelings.*

Wayne kept his in his pockets.

"Goodbye. Please let yourselves out."

19

"Do you think they could have been in on it together?" Asra asked.

It was the morning after every single one of their suspects refused their DNA requests. Gabriel hated the feeling that a murderer was laughing at him, but he could almost hear the cackle.

"Possible," he said. Indeed, a part of him was hoping that was the explanation. Conspiracies never held together. Like the old saying goes, a secret can only be kept between two people if one of them is dead. "But it sounds pretty unlikely. I mean, Jessica Sommers leaves her husband of seventeen years for another man, and then conspires with that same ex-husband to kill her new husband?"

"It makes sense if the only way to save their son was collecting on that insurance policy," Asra said. "But I still think it's more likely that Wayne Fiske did it alone. The wife was clearly hoping her husband would sell the artwork to fund her son's treatment. But the ex-husband, he might leap on a surefire way to get his son's treatment paid for. And if it means that the guy who stole his wife drops out of the picture, that sounds like a win-win to me."

"How'd he even know about the policy?"

"She probably told him. The policy had a cash surrender value. Maybe she mentioned to her ex that they could cash it in and put that toward the treatment cost, and he decided it would be better to off the husband and use the proceeds to pay for the whole shebang."

"And now she's protecting him?" Gabriel asked.

"Wouldn't you protect your ex-wife if she was a murderer?"

Gabriel considered that scenario. He couldn't imagine ever not loving Ella, and he also couldn't imagine ever cooperating with the police to put his wife behind bars, no matter what she had done. Not only because he loved his wife, but also for his daughter's sake. And if Ella's crime had been in furtherance of protecting Annie, he'd definitely stand by her, without a moment's hesitation. Which was why he concluded that, if faced with the same calculus, Jessica Sommers would opt to keep the father of her seventeen-year-old son, a son who was suffering from leukemia, in his life and out of jail. And that would include lying about whether he'd been in her husband's office recently, and giving Wayne a heads-up that the NYPD was coming to ask him that same question.

"So you're giving the first Mrs. Sommers a pass?" Gabriel asked. "Even with that voice mail? And why on earth doesn't Reid fill us in about Allison if Wayne Fiske is our guy?"

The questions hung in the air. Asra didn't have a good answer to either.

"Let's look at it from a different angle," Gabriel said. "Maybe the murder has nothing to do with insurance at all. It could very well be a business deal gone bad. If Allison was working on a multimillion-dollar drug deal, we wouldn't be thinking twice about spouses and ex-spouses. I'm not sure that this art transaction was any more legal."

"Expending all this energy on motive doesn't really matter at the end of the day," Asra said. "It's going to come down to the DNA match. Whoever left their blood when punching James Sommers is going to be our killer. We should just get subpoenas to collect DNA from all of them."

If only police work were so simple, Gabriel thought. He often believed crime could be eradicated if it weren't for the Constitution.

"No judge is going to give us a warrant to take DNA from every one of our suspects," he said. "But I was thinking that maybe we could use one of those ancestry websites. We take the DNA we have and see if it matches anyone in their database. My guess is that it's much more likely that our murderer has a relative who got into genealogy than one who's a felon."

"There's no way the websites cooperate with us," Asra said.

Gabriel knew that was true. Ever since the Golden State Killer was arrested in 2018, after police had tracked the DNA left at old crime scenes to the suspect's relatives using such sites, the technique had been at the intersection of civil rights and criminal investigation. The problem was that the major corporate players—Ancestry.com and 23andMe, among others—had vowed not to cooperate with law enforcement. It wasn't good for their business model if, in addition to helping people find unknown relatives, they were also making it easier for those relatives to be arrested. Which was why they refused even in the face of a subpoena. And so far, most courts had sided with them.

Gabriel had the distinct feeling they were running out of time. They had collected all the evidence by now. They had the forensics, they'd canvassed people in the area (which was how they knew about Haley's proximity to the murder scene that day), and they had timelines establishing the whereabouts of their people of interest. And yet no one stood out as any more likely a suspect than anyone else.

After a week, cases got cold. After two weeks, they were frozen solid.

———

Jessica spent the main part of her days at the hospital. Her visits with Owen were limited to ten minutes every two hours, but rather than go home in between, she stayed in the waiting area. She preferred to spend the time in the company of others, even if they were nurses or family members of other cancer patients, none of whom she knew. At least that way she didn't feel so alone.

Wayne would arrive after school let out, around four. Sometimes they would sit together for a while. So far, not a day had gone by in which he hadn't offered to take her to dinner. Either at the diner across the street for malts or someplace else.

Twice she accepted. Twice she declined.

She knew that her ex-husband was hoping that it was the beginning of something more for them. She laughed at the irony that he could so easily sweep away what she had done, when it was impossible for her to do likewise. Her affair with James would forever define her, and she could not imagine living a life in which her partner pretended that it had never happened. Or that it had simply been an inconsequential detour in her life's path, rather than the most actualizing choice she'd ever made.

The biggest reason, of course, was that James had showed her what true love was, and going back to anything less was unfathomable. Still, Wayne remained the one person who understood what she was going through. Not entirely, of course. He hadn't lost his spouse. But she knew that they were of one mind when it came to Owen, and that brought her the sole source of comfort she experienced these days. Like her, Wayne would do anything for their son, and that she did love about him.

———

Sometimes Owen couldn't remember if he'd been in the hospital for a day or a month. Nothing ever changed except the sky outside his window, and that only went from blue to black and back again.

He continued to follow his friends' group chats, which gave him a window into the life he had left behind. Occasionally he'd get a text from someone from school, checking in on him. Zoey Sanderson had actually DM'd him last week. It was only a heart emoji and a "feel better," but it had come with three exclamation points. Owen hadn't thought she'd even notice his absence. She certainly didn't talk to him much when they were in school, outside of sometimes asking him about the chemistry homework.

Maybe if he ever got out of here, he'd ask her out. Assuming, of course, that Zoey had a thing for bald teenagers who might die at any moment.

The other day he had tried to play a little violin. Nothing fancy, but it had felt good to have the bow in his hands again, the chin rest against his jaw. He thought that with the door shut no one could hear, but the moment he was finished, Owen heard the applause from the nurses' station and even some calls of "Bravo!" That felt good too.

———

Reid was holding tight to the portfolio case, a big black leather number he'd purchased for the occasion.

Allison had selected the St. Regis again. "I'll even cover the fifteen hundred dollars for a suite out of my end," she'd said with a smile.

Reid wondered if maybe they'd be able to use the room for more than selling some art. He even had visions that, after Allison's client left, the two of them would pour the cash out onto the bed and roll around in it naked, like they did in the movies.

Allison opened the door after a single knock and smiled when she saw Reid on the other side. She was dressed in a conservative suit but still looked stunning, which caused him to smile too.

"Welcome, Reid," she said. "Allow me to introduce you to my client, Harrison Ellis. Harrison, this is Reid Warwick."

The soon-to-be owner of three Jackson Pollock pieces was African American, which surprised Reid, although he realized it shouldn't have. No rule said that only white people should have expensive art, or the millions of dollars in cash it took to buy it.

The buyer was wearing a three-piece suit, which didn't mesh exactly with his goatee.

Reid shook his benefactor's hand. "Nice to meet you, Mr. Ellis."

"Please, let's be on a first-name basis. Call me Harrison. And may I call you Reid?"

"If you have the three million dollars we discussed, you can call me whatever you want."

It was Ellis's turn to smile. "It's in my car, being guarded by my driver."

Reid got that hinky feeling again. He'd brought the Pollocks, after all, and expected a simultaneous exchange. Nonetheless, he wasn't about to bail on the chance of walking out $3 million richer.

"Still don't trust me, do you, Allison?" he said.

"Why would you ever say that?" Allison replied with a butter-wouldn't-melt-in-her-mouth expression.

"So I guess one of us has to show the other his first, right?"

"I know you're not shy, Reid," Allison said. "Be my guest."

Reid brought his portfolio case over to the table. He unlatched the sides and opened it.

"If you don't mind, I would prefer you not touch them," he said. "But look as much as you like. As we discussed, there are three in total."

Ellis examined the first Pollock, hovering over it to get a closer look. He then turned to Allison, silently asking her to opine.

"Perfect," she said.

"May I see the others?" Ellis asked.

"Of course."

Reid carefully flipped over the first Pollock, revealing the second one beneath it. Once again, Ellis looked up at Allison after examining it. This time she merely nodded.

That was Reid's signal to flip the page. He repeated the ritual a third time.

"Three million dollars, cash," Ellis said.

Reid didn't sense that he was questioning the price. He was merely stating it.

"Yes," Reid said.

"Tell Mr. Ellis how you came upon these pieces, Reid. As you know, collectors always like hearing about that."

"The seller is a man who was very close to Lee Krasner, Jackson Pollock's widow, for much of Lee's later years. These were given to him by Ms. Krasner as gifts before she passed."

"And why is he selling now?" Ellis asked.

"He just feels it's time. He's an older gentleman, and he's considering estate-planning issues."

"Do you have any other questions, Harrison?" Allison asked.

"I don't. Do you?"

"No. I think we're all good here."

"All except the payment," Reid said.

That's when the door flung open. Even before Reid saw who was on the other side, he knew what was happening. And cursed the fact that he hadn't listened to that hinky feeling.

20

Captain Tomlinson knocked on Gabriel's half-open door.

"The pleasure of your company has been requested by our brothers and sisters on the federal side of the street."

Gabriel looked over at Asra.

"What about?" she asked.

"All they said was that they had some information that might be relevant to your investigation and wanted a sit-down."

"When and where?" Gabriel asked.

"They were kind enough to slum it over here," Tomlinson said. "They'll be here in fifteen minutes."

Gabriel hated these interdepartmental meetings between the FBI and the NYPD, but they were a fact of life in law enforcement. They didn't at all resemble the way they were portrayed on TV, however, like celebrity marriages gone bad with screaming on both sides about jurisdiction. In reality, they were simply a different constituency you had to manage. Like a boss you didn't necessarily like.

When Asra and Gabriel arrived in the captain's office, the feds were already there. A man and a woman.

Tomlinson's office wasn't quite large enough to accommodate four guests. Two squad room chairs had been pulled into the room for Gabriel and Asra, but it made for an awkward seating arrangement: Tomlinson behind his desk, the feds in his guest chairs facing him, and

Asra and Gabriel sitting behind them, as if they were the audience and Tomlinson was performing onstage. The feds, at least, twisted their seats to form something of a circle.

For most people, ADA and AUSA are interchangeable titles. They're all prosecutors. But much as the NYPD and FBI each have their types, so do local and federal prosecutors. As a general matter, those budding attorneys who had the choice chose to go to the federal side. The pay was better, and the level of criminal more sophisticated. That mattered more for lawyers than for cops because it made for an easier transition to the private sector later in their careers. On the other hand, the work was more interesting on the local side. Gabriel thought that being in federal law enforcement was all about financial crime, with the victims sometimes even less sympathetic than the perpetrators. Ella seconded that opinion, and she should know—unlike him, she'd had a choice of employers, and she'd chosen the DA's office without hesitation.

"I'm AUSA Parker Henderson," the man said.

He looked like a federal prosecutor. Young, clean-cut, probably from money, or maybe he'd had a big law firm job before going to work for the government.

"Special agent Allison Lashley," the female fed said.

Gabriel looked to Asra. From her smile, it had clicked for her too.

"We've been looking for you, Ms. Lashley," he said.

"Apologies for waiting so long for this reveal," Henderson said. "We wanted to see how things played out before we had this meeting."

"Someone want to tell me what it seems like you all already know?" asked Tomlinson.

"Special Agent Lashley here was the last person to see James Sommers alive," Asra said.

"Second to last," she said. "I didn't kill him."

Henderson said, "Mr. Sommers was, unfortunately for him, ensnared in a federal operation concerning stolen art. Special Agent

Lashley told Mr. Sommers about his misfortune only a few hours before his murder."

"I was undercover as an art appraiser for a client," Lashley said. "I accompanied my CI—a guy who had done a previous deal with Mr. Sommers a few years earlier—to do a buy. A Jackson Pollock to be purchased from Mr. Sommers and his partner, a man named Reid Warwick. After that went off without a hitch, I reestablished contact with Mr. Sommers and we arranged a more significant buy. A three-purchase sale. I met with Mr. Sommers and Reid Warwick in Mr. Sommers's office to discuss this sale. After Mr. Warwick left, I revealed myself to Mr. Sommers as a federal agent."

"Was Sommers going to flip?" Asra asked.

"He didn't have much choice. Under the sentencing guidelines, even for a first-time offender, he was looking at real time. And guys like James Sommers, they're not built for prison."

"So what happened that caused Mr. Sommers to crack his skull shortly thereafter?" Gabriel asked.

"Not sure," Lashley said. "Sommers and I discussed the next steps. The standard stuff. Not to tell anyone, even his wife. That he should pretend that the deal we were doing went off without a hitch. That he'd wear a wire for the payoff with Reid Warwick. And when we were done, I left him very much alive in his office."

"We figure that, despite our instructions, Sommers told Warwick, and Warwick killed him," Henderson said.

"Why is this the first we're all hearing about this?" Tomlinson said.

"That's on me," Henderson said. "We didn't want to jeopardize our investigation. Also, I thought we could help you all out a little better if we didn't disclose it right away. But this morning, Allison and another federal agent engaged in an undercover buy directly with Mr. Warwick. He's on tape. All wrapped up with a bow. We arrested him on the spot."

"Arrested him for what?" Asra said.

"Trafficking in stolen art. There'll be other charges to follow. Money laundering, wire fraud. It'll be a decent chunk of time he'll be facing when it's all added up."

"Where is he now?" Asra asked.

"Federal custody. Over at the MCC."

"How does keeping one of our prime suspects in a murder investigation on ice in federal lockup help us out?" Gabriel asked.

"Our initial thought was that maybe if we questioned him, you know, focusing on the federal crimes, he might let down his guard and give us something on the murder," Henderson said.

Gabriel actually laughed. "Yeah, how'd that work out for you?"

"About how you figured it would, based on your sarcasm. He lawyered up instantly. We're still going to hold him for the full forty-eight hours. Hoping that a taste of prison life might soften him up a bit. But once he appears for arraignment, we expect him to make bail on the art charges."

"Well," said Asra with a shrug, "at least we can take Allison off our suspect list."

"And put Reid Warwick at the top," Gabriel added.

———

Reid did not like a word of what Steve Weitzen was telling him.

He had been sitting in a prison cell for more than six hours now, clinging to the idea that he'd be out as soon as his mouthpiece showed up. Now that mouthpiece was telling Reid that he'd be staying put for a while.

In Reid's line of work, keeping a guy like Weitzen on retainer was the equivalent of visiting the dentist twice a year. You wanted to check in every so often to make sure you were not going to have a more serious problem down the road, and if something came up in the middle of the night that needed immediate attention, you had someone at the ready to take care of it.

Reid had first retained Weitzen's services ten years earlier, regarding a money-laundering investigation in which he had become enmeshed. He liked Weitzen's bedside manner. The way he told it to Reid straight, and didn't seem to judge him. Of course, he mainly liked the fact that he hadn't been indicted that time around. Some of his associates hadn't been so lucky.

Over the next decade, the advice of a criminal defense lawyer had come in handy in probably half a dozen instances. Usually they concerned Reid's principal business, which was money laundering. Occasionally, they involved his side hustles, like trafficking in stolen art. None of them had ever involved murder, however.

This was also the first time he'd been in the unfortunate position of talking to his lawyer while incarcerated.

"I'm sorry, Reid," Weitzen said. "I can't push up the arraignment date. By law, they can hold you for forty-eight hours. I think they want to squeeze you a bit on the Sommers murder."

"I don't know anything about the murder," Reid said.

Weitzen showed no emotion. Reid knew he didn't care one way or the other about whether his client was a murderer, a money launderer, or an art thief.

"I hear you. The good news is that you'll get bail when we get before the judge. The bad news is that they think you do know something about the murder, and that means you're inside for two more days."

"What if I give them my DNA? Will that give us some leverage with them to push up the bail hearing?"

Weitzen considered this for a moment in his lawyerly way. "It can't hurt," he finally said. Then he caught himself. "Are you absolutely certain that your blood isn't going to be a match?"

Reid looked at him. "I'm not stupid, Steve. I wouldn't be suggesting this if I had actually murdered the guy. My DNA will be at his office because I was there. But that's not a secret at this point. I don't know what they're looking for with my DNA, but it's not going to show I killed James because I didn't."

———

Jessica had been told that once she invoked her right to counsel, the police wouldn't bother her anymore. Yet there they were, standing on the other side of her front door.

Even before she could tell them to leave, Lieutenant Velasquez said, "We have some news about the woman who was doing the art deal with your husband. The woman named Allison."

She considered telling Lieutenant Velasquez that she didn't care anymore, just like she'd said the other day. But that hadn't been true then, and it wasn't true now.

She opened the door. No harm in simply listening, she figured.

"Okay. So tell me about Allison."

"It turns out Allison is Allison Lashley. She's an FBI agent."

If they had said Allison was Bigfoot, Jessica would have been no less surprised. "Why was an FBI agent involved in selling art?"

Detective Jamali smiled at Jessica's mistake. "She was working undercover. The FBI was investigating stolen art. The pieces that your husband was selling with Reid Warwick—the Pollocks—were stolen."

When Jessica finally made sense of what the detective was telling her, her sole takeaway was that James hadn't been unfaithful. Of course he hadn't. She was annoyed with herself for ever doubting him and hoped that, wherever he was right now, he forgave her.

"Did you hear what I just said, Mrs. Sommers? Your husband was trafficking in stolen art."

Instinctively, Jessica wanted to defend James; then she remembered that he didn't need her help. He had the best defense possible—he was dead.

———

Wayne looked forward to seeing Jessica when he arrived at the hospital. He was hoping that she might agree to have dinner tonight. She'd declined his offer the previous night, and he thought she was working on an every-other-night pattern.

Much to his disappointment, however, she was not in the waiting area when he got there. He assumed that he'd find her with Owen, yet when he entered his son's room, he saw that was not the case. Wayne's spirits were nonetheless lifted by the fact that Owen was awake, which was not a common occurrence. In fact, Owen seemed to be on some type of sleep cycle that made 4:00 p.m. to 8:00 p.m. the middle of the night.

"So how are you today? Scale of one to ten."

Wayne had read that this question was a good way to get information about Owen's health. Asking "How are you?" was invariably met with "fine," whether Owen was or not. At least a numerical evaluation gave Wayne a way to measure Owen's progress.

"What was I yesterday?"

"Two, but almost three."

"Holding steady, then."

"I'll take that."

"Good, because that's what I'm giving you."

"You know, now that your mom isn't here, and you're lucid during one of my visits, I thought maybe we could talk about something."

Wayne stopped, gauging Owen for some sign that he was receptive to the idea. As usual, his son provided little visual evidence of his thoughts.

"I'll take that as a yes," Wayne said with a smile. "One of the things about being a teenager, if I remember, and I think I do, is that you pretty much have the perspective about life that you're always going to have. Of course, it'll change a little bit; the importance of certain things will grow or decrease. You won't be as passionate about playing video games, for example. But who you are, how you feel about people . . . you already have a clear sense of that. Even though, as far as I know at least, you've never been in love, I suspect you have some sense about what that's going to feel like."

Another pause. The same blank stare from his son.

"But the one thing you don't know, which you can't know, is what it's like to have a child. It utterly transforms you, in a way that nothing else ever could. And that's not hyperbole, O. It's the truth. We humans are hardwired in certain ways. As a biology teacher, I can speak with some authority about this. There is a biological imperative for survival. So much of what we do is to protect ourselves from pain or death. You with me so far?"

"Yeah, I think so."

"Good. So I think that's the first order for every living species on this planet. There's something inside that's constantly telling you, *Don't die. Avoid pain.* But then you have a child, and all of a sudden, it's like a switch is flipped. Now that voice says something different. It says, *Don't let that child die. Don't let that child suffer any pain.*"

"Okay."

"And the things that you'll do to make sure that doesn't happen, they may be things you never thought yourself capable of doing. People who run into burning buildings. Or those stories of fathers who know they can't swim but still dive into the pool to rescue a child, which almost always leads to both of them drowning."

"I'm not sure why you're telling me this, Dad. Are you going to die for me?"

Owen said this with a chuckle, but Wayne could tell his son understood that it was not a laughing matter. In fact, he was reasonably sure his son understood exactly what he was saying to him.

———

Taxi TV is the service that plays in the back of New York City taxicabs. It's annoying as can be, with its Jimmy Kimmel segments and easy *Jeopardy!* questions. Haley always muted it as soon as she got in a cab.

She followed that pattern for today's ride as well. First, she told the driver where she was going; then she pressed the button to turn off the sound. As she did, however, a photograph of Reid popped up on the screen. In it, Reid looked tanned and slightly drunk. In other words, like Reid.

Haley turned the sound back on. The coverage was from NY1, the city's local news station. A woman's voice was providing the narrative.

"FBI agents said that Mr. Warwick, shown here, was selling stolen Jackson Pollock paintings. Jackson Pollock holds the record for highest sale price of an American artist's work. In 2015, his painting titled *Number 17A* was sold for a whopping $200 million in a private sale. The US Attorney said that Mr. Warwick faces up to fifty-seven years in prison."

The story lasted all of fifteen seconds before the screen morphed into an advertisement for a local steak house. By then, Haley was trying to find more information about Reid's arrest on her phone.

She searched "Reid Warwick." Too many hits. Then she filtered it to the last twenty-four hours.

The top hit was the website of the United States Attorney for the Southern District of New York. A press release told the story in a bit more detail:

Press Releases
Department of Justice
US Attorney's Office
Southern District of New York

FOR IMMEDIATE RELEASE

Art Dealer Charged with Trafficking in Stolen Art, Money Laundering

Abby Freedman, the United States Attorney for the Southern District of New York, announced the arrest today of REID WARWICK on charges of grand larceny, wire fraud, mail fraud and money laundering. Specifically, WARWICK has been charged with the attempted sale of several Jackson Pollock works stolen more than 40 years ago from the home of Lee Krasner, Pollock's widow.

Freedman said, "Reid Warwick, an art dealer, claimed that he was representing a client who had lawfully acquired numerous Jackson Pollock drawings, each worth approximately $1 million. In fact, Mr. Warwick was well aware that these works had been stolen."

Freedman praised the outstanding investigative work of Assistant US Attorney Parker Henderson and FBI special agent Allison Lashley.

The charges contained in the Complaint are merely accusations, and the defendant is presumed innocent unless and until proven guilty.

Haley found it gratifying that she had been right all along. James's deal with Reid was illegal. If he hadn't been murdered, James would be in handcuffs now too.

Reid hadn't been charged with murder, though. That meant they were still investigating. Which left open the terrifying possibility that they still could be coming for her.

21

Once Reid Warwick was in a talking mood, the man let loose like an open spigot. Information flowed out of him. Unfortunately, Gabriel already knew all of it.

Nonetheless, Warwick confirmed Gabriel's suspicions about the Sommerses' money problems. Warwick also told them that the reason James Sommers had agreed to sell the Pollocks in the first place was to pay for his stepson's treatment. "Without the money from those sales, James knew that boy was fucked," was Warwick's eloquent summation of the situation.

Warwick was most forceful in pointing the finger at Haley, however. He admitted that they sometimes slept together and that he thought she was angry enough at her ex-husband to kill him.

"There's something not right about that girl," he said. "She could go on and on about how much she wanted to kill James. If I were you, I'd focus my attention on her."

Gabriel hardly needed the advice of a felon. But he did appreciate being able to cross Reid Warwick off his list of suspects. Warwick's DNA didn't match the blood left at the scene. And, of course, the man had an alibi courtesy of Agent Lashley, who'd confirmed that when Reid left James's office, she remained behind to talk to James, and the victim was very much alive.

"It's beginning to feel a little like that board game Clue," Asra said. "We're not any closer to finding out who did it, but at least we're eliminating suspects."

———

Every time his parents came to visit, the first thing they asked was how he felt. Owen understood why they did it. It was the standard question under the circumstances. The problem was that he didn't know how to answer. At this point, it was almost a metaphysical query.

He felt terrible. About as bad as someone could be and still be alive. And yet, life continued to cling to him.

Telling that to his parents didn't seem right, though. So he made something up about getting stronger, or not feeling too bad, or whatever else he thought they wanted to hear.

He did, in fact, reek of garlic. And just like Dr. Cammerman had suggested what now seemed like eons ago, Owen sucked on Life Savers to get that god-awful taste out of his mouth. And he remained terribly weak.

Despite how he felt, the doctors claimed that he was getting better. The stem cells were "taking" and "reproducing," whatever that meant. Sometimes he wondered if they weren't just feeding him the same sort of BS he was telling his parents. A never-ending cycle of lies.

———

"Every day that goes by is a good day," Wayne told Jessica one afternoon at the hospital.

Four weeks had passed since James's death. Two and a half since Owen's operation.

It was typical Wayne, Jessica thought. Putting a happy face on a situation that was anything but.

"That's one way of thinking about it," she said. "The other is that the day of reckoning is that much closer."

"I prefer my way," Wayne said with a smile. "Maybe you should try it too."

"Maybe," she said.

"Focus on the positive, Jess. We've fully paid for Owen's treatment. We didn't think we'd be able to at the beginning of all this. Remember how desperate we were back then? And now the doctor says Owen's doing great. He might be able to come home in a couple of weeks."

The statement made Jessica's blood boil. She knew Wayne hadn't meant to directly equate James's death with Owen's life, but that's all she heard out of his little pep talk.

"We paid for his treatment with James's life insurance," she said loud enough that the others in the waiting room took notice.

Wayne tried to calm her, but it was too late. That dam had broken, and feelings Jessica had held inside for weeks burst through. "I never begrudged you for hating him. And I give you high marks for always putting those feelings aside and doing what's in Owen's best interest. Not every man would. But you can't imagine what it's like to lose someone you loved so much, suddenly, and under such terrible circumstances. Someone that you thought you'd grow old with."

She knew she had gone too far the moment the words left her mouth. Maybe even before, which was why she'd said them.

"I think I do," Wayne said, then walked away.

———

Wayne told himself he needed to remain in control. Sometimes he felt like Bruce Banner, struggling with his alter ego, the Hulk. He had to control that beast within him.

As much as he told himself that he and Jessica were going through this together, today's rebuke revealed it for the fantasy it was.

223

He was alone.

If that was the case, he might as well get used to it. So, after leaving Jessica at the hospital, he went home, popped open a beer, and turned on a college basketball game.

Shortly before the first half ended, Wayne heard the sound of cars in his driveway. Then the slamming of multiple car doors.

They were coming for him.

The knocks on the door were followed by, "Mr. Fiske, this is Lieutenant Velasquez of the NYPD. We have a warrant and will forcibly enter if you do not immediately open the door."

From the window his eyes confirmed what his ears had already told him. There were two cars in his driveway. One a dark sedan, the other a marked police vehicle.

Opening the door, Wayne saw that his visitors matched their modes of transportation. Lieutenant Velasquez and Detective Jamali were in plain clothes. Behind them were two uniformed cops.

"Mr. Fiske, you're under arrest for the murder of James Sommers."

The cop kept talking, reciting the Miranda warning that Wayne knew by heart from television. As the lieutenant uttered the words, the female officer grabbed his arms and applied handcuffs.

Wayne didn't say a word.

"Does the name Howard Fiske ring any bells?" Lieutenant Velasquez said.

Wayne remained mute. When Lieutenant Velasquez realized that Wayne was not rising to the bait, he smiled, and said, "He lives in Portland, Oregon. We found him courtesy of a genealogy database. Unfortunately for you, your cousin Howard's DNA was a partial match for the blood left at the crime scene.

"This is your last chance to get out in front of this thing," Lieutenant Velasquez continued. "Admit what you did. Accept responsibility. Explain how it happened. Show some remorse. All of that will help you, come sentencing time. But if you keep quiet, once your blood matches the blood found at the crime scene, there'll be no coming back from that."

Wayne wanted to say something like he imagined they would in a movie: *You're way off base,* maybe. Or, *You don't scare me.*

But neither of those really applied, so he kept silent.

They were on the right track. And he *was* scared. Petrified actually. Goddamn cousin Howard.

———

After the indignity of being booked and processed, Wayne was told his lawyer was here to see him. He was brought to a small room where Alex Miller was waiting.

Alex was Wayne's age and looked like a lawyer in that he had a certain Atticus Finch vibe, mainly because he was tall and thin and wore round wire-rimmed glasses. Wayne had retained Alex a few weeks earlier. Now he was awfully glad that he had.

It had been Alex who emphasized that Wayne must invoke his rights to counsel immediately upon his arrest. More importantly, Alex had predicted it would unfold exactly as it had. First, they'd find the link in the DNA to Wayne somehow, he'd explained. Then they'd arrest him. Once he was in custody, they'd get a warrant to confirm his DNA matched the blood at the crime scene.

"Here's how it's going to work," Miller said. "Tomorrow morning you'll be arraigned. That's like on TV. Thirty seconds. You say 'not guilty.' The prosecutor will say that given the severity of the crime, bail should be high. I'll ask for a bail you can afford. Then the judge imposes some amount. After that, a trial judge is selected. That's important because we're going to go straight to the trial judge's courtroom from the arraignment to fight out the DNA request."

"Any chance I won't have to give the DNA?" Wayne asked.

"None," Miller told him.

22

Jessica came to the hospital early the next morning. She wanted to tell Owen about his father's arrest before he read about it online.

She knew from the look on his face that she was too late.

"I'm sorry," she said.

"Dad didn't kill James," Owen said, a pleading sound to his voice.

"I know he didn't. He's got a good lawyer. Hopefully, he'll be able to convince the judge of that."

"What if he can't?" Owen asked.

"Let's take things one step at a time, okay?"

———

Wayne was wearing the prison jumpsuit, which was as uncomfortable as it was ugly. He also hadn't showered, which made his skin itch that much more.

Alex Miller stood beside him behind the table for defendants. Across the room was a young woman who barely looked older than Owen. Alex had explained that she was the arraignment ADA but wouldn't be the prosecutor on the case. The same was true of the arraignment judge. Wayne thought that was good because he doubted the man would live to see the trial. He looked to be the age of everyone else in the court-room combined.

"What's the People's position on bail?" the judge asked.

"Remand," the young woman said. "This is a murder indictment, and while Mr. Fiske does have a teenage child, we believe he nonetheless remains a flight risk."

"Mr. Miller, what say you?"

"Your Honor, we request bail that this defendant can post, which is somewhere in the neighborhood of a hundred thousand dollars."

"On a murder indictment?" the judge asked incredulously.

"He's not a rich man. Which also means he's unlikely to be a flight risk. Mr. Fiske has never been arrested. He's a teacher at the Sheffield Academy in New York City. He lives in Queens. Most importantly, the son that the ADA mentioned is in the hospital at Sloan Kettering, having just undergone a very serious operation to treat leukemia. Mr. Fiske very much wants to be able to continue to visit his son. Not for himself, but for his son. This is a situation that demands the court's leniency and compassion."

"The most compassion I can summon on a murder indictment is two million dollars," the judge said. "Roll the wheel."

Wayne winced at the number. It might as well have been two trillion. But even two hundred thousand wouldn't have mattered. He wouldn't be able to raise bail, which meant prison would be his home for the foreseeable future.

The law clerk did as requested, turning a crank that looked like the kind used in a retirement home bingo tournament. He then reached inside the cage and pulled out a tile.

"The Honorable Margaret A. Martin," the law clerk yelled out.

Wayne was still lamenting his predicament when Alex whispered in his ear, "The trial judge is a good pick for us. I'll meet you in her courtroom."

For the hearing to obtain Wayne Fiske's DNA, Gabriel and Asra had to hand the reins over to Joe Salvesen, the Assistant District Attorney assigned to the matter.

Gabriel had asked his wife, Ella, about Salvesen. Ella had spent much of her legal career in the Manhattan DA's office, and as a result, she knew just about every prosecutor there.

"He's okay," she'd said.

Gabriel knew that meant he was well below average. Ella rarely criticized her fellow ADAs. But like they tell kindergarteners, when the assignment of an ADA is made, you get what you get and you don't get upset.

Gabriel had assumed as much about Salvesen even before asking Ella. The man had crossed fifty and was still a line ADA. By the time you reached the downslide of middle age, you either had been given management responsibility or should have moved to the defense side to make real money. Those who stayed without advancement were, by and large, lazy lawyers.

It was therefore completely on brand when Salvesen claimed he didn't have time for a proper meeting with Gabriel and Asra before the hearing. "I'll try to get to court a few minutes early, and you can give me the skinny then," he said.

And it was also no surprise that Salvesen didn't get to court early. Luckily, Judge Martin was also late, so Gabriel had a few minutes to debrief Salvesen before the case was called.

He tried to explain the facts of the case in that limited time. If Gabriel had to guess, Salvesen grasped 25 percent of it. If that much.

"No, I got it," Salvesen said when Gabriel suggested they go over it one more time.

It didn't matter. The clerk was cutting short their opportunity with her three knocks on the doorframe to the judge's chambers. Then she said, "All rise! The Supreme Court for the State of New York, County of New York, Criminal Division, the Honorable Margaret A. Martin presiding. Come forward and you shall be heard."

Gabriel and Asra sat in the gallery's first row. They'd be spectators for this event, unless Judge Martin wanted to hear from witnesses. If not, it would all be up to Salvesen.

Wayne Fiske was wearing the prison orange, with his back to the gallery. The man hadn't even looked back at Gabriel yet. He had been brought in wearing handcuffs, and the court officers and prison guards stood close by as soon as he was uncuffed, per courtroom protocol.

Judge Martin was relatively new to the bench. Gabriel's phone Google search had revealed that she was a former ADA, which generally boded well for the good guys, but her tenure as a prosecutor had ended a long time ago. The bulk of her legal career had been spent doing immigration work for a nonprofit. That cut the other way: do-gooder types tended to be more suspicious of law enforcement than cops preferred.

The court clerk said: "Counsel, please state your appearances."

"Assistant District Attorney Joseph P. Salvesen, on behalf of the People, Your Honor."

"Alex Miller of Peikes Schwartz, representing Wayne Fiske."

"Thank you both," Judge Martin said. "And my sincerest apologies for running a few minutes behind this morning. Mr. Salvesen, are the People prepared to present witnesses today?"

Salvesen came back to his feet. "Good morning, Your Honor. Present in the courtroom are the two detectives that have been handling this case. They are the experts here, not me. So the answer to the court's question is *yes*. I would very much like to call Gabriel Velasquez to the stand. He can explain to Your Honor precisely why execution of the warrant is critical to apprehending a murderer."

Gabriel was pleased that he'd be telling the judge what was going on instead of Salvesen. He was less pleased that Salvesen had set it up to suggest that the DNA results alone would solve the case.

"Good," the judge said. "I'm ready to hear from the witness now, unless you have something you want to address before then, Mr. Miller."

Gabriel had never met Alex Miller before today. That was not uncommon. Most of the people prosecuted in Gabriel's cases were too poor to have private lawyers. Ella had told him that Miller was "good . . . very good, in fact." The same way he knew that his wife's "okay" regarding Salvesen was unqualified shade, her review of Alex Miller was an absolute rave. As rarely as she criticized her colleagues in the DA's office, Ella was even stingier in her praise for members of the defense bar.

"Thank you, Your Honor," Miller said, coming to his feet. "I'm as interested in hearing the People's evidence as everyone else. For the life of us, we don't understand why they have come to the conclusion that Mr. Fiske murdered Mr. Sommers. As far as we know, there is absolutely no evidence supporting that position."

"Then I guess we'll all find out together," the judge said. "Mr. Salvesen, call your first witness."

———

Gabriel stepped to the witness stand and raised his right hand before the request was made by the clerk. He knew the drill. This wasn't his first rodeo.

Once he had sworn to tell the truth and nothing but the truth, so help him God, Salvesen said, "Before I ask you about the reason we're all assembled today—the request for a DNA sample from Wayne Fiske—please give the court a brief description of your background with the NYPD so the judge knows a little bit about you, Detective."

"First of all, I'm a lieutenant, not a detective, with the NYPD. I've been on the force for about twenty years now and assigned to major cases since 2014. In my career with the NYPD, I would estimate that I have handled two dozen homicide cases. Probably more."

"Thank you, *Lieutenant*," Salvesen said. "Please explain to Judge Martin the nature of the crime that has brought us here today."

"The crime is the homicide of a man named James Sommers. He was involved in an altercation at his place of business, and died when he was punched and fell, sustaining a blow to the head. Blood not belonging to Mr. Sommers was found at the crime scene. We believe that the person who left that blood is responsible for Mr. Sommers's death."

He came to a stop, as Gabriel was told long ago that a good witness did when he was about to change subjects. The equivalent of a paragraph break in a story.

"There were no matches in the police database for the blood at the crime scene," he continued. "We therefore submitted the blood to a private genealogy database. The result was a partial match indicating that the blood at the crime scene was left by someone related to a man named Howard Fiske, who lives in Portland, Oregon. The defendant, Wayne Fiske, is a cousin of Howard Fiske and the ex-husband of Jessica Sommers, the wife of the victim. Mr. Fiske's fingerprints were also found at the crime scene. We learned in the course of our investigation that Jessica Sommers's relationship with James Sommers began when she was still married to Mr. Fiske, so jealousy is one motive. We later learned that Mr. Fiske's son was undergoing a very expensive experimental medical treatment, and the cost of that treatment was well beyond the means of Mr. Fiske or that of his ex-wife. However, after James Sommers was murdered, his wife, Jessica Sommers, collected half a million dollars through an insurance policy on Mr. Sommers's life, and those proceeds were used to pay for the lifesaving treatment for their son. We believe that Mr. Fiske killed Mr. Sommers in order for his ex-wife to collect on that life insurance policy because he knew that she would use the proceeds to save their son."

Gabriel glanced up at Judge Martin when he was finished. She nodded back to him. As far as Gabriel was concerned, this one was in the bank. There was no way she wasn't going to order Wayne Fiske to provide his DNA. And once that happened, they had him dead to rights on the murder.

"Thank you, Lieutenant," Salvesen said. "Did you ask Mr. Fiske to provide DNA voluntarily?"

"We did. He refused."

"Was there anything else that caused you to view Mr. Fiske as a potential suspect, aside from what you have already testified?"

"Yes. Based on the forensics, we believe that Mr. Sommers's murderer struck Mr. Sommers in the jaw. As a result, we suspect that the murderer scratched the knuckles on his fist, consistent with delivering such a blow. Mr. Fiske refused to allow us to inspect his hands upon request."

Salvesen wore the smug expression of someone who had just killed it, even though all he'd done was ask Gabriel to provide a narrative. He turned to look up at the judge and said, "Your Honor, I have no further questions."

"Let's recess for fifteen minutes," Judge Martin said. "When we resume, Mr. Miller, you can conduct your cross-examination."

23

The court officers would not allow Wayne to leave the courtroom during the recess. Instead, he was permitted to caucus with Alex in a room designated for witnesses, which adjoined the courtroom. The court officers waited outside to give Wayne and Alex some privacy but wouldn't unlock Wayne's handcuffs.

"Having fun so far?" Alex said.

Wayne knew it was to break the ice. Still, he couldn't even smile in response.

"I don't expect the cross to last more than half an hour," Alex said. "Probably less."

"And you're not going to call me to the stand?"

"Not a chance."

They had discussed this several times, the night before being the last. Alex had never wavered that it would be a serious mistake for Wayne to testify.

"The DNA hearing is a one-way street," he had said. "They're going to put on some evidence, so we'll learn what they have. Then the judge will order you to provide DNA, and we'll take it from there. Remember, this is not the war. This is just the first battle."

Wayne knew that was true. Still, he wasn't eager to lose this battle or wage the war to follow.

He wished that Jessica had been in the courtroom. He understood why she wasn't, of course. But her absence made him feel completely alone.

―――

Gabriel liked cross-examination. He viewed it as a battle of wits. Of course, he always had the advantage. Not because he was smarter than his inquisitors, although that was often true, but because his job was simply to tell the truth, and their job was to make it seem as if he weren't, and that was never the case.

Alex Miller stepped up to the lectern some ten feet away from the witness box. "Good morning, Lieutenant. I do not have a lot of questions for you, but the ones I will pose are very important. Let me start with the biggest one. How confident are you that Mr. Fiske killed Mr. Sommers?"

Gabriel was surprised by the question. Open-ended queries were rarely used on cross-examination. Most good questioners tried to maintain control over the witness, trying to ask questions that could be answered with only a yes or no.

"Extremely."

"And you make that assertion based on your . . . I think you said twenty years as a New York City police officer?"

"And the evidence present in this case."

"Ah, the evidence. What evidence do you think points to Mr. Fiske's guilt?"

"DNA doesn't lie, counselor."

"But this hearing is for you to obtain Mr. Fiske's DNA. Isn't it a bit circular that you're asking for Mr. Fiske's DNA because you are already convinced that his DNA will prove his guilt?"

"Not at all. As I explained, we are asking for his DNA to confirm the match. The evidence we've already obtained all points to Mr. Fiske. Fingerprints also do not lie, and they place Mr. Fiske in Mr. Sommers's office. His biological cousin's DNA is a partial match for the blood left at the scene, which causes us to believe that Mr. Fiske's blood will be a complete match. We further believe that Mr. Fiske spilled that blood when he struck Mr. Sommers's jaw, which directly led to Mr. Sommers's death. And finally, Mr. Fiske has not cooperated with our investigation and has a very strong motive, as I previously testified."

"Let me ask you a little about your testimony, Lieutenant. There are some things that . . . well, let's just say that they would benefit from some context."

Gabriel looked over to Salvesen. He should have objected to Miller's editorializing, but he didn't.

"First, you said that Mr. Fiske didn't cooperate with your investigation. But that's not entirely true. When you first spoke with him, he told you where he had been at the time of the murder—which was at his home. Didn't he?"

"He said that but—"

"No need for buts, Lieutenant. Just answer my question, please. If there's more context you want to provide, I'm sure the ADA will ask you to provide it. So Mr. Fiske told you that he had gone straight home after work that day?"

"That's what he told us, yes. We didn't believe him."

"Not quite a shocker, is it? The police not believing the person they ultimately arrested."

"No need for the sarcasm, Mr. Miller," Judge Martin said. "There's no jury here."

"Apologies, Your Honor," Miller said, then turned his attention back to Gabriel. "And the fingerprints at the scene . . . Didn't Mr. Fiske tell you that he visited Mr. Sommers's office at certain times?"

"Yes, he said that, but he would not tell us when he had last been there."

"But his ex-wife corroborated that he visited Mr. Sommers's office from time to time, didn't she?"

"She did."

"So even though you were suspicious of Mr. Fiske being in Mr. Sommers's office, she wasn't."

"I can't speak to her motivations regarding what she told me."

Gabriel thought for a quick second about adding that Jessica Sommers might have lied to keep her son's father out of jail but decided there was no need. Miller hadn't landed any punches.

The lawyer still hadn't done any damage five minutes later when he informed the judge that he had no further questions. Salvesen obviously also concluded that Gabriel had emerged unscathed because he declined to conduct any redirect. Gabriel left the witness stand and reclaimed his seat beside Asra in the gallery.

Judge Martin said, "Any further witnesses, Mr. Salvesen?"

"No, Your Honor."

She turned to Miller. "For the defendant?"

"No witnesses, Your Honor."

"Very well. I'm going to issue my ruling, then."

Gabriel knew that the fact that the judge was ruling from the bench meant she had already decided the issue before she even took the bench. Judges would often write out their ruling beforehand, and it was only if something came up unexpectedly during the hearing that they'd reserve judgment and issue a written order later.

Sure enough, Judge Martin put on her reading glasses.

"In this matter, the People request a DNA sample from Wayne Fiske. The legal standard that applies when a biological DNA sample is obtained by court order is well established and designed to reflect the United States Supreme Court's directive that an individual has a privacy interest to his or her bodily fluids. See Maryland v. King, 569 U.S. 435, 446 (2012). A court order allowing the government to procure evidence from a person's body constitutes a search and seizure under the Fourth Amendment of the United States Constitution. Such court order may be issued if the three-prong standard of Abe A. is met. Matter of Abe A., 56 N.Y. 2d 288."

The court reporter asked the judge to repeat the citation to the case she had referenced, to which the judge replied that she'd go one better and allow the court reporter to review her notes when the order was fully read into the record.

With that, she continued: "This well-established test decided by the New York State Court of Appeals held a court may order a suspect to provide a sample for DNA profiling, provided the People establish: (1) probable cause to believe the suspect has committed the crime; (2) that relevant material evidence will be found; and (3) the method used to secure it is safe and reliable. The Court of Appeals also stated that the worth of the evidence to the case must also outweigh the intrusion to the individual.

"It is the ruling of this court that the People have satisfied all of the prongs required by the Court of Appeals. First, I am convinced that there is sufficient probable cause that Wayne Fiske committed the crime for which he has been charged. Second, I further believe that the DNA test will lead to the discovery of material evidence. To wit, his blood at the crime scene. Third, there has been no showing by the defendant that there is any risk to him if he were compelled to provide DNA evidence. And finally, I hold that the stated worth of this evidence outweighs the intrusion to Mr. Fiske. Nonetheless, to ensure Mr. Fiske's safety through the DNA retrieval process, I order that the DNA be procured through a licensed medical professional. That is the order of the court."

———

Wayne was immediately brought back into the witness room. He waited in handcuffs for a nurse to arrive. Once she did, the police unlocked the shackles but then reapplied the right one to the chair leg.

The entire process lasted only a few minutes. The nurse put the rubber band around his bicep and told him to make a fist. Then she stuck the needle in his arm and drew two vials of blood. When she was done, she even put a Band-Aid over the puncture.

24

It was an old cop adage to claim that you'd seen it all. After a couple of decades on the force, Gabriel thought he'd earned the right to apply it to his own experiences. He'd seen a man who beheaded his wife with a samurai sword. A woman who poisoned her husband by sprinkling crystals from a dishwasher pod on his breakfast cereal. A man who slaughtered his brother and two cousins while they ate Thanksgiving dinner because, according to the murderer, the Detroit Lions failed to cover the spread.

But a child murdering a parent was a first for him. Even if it was a stepparent.

Gabriel knew it happened, of course. The Menendez brothers sprang to mind. Lizzie Borden. Oedipus, although he didn't count because he wasn't real, and besides, in the play he didn't realize it was his father.

Owen Fiske knew, however. For some reason, he had decided to go to his stepfather's place of business after school, and however it happened, his stepfather's head hit the coffee table, and Owen fled the scene while James Sommers lay dead.

That was the only conclusion Gabriel could reach after the DNA test showed that Wayne Fiske was only a partial match. Their killer still had to be a DNA-linked member of the Fiske family, and Owen was the only possible relative left.

It also explained why Jessica Sommers and Wayne Fiske had done a complete one-eighty, going from full cooperation to refusing to talk to the police at all. They had closed ranks to protect their son.

"Damn," was Asra's reaction upon hearing the news.

Gabriel understood that his partner's disappointment wasn't solely because she preferred to send a full-grown man to jail rather than a teenager with cancer, although that might have had something to do with it. More likely, however, Asra was mainly reacting to the fact that it would be much harder to secure a conviction of Owen Fiske based on the DNA match alone.

Gabriel believed Wayne Fiske would have been convicted in a heartbeat if the DNA had matched. After all, his fingerprints were at the scene, he needed James Sommers to be dead so his wife could collect the insurance money to save his son, and he undoubtedly hated the man.

But making a case against Owen Fiske was a tougher sell, even if they could prove that the boy had left his DNA at the scene. The motive, of course, still fit. It was equally logical to assume that a seventeen-year-old would commit murder to pay for his own lifesaving cancer treatment as it was to imagine his mother or father doing it to save him.

But it still took something of a suspension of disbelief to come to terms with a child killing a parent, even if it was for self-preservation. Added to that, the physical evidence linking Owen to the crime was equivocal, as opposed to when it came to his father. For example, there could have been any number of reasons for Owen to have visited his stepfather at work. And Gabriel knew that a smart defense attorney would come up with some innocuous reason for why Owen had left his blood at the scene that didn't have anything to do with him punching his stepfather in the jaw.

Beyond that, because Gabriel hadn't considered Owen a suspect, they had no idea where he had been at the time of the murder. They'd never gotten his statement, or even examined his hands. That was on Gabriel . . . A seventeen-year-old boy *should* have registered as a possible murderer, even if he was white, sick, and a good student.

"I should have thought to question him," Gabriel said.

"It never occurred to me either. Or Tomlinson," Asra said. "Why don't we take a run at him now? Worst thing that happens is he declines."

Gabriel knew that was a nonstarter. Even if Owen agreed to provide a DNA sample, they'd need parental permission. Same thing even to ask him for an alibi. There was no way that they'd get anything voluntarily at this point. Jessica Sommers and Wayne Fiske had shut it all down even when they knew their DNA wouldn't be a match; now, they'd be twice as adamant when it came to protecting their son.

"No. We missed the window. We'll need a warrant."

An hour later, Gabriel was cooling his heels in the hallway outside the chambers of the Honorable Margaret Martin. Alex Miller sat beside him.

The request for a warrant was usually done *ex parte*, a Latin term that literally meant "without the other part." Yet Joe Salvesen had said that the other part—Alex Miller—should be notified so as not to upset the judge. Salvesen then added that he had complete confidence that Gabriel could handle the matter on his own, so there was no need for him to trek to Judge Martin's courtroom.

It likely didn't matter who was sitting outside the chambers because no one would say a word, or even be granted entry inside. The process was for the application to be submitted to the judge's law secretary, who then brought the papers to the judge. A few minutes later, the clerk would be back in the hallway and would hand the warrant to Gabriel, at which time he'd flip to the last page to see if the judge had signed it.

This time, however, when the clerk returned to the hallway, she was empty-handed. "The judge wants to see you both," the clerk said.

The moment Gabriel and Miller stepped inside her chambers, Judge Martin said, "Lieutenant, didn't we just go through this exercise not even a week ago?"

"That was for the father. Mr. Wayne Fiske. This is for his son, Owen Fiske," Gabriel said.

"I know that. The name is on the warrant. What I'm saying is, didn't you tell me just a few days ago that you had probable cause that it was the father who had left the blood at the crime scene? That's why the man was arrested, after all. And it was on the basis of that representation that I issued the prior warrant."

Gabriel figured that this tongue-lashing was likely the reason Salvesen had made himself scarce. With no other option, he apologized, even though he had done nothing wrong. That was what you did with judges when they were angry and you wanted something from them.

Miller took full advantage of having the upper hand. "That's precisely why this warrant should not be issued, Your Honor."

"I'll get to you in a moment, Mr. Miller," Judge Martin snapped. "Right now I want to hear from Lieutenant Velasquez about the sudden change in direction."

"We knew the DNA was left by someone related to Howard Fiske," Gabriel said. "We came to that conclusion, as Your Honor will recall, because a search of a private genealogy database revealed that the blood was a match for someone in the Fiske family. We got the results back of Wayne Fiske's DNA this morning, and he's only a partial match. That means that someone else in his family left blood at the crime scene. Wayne Fiske has no siblings or parents and only one son. The pending warrant seeks to allow us to do a DNA test on the son."

"How old is he? The son."

"Seventeen."

"And he's very sick," Miller said. "Leukemia."

"Mr. Miller, do you represent the son too?"

The question seemed to catch Miller off guard. "I guess I do."

"Guess again, Mr. Miller. It seems to me you have a conflict. If I understand Lieutenant Velasquez here, he's looking for evidence that might exonerate your client, Wayne Fiske. That suggests to me that you should not be the person arguing that the police not be allowed to obtain that evidence from Owen Fiske. Does his mother want to hire a lawyer for her son, or should I appoint one for him?"

Miller said, "I think she'll want to pick the attorney."

"Very well, then. She has until Wednesday morning. Because at that time, I want to see everyone—you, the ADA, and counsel for Owen Fiske—in my courtroom and we'll thrash this out."

———

Jessica understood the logic of what Alex Miller was telling her. He had just returned from the judge's chambers, had explained what was going to happen on Wednesday morning, and told her that they needed to find a lawyer to represent Owen between now and then.

Needless to say, she didn't know another criminal defense lawyer, but Alex had that covered too. He recommended a friend of his named Lisa Kaplan.

"She's very good," Alex said. "A former ADA."

After Miller left, Jessica explained the situation to Owen. Just like he behaved in every interaction they'd had since his father's arrest, Owen took the news that the DA now wanted his DNA without any show of emotion. Almost as if it involved someone else.

"Your lawyer's job will be to fight the subpoena," Jessica explained. "If she's successful, they won't get to take your blood at all."

"Why don't I just give them my blood and get it over with?" Owen said. "It'll get Dad out of jail."

"Trust me, this is the right thing to do," she said. "Dad agrees."

"Okay," Owen said, not sounding too convinced.

Jessica had no such mixed emotions. She would walk on broken glass that was on fire to protect her son. Even for the murder of her husband.

She wondered what James would think about what she was doing. She thought she knew the answer. He'd understand. Of everyone, James would understand.

———

If it had been up to him, Owen would have simply complied with the DNA request. He'd said as much to his mother, but she wouldn't listen.

That was the problem right there: no one ever listened. Everyone was making decisions about what they thought was in his best interest, paying at most lip service to his thoughts and desires.

25

Judge Martin couldn't hide a smile. "It's like déjà vu," she said.

Wayne sat at the defense table with Alex Miller at his side. Like before, he was in prison garb. Unlike the last time, Jessica was in the gallery. Also different this time was that Lisa Kaplan sat at the end of the table.

Wayne didn't smile at the judge's quip. To his mind, there was nothing amusing about what was about to unfold.

Salvesen came to his feet. "The DNA test that the court ordered Wayne Fiske to undertake came back as only a partial match," he said. "That means that the person who left blood at the crime scene is a blood relative to Mr. Fiske, but not Mr. Fiske. We are here today to seek an order to compel Mr. Fiske's only child, Owen Fiske, to provide DNA. We believe that Owen Fiske will be a match."

"Believe or hope, Mr. Salvesen?"

"More than hope. The police can't be faulted for assuming that the family member who matched the DNA was Wayne Fiske, not his teenage son."

"Tell that to Mr. Fiske, who has been in prison while all this was sorted out. On that point, why haven't the charges against Mr. Fiske been dismissed?"

"We're not yet prepared to do that," Salvesen said. "His fingerprints at the scene suggest that he might have acted in concert with his son in this crime."

Miller came to his feet. "I request that the court dismiss the indictment against Wayne Fiske. There simply is not enough evidence to satisfy probable cause for the arrest. In fact, all they have is that the man's fingerprints were found at the crime scene, but that is easily explained by the fact that Mr. Fiske often met his son at Mr. Sommers's office. There is absolutely no other evidence linking him to the crime. None."

"That's not true," Salvesen said, now also standing. "He has a strong motive and no alibi."

Miller was right on cue. "The police don't know where I was at the time of the murder either. Is there probable cause to arrest me if I had once been in Mr. Sommers's studio? Because it's pretty much the same case they have against Mr. Fiske."

"Careful what you wish for, Mr. Miller," Judge Martin said with a grin, "but I get your point."

Wayne could barely breathe. Alex had told him that he thought the judge would likely dismiss the charges, but he cautioned it was a close call.

"Mr. Salvesen, let me ask you this: Is it now the People's position that the blood at the crime scene was left by Owen Fiske, and not his father?"

"Yes."

"But you think that father and son might have conspired together to commit this crime?"

"That is a strong possibility."

"What evidence of this conspiracy do you have?"

"As I stated, there's motive, there's lack of cooperation, there's lack of an alibi, there are the fingerprints, and there is the DNA, which we believe will prove a match to Owen Fiske."

"All that tells me is that Mr. Fiske is exercising his constitutional rights and had at one time been in the office of his ex-wife's husband. I see nothing to support the idea of a conspiracy between the son and the father. The initial arrest warrant was premised on the claim that Mr.

Wayne Fiske's DNA would match the blood at the crime scene. We all now know that is not the case. Therefore, the People have not met the probable-cause standard for an indictment against Wayne Fiske. The indictment is dismissed."

The air came back into Wayne's lungs. He was being set free. The only problem was that now his son was the one in harm's way.

———

The judge ordered a recess after her ruling, providing time for Wayne to change out of the prison jumpsuit and into the business suit that Jessica had brought for him. Away from watchful eyes, Jessica embraced her ex-husband.

"You ready for round two?" Miller asked.

"No," Jessica said.

"I understand," Miller said. "There's a better shot this time to defeat the warrant than there was before. Owen's illness provides a hook that wasn't present when they wanted to get DNA from Wayne. And Lisa will go all out in the cross. So keep the faith just a little while longer."

———

When court resumed, Salvesen wasted no time calling Gabriel back to the stand. Just like when they sought Wayne Fiske's DNA, the prosecutor had decided he was going to let Gabriel do the heavy lifting, which once again suited Gabriel just fine.

The other players had rearranged, however. Whereas before Alex Miller and Wayne Fiske sat at the defense table, their seats were now occupied by Jessica Sommers and Lisa Kaplan. Miller and Fiske were in the gallery.

"Lieutenant Velasquez, please tell Judge Martin the result of the DNA test you administered on Wayne Fiske?"

"It was a partial match."

"What does that mean?"

"It means that the person who left blood at the crime scene is a blood relative of Wayne Fiske, but not Wayne Fiske."

"Does Wayne Fiske have any other biological children aside from Owen Fiske?"

"Not to our knowledge."

"Brothers or sisters?"

"Again, we have no knowledge of that."

"Parents who are living?"

"No."

"What conclusions, if any, did you draw from those facts?"

"That his son, Owen Fiske, left the blood at the crime scene."

"Is there anything else you'd like to add, Lieutenant?" Salvesen asked.

"No."

"That's my examination, Judge," Salvesen said, seemingly pleased to be done working. "We ask the court to take judicial notice of Lieutenant Velasquez's prior testimony regarding motive, which applies now to Owen Fiske."

"Understood," Judge Martin said. "No need to replow that field. Ms. Kaplan, the witness is yours."

Lisa Kaplan stepped up to the lectern. She was familiar to Gabriel from her days as an ADA. He liked it better when they had been on the same team and knew he was in for a grilling every bit as intense as Miller had done the last time.

"Good morning, Lieutenant. Let's start with the people you considered suspects in the murder of Mr. Sommers. Before you arrested Wayne Fiske, how many serious suspects were in the mix?"

"'Serious suspect' is not a term I use—"

"I don't want to spar with you, Lieutenant. We're just talking normal usage of words here. How many people did you think might have killed James Sommers?"

"In any murder case, the spouse is the first suspect."

"Let me stop you there, Lieutenant. You're talking about Ms. Jessica Sommers, the widow of James Sommers—who is not to be confused with Mrs. Haley Sommers, his ex-wife."

"That's right. Jessica Sommers."

"Jessica Sommers did not have an alibi, right?"

"That is correct. She told us she was at home, alone, when the crime was committed."

"Did you know then that Ms. Sommers was the beneficiary of a five-hundred-thousand-dollar life insurance policy on her husband?"

"We discovered that in the course of our investigation, yes."

"I assume that you also discovered in the course of your investigation that the life insurance proceeds that Jessica Sommers recently received were desperately needed to pay for her son's lifesaving cancer treatment."

"We knew that Owen Fiske was undergoing a medical procedure, yes. We also knew it was expensive, and beyond Jessica Sommers's and Wayne Fiske's means, absent the insurance proceeds."

"And even aside from the obvious motive to save her son, isn't it also the case that the reason the wife is always the first suspect is that there's always a possible motive between spouses, even if it isn't known to anyone outside of the marriage?"

"Yes."

"And here you didn't even have to speculate as to that motive. She was essentially choosing between the life of her seventeen-year-old son or that of her husband of barely a year."

It was about as improper a question as Gabriel could imagine. He shot a look in Salvesen's direction, but the prosecutor's head was down. With Kaplan on her A game, it would have been nice if Salvesen rose to the challenge too . . .

"Is that a question or an invitation for me to speculate about Ms. Sommers's mental state?"

Kaplan smiled. The defense-lawyer equivalent of telling Gabriel, *Well played*.

"Who else was a suspect, Lieutenant?"

"We also considered Wayne Fiske—"

"I'm sorry to interrupt, but I just thought of a question I forgot to ask about Jessica Sommers. Apologies for jumping around on you, but before we discuss all the reasons why Wayne Fiske was considered a suspect by the NYPD, I wanted to ask whether Jessica Sommers cooperated with your investigation into the murder of her husband?"

"At first she did, but then she declined to provide a DNA sample upon request."

"Just so we're all on the same page . . . Jessica Sommers: No alibi. She had a motive because she needed the life insurance money to save her son, and she was not cooperating. Got it. Now, tell us about Wayne Fiske. In fact, let's move this along. We know you thought he was such a good suspect that you actually arrested him, right?"

Gabriel had to hand it to Lisa Kaplan. She knew how to cross-examine a witness. Ask only questions that you knew would elicit the response you wanted, keep the witness off balance, and do as much testifying yourself as the judge would allow.

And he had to give credit where credit was due. Wayne Fiske and Jessica Sommers had hired a pit bull to represent their son so that she could blame them for James Sommers's murder.

"Yes."

"And that was because his fingerprints were at the crime scene, he had no alibi, he had motive in the form of the insurance proceeds, and you believed that the blood at the scene was going to be a match for him."

"Yes. And as it has been already stated, it turned out he was not a match for the blood, but a biological family member definitely was."

If Gabriel's counterpunch landed, Kaplan didn't show it. Like a boxer, she smiled and prepared for her next combination.

"So to recap. Wayne Fiske. No alibi. Strong motive. Not cooperating. Fingerprints at the scene."

Even though there was no question pending, Gabriel said, "All is equally true of his son, except we also believe we have his blood."

"We'll get to Owen Fiske in a minute, Lieutenant. But I'm still not done going through all the other suspects with motive, who lack an alibi, and who refused to provide DNA. In fact, this is a good time to talk about Haley Sommers, who is James Sommers's ex-wife. You mentioned that James and Jessica Sommers had an anniversary party. Something really strange happened at that party, isn't that right?"

"Haley Sommers crashed the party. She interrupted the toasts that were being made."

"You're underselling it, Lieutenant," Kaplan said.

Salvesen could have objected to the characterization but remained firmly in his seat. That was just as well. Gabriel could handle it.

"I'm not selling, counselor. She crashed the party. She interrupted the toasts. If you want more detail, all you have to do is ask."

"Counselors," Judge Martin said. "Let's remember everybody's job here, shall we? Ms. Kaplan, you ask questions. Lieutenant Velasquez, you answer questions. I tell everyone what they should or shouldn't do. Proceed, Ms. Kaplan."

"Thank you, Your Honor," Kaplan said, quickly regaining control of the examination. "My apologies, Lieutenant. You're exactly right. I should have been more specific. Let me ask you this: How would you characterize Haley Sommers's relationship with her ex-husband?"

Another open-ended question chosen by Kaplan because there was no good way to answer it. No matter what Gabriel said, Kaplan would say it was worse than that.

"There was evidence that she was still angry with her ex-husband," he said, deciding that less was more.

"What brought you to the conclusion that Haley Sommers was—in your words—*angry* at her ex-husband? Was it the restraining order that

James Sommers took out that required Haley Sommers to stay away from him and his family? Or was it the fact that she repeatedly violated that order? Or was it because Haley Sommers threatened to murder James Sommers a week before he was, in fact, murdered?"

Once again, Salvesen should have objected. Compound questions were always impermissible because they required multiple responses. Kaplan had just asked four different questions, but the ADA looked on with a bored expression, not making a peep.

"All of the above," Gabriel said.

"So you knew that Haley Sommers violated the protective order by calling Mr. Sommers and his wife and threatening them with bodily harm?"

"I am aware that she made such threats."

"Isn't it the case that just a few days before the murder, on the day of James and Jessica's first wedding anniversary, in fact, Haley Sommers called James Sommers and left a voice mail in which she said, and here I am quoting: 'James, you miserable fuck. I hope you and that skank bitch of a wife of yours both die. But don't worry, after you're dead, I'll be sure to dance on your graves.'"

"Yes. I heard that voice mail. I can't be sure you said it verbatim, but I have no reason to doubt it if you make that representation."

"Oh, I make that representation, Lieutenant. That's what she said. Can we agree that was only the latest of many threatening statements Haley Sommers had made toward James Sommers prior to his death?"

"Yes."

"And I suspect that a man with your experience on the NYPD takes that type of threatening language very seriously."

"Yes."

"Okay. So, with respect to Haley Sommers, she checks off a lot of boxes, right?"

Gabriel knew exactly what Kaplan meant but said the opposite. "I don't think about suspects as checking off boxes."

"The terminology hardly matters. Let's just talk facts. Haley Sommers had motive, right?"

"Yes."

"She refused to provide DNA too, right?"

"That is correct."

"In your experience, Lieutenant, do innocent people usually refuse to provide DNA?"

This, of all things, caused Salvesen to come to his feet. "Objection."

Judge Martin shrugged. "Overruled. Lieutenant, you can answer."

"Not usually, no," Gabriel said.

"What about an alibi? When you first spoke to Haley Sommers, what did she tell you regarding her whereabouts at the time of this crime?"

Clever question. In fact, for Kaplan it was better than that. It was a twofer. The answer would prove that Haley Sommers had no alibi *and* that she had lied to the police.

"She initially provided an alibi that she was with a friend during the time in question."

"As a police lieutenant with more than two decades on the job, did you believe that alibi?"

"I was skeptical."

"Did you later learn that Ms. Haley Sommers had lied to you? That, in point of fact, she wasn't with a friend when this murder occurred, but at the scene of the crime?"

"We can verify that Ms. Sommers was in a restaurant next door to Mr. Sommers's place of business during the window in which he died inside that place of business."

Gabriel watched Kaplan replay the last question and answer in her head. Apparently, she had gotten enough, because she went on to a different subject.

"So we have three suspects so far," Kaplan said. "Each with motive. Each refusing to provide DNA. Each with no alibi. Anyone else? Maybe a business partner who was afraid of going to jail if Mr. Sommers cooperated against him. Does that ring a bell, Lieutenant?"

"Reid Warwick was working with James Sommers to sell stolen art. Mr. Sommers had been caught in an FBI sting. So, anticipating your next question, Ms. Kaplan, *that* told us that Mr. Warwick also had a motive. But he did ultimately provide a DNA sample, and it wasn't a match for the blood at the crime scene. And he did end up giving us an alibi, which checked out. Reid Warwick is no longer a suspect in this crime."

It was possible that Kaplan hadn't known about Warwick's alibi until Gabriel testified about it. Nonetheless, the attorney acted as if nothing could have mattered less.

"Good to know Mr. Warwick is only an art thief, and the NYPD has chosen to believe what this *criminal* told you about his whereabouts at the time of Mr. Sommers's murder."

Gabriel would have countered the assertion, but Kaplan quickly segued. "Am I correct that you never considered Owen Fiske a suspect until a few days ago?"

"He was not among the first people we questioned, that's right."

"In fact, you never questioned him at all. Isn't that correct?"

"Yes. It is."

"Why was that?"

Another *why* question.

"We had other initial suspects. Their motives, on first consideration, seemed stronger . . . until we had the forensic evidence regarding the possible DNA match."

"You've just said the million-dollar word, Lieutenant. Actually, three letters and one word: *DNA match*. That's why we're here, after all. So let's talk about that. You found some blood at the scene, right?"

"Yes."

"And your investigation led you to a private genetics company that indicated the blood matched, at least in part, a fellow named Howard Fiske, who lives all the way in Oregon. Do I have that right?"

"You do."

"Good. Is Howard Fiske a suspect too?"

"No. He is not."

"I'm glad to hear that. We have quite enough of them already, don't you think?"

Gabriel looked over at Salvesen. The guy really sucked at his job.

"I'm sorry, was that a serious question?" Gabriel asked, still staring at Salvesen.

"No. I guess it wasn't," Kaplan said with a smile. "So this private company—which one was it, by the way?"

"FamilyTreeDNA."

"So FamilyTreeDNA tells you that the person who left the blood in Mr. Sommers's workplace is related to this Howard Fiske. Do I have that right?"

"Yes. The DNA left at the crime scene was a match for a blood relation to Howard Fiske."

"I'm going to ask for a clarification, Lieutenant. This is important because I know you want to be precise in your testimony. You keep saying that DNA was left at the crime scene. But that's not really accurate, is it?"

Gabriel knew where this was going and made a split-second decision to get out in front of it.

"Blood was found at the crime scene that did not come from the victim, Mr. Sommers. But if you're asking whether we can prove that this blood was left at the exact time that Mr. Sommers died, the answer is we cannot."

"That is my point precisely, Lieutenant," Kaplan said. "There was blood found at James Sommers's workplace. And his workplace ended up being a crime scene. But you cannot prove that the blood found there was left during the crime, isn't that right?"

Gabriel decided it was time to push back. "Yes and no. You are correct that there is no way to prove when blood was left with the precision you seem to be seeking. So even Mr. Sommers's blood, of which there was quite a bit found at the crime scene, can't be proven to have spilled during the murder, precisely. However, we can make that deduction because the blood was relatively fresh when we arrived at the scene, which was one of the ways the medical examiner determined the time of death. That same analysis is reached by virtue of the fact that the nature of the crime resulted in Mr. Sommers losing a lot of blood. So, I don't mean to nitpick, but since you made a point of wanting me to be precise, I am trying to be precise. DNA doesn't reveal all. It's one piece of a larger puzzle. So while it is true that DNA testing does not tell us the precise moment when the blood is spilled, other investigative modes do give rise to the conclusion that all the blood left at the scene was left during the commission of the murder."

"Or maybe it was old blood and Mr. Sommers just never noticed the blood left the day before. Maybe Mr. Sommers was a messy guy."

Before Gabriel could respond, Kaplan went in a different direction. "Lieutenant, you are aware that Owen Fiske is a very sick boy, correct?"

"I'm not a doctor. I know he's in the hospital. His mother told me that he has leukemia."

"You're not suggesting that your lack of medical training makes you ignorant of whether a boy in the hospital for leukemia is very ill, are you?"

"Let me stop you there, Ms. Kaplan," Judge Martin said. "Is either side going to call any medical personnel on this issue?" She was looking at Salvesen.

"We could if you wanted, Judge," he said without coming to his feet.

"I do want. Right now, in fact. Let's recess for an hour, at which time I expect there to be a doctor in the house."

26

An hour later, Dr. Cammerman took the stand. He looked as if he'd come straight from the hospital, to the point he was still wearing a white lab coat.

Wayne had never thought about Cammerman's credentials. Dr. Goldman had told them about the treatment, and that was all Wayne had ever considered. But at the start of his testimony, Cammerman testified that he had graduated from Yale University and Harvard Medical School. He ticked off some prestigious-sounding fellowships and a litany of positions with hospitals before arriving at his current job at Memorial Sloan Kettering.

"Dr. Cammerman, please explain a little bit about AML, the disease afflicting Owen Fiske," Salvesen asked.

Judge Martin cut in before Cammerman could answer. "Mr. Salvesen, I know that Owen Fiske has leukemia, and I know that it is a serious disease. We can move this along a little faster. All I really need to know is the risk to him if he provided a DNA sample."

"Let's get right to that, then," Salvesen said. "Dr. Cammerman, are you familiar with the taking of DNA samples?"

"I'm not an expert in the area, but I know it's typically done by drawing blood or a cheek swab."

"And with a healthy person, is there any risk in such a procedure?"

"Again, with the caveat that I'm not an expert in this area, I suspect that there is not. Or it is minimal."

"Now, I get that Owen Fiske is not a healthy person, but let me ask you the question that Judge Martin said she wanted answered: If the police follow the hospital's precautionary procedures, will Owen Fiske's recovery be compromised by his giving a DNA sample?"

"That is unlikely. He has a CVC already in place." Dr. Cammerman looked up to Judge Martin to explain. "That's a catheter for the withdrawal of blood."

"In fact, the doctors and nurses at the hospital often take Mr. Fiske's blood, do they not?" Salvesen said.

"They do."

"In other words, what the police want to do through the execution of this warrant is already being done to Owen Fiske on a fairly regular basis. Isn't that right?"

"Yes."

"Your witness," Salvesen said.

———

Lisa Kaplan returned to the podium.

"Dr. Cammerman, please explain the treatment you have been providing to Owen."

"Owen was diagnosed with AML when he was thirteen. He was treated at that time with chemotherapy and radiation, and the cancer went into remission. However, it returned earlier this year. When it did, the decision was reached that additional chemotherapy alone was not recommended because his cells would continue to produce leukemia. Instead, we suggested he undergo what is called an allogeneic transplant, by which donor stem cells are implanted into the bone marrow."

"Prior to the transplant, a process called myeloablation occurs, correct?"

"Yes. Myeloablation is a particularly aggressive round of chemotherapy, in which the patient's existing stem cells are largely destroyed to make way for the transplanted cells."

"Was that process completed?"

"Yes."

"And did you immediately begin the transplant?"

"No. We waited forty-eight hours."

"Why was that?"

"It's the standard protocol. The myeloablation is severely debilitating to the patient. We want them to get their strength up before the transplant."

"Did there come a time when you performed an allogeneic transplant on Owen?"

"Yes."

"Did it work?"

"It was a successful procedure, but it is still far from clear whether it will, as you say, *work*. Or even what *working* means in this context. We deal with five-year survival rates, and our patients, of course, hope for much more than that. So it hasn't, quote, unquote, 'worked' until we pass at least that milestone."

"So there is still a possibility that Owen Fiske could die from his leukemia?"

"Yes, of course."

"What are the risks that Owen faces now that the transplant has been completed?"

"There are many, but the thing we're most concerned about after a transplant is a rejection of the transplanted cells. After that, the focus turns to the elevated risk of infection. The myeloablation process eliminates the entirety of the patient's white blood cells. The white blood cells are the body's defense against infection. It can take up to a year before the new stem cells—the stem cells that have been transplanted—are producing sufficient white blood cells to fight infection. During this period, we monitor the patient very closely and take precautions to ward off infection."

"What precautions do you take?"

"The patient remains hospitalized after the procedure for about a month. Sometimes a bit shorter, sometimes a little longer. During that period, visitation is limited, and we require anyone who has contact with the patient to wear gloves and a mask."

"Is Owen still in that phase of the treatment?"

"He is. And he will be for at least another week. Maybe longer."

"What are the other risks?"

"The medicines we provide to fight off other risks unfortunately increase the likelihood of the patient contracting a fungal infection. Even mold is a serious risk for these patients."

"How serious are these risks?"

Dr. Cammerman hesitated for a moment as he considered the question. "They run the gamut from mere annoyances, like a skin rash, to fungal pneumonia, which is potentially fatal."

"Thank you, Doctor," Kaplan said. "No further questions."

———

After Dr. Cammerman was excused, Judge Martin asked whether either side had any further witnesses to call. Both lawyers answered that they did not.

Jessica held her breath. She knew that a decision might come immediately, just as it had when the judge considered the DNA issue with regard to Wayne.

Judge Martin said, "Thank you. I will take the matter under advisement and issue a written ruling with all deliberate speed. I understand the importance of the issues for both sides, so you will not wait long."

Once they had left the courtroom, Wayne opined that it was a good sign that the judge hadn't ruled from the bench. Jessica didn't have the strength to disagree.

27

Jessica was at home, seeking comfort in a bottle of chardonnay, when her phone rang. It was Alex Miller.

"Is there a decision?"

"There is. I have Wayne on the line too. I conferenced him into the call before calling you so I could tell you both at the same time."

"Hi, Jessica," Wayne said.

She didn't return the greeting. She didn't want to say anything to delay Alex's reveal of the judge's ruling.

"I'm sorry to report that Judge Martin went against us and is allowing the police to get Owen's DNA," Alex said. "Lisa asked me to convey her disappointment as well. But as I told you from the beginning, these motions are real long shots. Judges like to grant the police every benefit of the doubt. And Dr. Cammerman didn't help our cause by saying that compliance with the warrant wouldn't put Owen's recovery at any risk."

Jessica wasn't listening. She didn't care why they'd lost. All that mattered was that the police were now going to get Owen's DNA. And once they had it, they'd be able to prove that her son had left his blood at the crime scene.

"When will it happen?" she asked.

"Lisa called the ADA and told him that she needed twenty-four to forty-eight hours to decide whether to make an emergency stay application. He agreed to hold off executing the warrant until then."

"So we're going to appeal, then?" Wayne asked. He sounded hopeful, as if he wanted to continue to fight until the bitter end.

"We can," Alex said, which Jessica recognized was not the same as a recommendation that they should. "It's your right. And maybe we even get a stay of the order while the appeal is pending. But all that does is kick the can down the road. And to what end? At the end of the day, they're almost certainly still going to get Owen's DNA. Our best shot to block that was with Judge Martin. Appellate courts are very reluctant to overrule a trial judge who has heard live testimony. All that being said, the only real downside to appealing is the legal cost. So I'm happy to make that filing and play the delay game. But it doesn't come cheap."

"How much?" Wayne asked.

"Somewhere in the neighborhood of fifty grand? Maybe a little less. But in that ballpark. But to be perfectly frank, you'd be throwing good money after bad. My advice would be to preserve your resources for the trial. I've spoken to Lisa and she agrees. You need to be thinking about the long-term defense, not every battle. A trial is going to cost you at least two hundred grand. Unless you are really liquid, I wouldn't spend any money you could put toward the defense on a near-hopeless appeal."

Jessica was now in tears. All she heard from Alex's legal analysis was the word *hopeless*.

"Are they going to arrest him?" Jessica asked. "I mean, when they find that his DNA matches."

Alex didn't answer at first. It was almost as if the question had surprised him, although it couldn't possibly have. This was the only question that mattered, after all.

"I assume they will," he finally said. "They'll have the same evidence against Owen that they had against Wayne at that point. No, they'll actually have more because they'll have the DNA match too. So, yes, I think you need to prepare yourself for Owen being arrested after the DNA comes back as a match."

Adam Mitzner

Jessica sobbed into the phone, wishing she hadn't asked the question.

"But—and this is the key thing, Jessica. And you too, Wayne. You need to focus on the positives. If Owen is arrested, we'll fight like hell for him to stay confined in the hospital and then be released on bail, or, at worst, kept under house arrest. The prosecution will resist. They don't want it to look like white kids of means get to stay at home and kids of color rot on Rikers Island. But, at the end of the day, I'm confident that we'll be able to keep him out of jail pending trial. At the same time, it isn't too early to start thinking about a plea. Involuntary manslaughter carries a three-and-a-half- to fifteen-year sentence."

"Oh my God," Jessica said.

"What's the charge going to be if he doesn't do a plea?" Wayne asked.

"Murder in the second, which is the most serious charge for a murder that is premeditated but not involving a police officer. That carries a life sentence, no possibility of parole. The DA will probably hedge its bets and also include a first-degree manslaughter charge as a lesser included offense. If convicted on that, Owen would get a sentence of five to twenty-five years."

Jessica could barely comprehend what Alex was telling them. All she heard was that her son would be in jail for a very long time.

"Just tell me one thing, Alex," Jessica said. "Can Owen win at trial?"

She heard their lawyer sigh. Never a good sign.

"I'll do everything I can to make that happen," he said.

No one said anything for a good ten seconds, then Alex continued, "I know I've given you a lot of information all at once, and I also know that the stakes couldn't be higher. You don't have to make a decision about even the appeal now. And as for the plea, that's premature right now too. So let's do this one step at a time. Talk to each other about the pros and cons of the appeal on the DNA warrant. On that, I need to

262

hear from you no later than tomorrow. If you decide not to pursue the appeal, there's nothing for us to do until Owen's DNA comes back as a match. At that time, we can turn to discussing the best time to raise a plea discussion or if we want to go that route at all. And, of course, Owen is the decision maker here, so I'm going to need to get his sign-off on any plea."

Wayne called Jessica back right after they got off the phone with Alex.

"We should get Owen out of the country," he said. "To Paraguay or Venezuela or some other place without an extradition treaty with the United States."

"That's just not possible, Wayne," Jessica said. "He's in the hospital, and will be for the foreseeable future."

"So what are we supposed to do? Just let them convict our son of murder?"

———

Owen's parents told him that the police were coming. In fact, that was why his mother and father were both in his room, like sentries on the castle walls. They'd told him that they couldn't do anything to prevent him from being forced to provide a DNA sample, that they'd done everything they could, and the judge had ordered it to happen.

The exact day and time for Owen to provide his DNA had been agreed upon in advance. Even with the warning, Owen was still startled when he heard "NYPD" following two loud knocks on his door.

"Come in," his father said.

His mother held his hand, their skin-on-skin contact prevented by her latex glove. He could tell that she was terrified. His father too, despite the bravado.

The man at the door was wearing hospital scrubs. He looked no different from any of the dozens of doctors Owen had seen but for the shimmer of silver around his neck. Owen's memory flashed back to the crime scene and the cop with the swagger who had worn his badge on a chain.

"I'm not going to come inside, but I'm sure your mother explained why I'm here, Owen. My name is Lieutenant Velasquez. I'm a police officer with the NYPD. A judge has granted us permission to take a sample of your DNA."

"Please don't talk to my son," Wayne said, firmly. "Just do what you came here to do and then leave."

"You won't have to do anything," the cop said to Owen, ignoring his father's tough-guy line. "A nurse is going to come in and take some blood. Okay?"

His parents had told Owen not to say a word. But it just seemed wrong not to answer him.

"Sure. Whatever."

The nurse came in. It was just like any of the countless times before when he had given blood through the CVC.

After she left, Velasquez said, "The warrant also permits us to inspect and photograph your hands."

Without waiting for permission, a man in full hospital garb entered, including a mask. Owen couldn't tell anything about him other than that he had blue eyes.

"Please hold out both your hands," he said.

Owen looked to his mother, but she had turned away. Out of his peripheral vision, he saw his father nod.

Owen pulled his right hand from beneath the covers. The photographer took pictures of the now-faint but still visible scratches across Owen's right knuckles. Yet another wonderful by-product of having leukemia—scars were slow to heal.

———

Haley still couldn't wipe from her mind's eye what she'd witnessed the day James died. She doubted she ever would. Sometimes she wondered why she had even entered James's office in the first place. She knew James was still there, after all, and that should have dictated that she stay far away. But after watching Reid leave and the skinny, short-haired woman follow him, and then James's stepson enter right after the woman left, only to flee like a bat out of hell a few minutes later with blood on his hands, she knew something was seriously wrong.

Had she entered the office to help James? Or was it only curiosity? Maybe she wanted to see James suffer. She honestly still did not know.

Whatever her motivation, when she entered, she saw James lying on the floor, facedown, blood pooled around his head. She was surprised by just how dark his blood was. She had always imagined blood to be red, like marinara sauce. Turned out it was more akin to the dark purple of a cabernet.

Instinctively, she checked his pulse—no doubt leaving evidence of her presence on his body—but he was already gone.

She hated to admit this, even to herself, but at that moment, she felt nothing but sorrow. She hadn't wanted James to die, despite all the times she'd soothed herself with thoughts of his death. What she really wanted was for him to regret leaving her. Now that could never happen.

And then the moment after that realization, her instinct for self-preservation kicked in. She had made herself the prime suspect in James's murder. From her antics at the party, to when she spotted James with the skinny, short-haired woman, to her persuading Malik to call Jessica, to her fingerprints putting her at the scene of the crime, the police wouldn't have to look too far for evidence to arrest and even convict her.

She could have told the police what she had seen that day, but she quickly realized that was very weak tea. Which meant that she had to figure out a way to put other suspects into the mix. But who? Pointing the finger at Reid would only cause him to tell the police that she was a scorned ex-lover. The skinny, short-haired woman was hardly a more inviting target, since there might not be any way for the police to prove she even existed.

But the boy, he was an entirely different kettle of fish. Pointing the finger at him was a game changer.

The irony wasn't lost on Haley that she wasn't even sure Owen had killed James when she made that very accusation to Jessica at the funeral. For all Haley knew, it could have been Reid or the skinny, short-haired woman. Or both of them in cahoots. Maybe they killed James, and Owen only came upon the body. In that way, he would have been no different from her: someone in the wrong place at the wrong time.

But Haley knew that Jessica would not stop accusing her unless Haley had something to hold over her as leverage. Threatening that she'd tell the police Owen had entered James's office, then left covered in blood, was more than enough to do the trick.

It worked like a charm. After confronting Jessica at the funeral, Jessica and Wayne presented a united front to stonewall the cops. Haley hadn't expected Reid to join the party, but of course he did. That guy didn't do anything that wasn't shady, so the last thing he was going to do was cooperate with the police, even about something he hadn't done.

With everyone else not cooperating, Haley's own refusal didn't seem so bad.

From what she'd read, the police made their way to Owen Fiske on their own. She couldn't even begin to comprehend why that kid had murdered James, but that wasn't her concern.

This summer would mark two years since James had left her. It was time to put her life back on track and stop blaming a dead man for her troubles. Well past time, in fact.

She needed to get a job and deal with her obsessive tendencies, her probable drinking problem, and definitely her anger issues. She thought she could do that. After all, she didn't have much choice in the matter.

———

Reid's lawyer was urging a plea deal. He thought he could get the feds to agree to less than five years.

"I'm not agreeing to spend even a day in jail," Reid said.

He'd made bail and was now living at home, albeit under some restrictions. Nevertheless, it was much more pleasant than life in a prison cell.

"They're not going to end up giving you the key to the city on this one, Reid," Weitzen said. "Murcer has already flipped, and they have you on tape negotiating the deal. And I don't have to tell you that without a deal, you'll be looking at ten years. Maybe more."

Reid knew he'd eventually have to take a plea. The strategy now was to delay that for as long as possible. In the meantime, he'd work his own lawyer so that Weitzen would work the prosecutors.

Negotiating jail time was just like any business deal. When Reid finally believed he was getting their rock-bottom offer, he'd accept it and plead guilty. He had no other choice.

———

Three days later, the DNA results from Owen Fiske came in. Gabriel found out via a call from Erica Thompson.

"Fuck," he said when she told him.

28

In Greek mythology, Chimera was a fire-breathing monster. She combined the head of a lion and midsection of a goat with a dragon's tail and hind legs. Sometimes the dragon tail was depicted with a snake's head on it. The legend was that Chimera destroyed the cities of Caria and Lycia before being slain by Bellerophon.

Owen was a chimera. Literally. Well, not literally. He did not breathe fire or have the head of a lion, the midsection of a goat, or the tail of a serpent. Nor had he ever destroyed a city. But in AML circles, his condition was actually called a *chimera*.

He was frankly surprised that no one else knew that. Apparently, neither his parents nor the NYPD were as devoted to googling "AML allogeneic hematopoietic cells transplantation" as he was. If they had been, they would have learned that in these types of transplants, the donor cells mix with the host's cells to create two separate sets of DNA.

Which was why, although the blood that Owen spilled when he punched James in the mouth was 100 percent his, it did not match the DNA in the blood sample the NYPD had taken from him following the stem cell transplant.

After his mother confronted him about what James's crazy stalker of an ex-wife told her at the funeral—that she'd seen Owen entering and leaving James's office at the time of the murder—he'd lied straight to his mother's face. Given all the lies his parents had told him over the past few years, Owen didn't feel too guilty about returning the favor.

Besides, what choice did he have? He wasn't about to confess to what had actually happened. He couldn't. Sometimes not even to himself.

"Haley's lying," he'd said. "You know that's what she does, Mom. She tries to get you all worked up by telling you whatever she thinks is what you're most afraid about."

He told his father the same thing a few days later. "I was hanging with friends after school, Dad, and then I came straight to your house."

His father had believed him. He could be counted on to accept whatever Owen said, without fail. If Owen had tried to peddle his old man a story that Martians had come to earth and shape-shifted into his body, and that's whom Haley had seen enter James's office, his father would have accepted it, no questions asked.

His mother, however, was not so gullible. She said she believed him, but Owen knew otherwise. She could always see through him.

His lie held up for a while. In fact, he thought it might carry the day. He hadn't considered that the police would be able to trace the DNA to him.

The day after his father was arrested—before his father had even provided his own DNA sample to the police—his mother had come to the hospital and told Owen that she had something important to discuss. He knew before she said a word that the jig was up.

Nevertheless, when she explained that DNA found at the crime scene matched his father's family, Owen initially held tight to his lie.

"What does *that* mean?" he had said.

His mother looked at him with disappointment.

"Your father didn't kill James," she said. "But someone who shares DNA with him did. I think you know what that means."

———

Jessica would never forget the second time she confronted Owen about his role in James's murder. The first time was after the funeral, when he flat-out denied Haley's claim that he had been inside James's office on the day he was killed. She wasn't sure what to believe then, but even the remote possibility that Haley was telling the truth and Owen was lying was enough for her to change her tack with the police and convince Wayne to do likewise.

She was content to let Owen's denial stand unchallenged until the police obtained her son's DNA. But once they had, she needed for Owen to tell her the truth before the science left no doubt that her son had been lying to her.

Yet when she confronted him, Owen didn't initially react. She had just accused him of murdering his stepfather, and he remained silent.

His refusal to admit what he'd done overwhelmed her, and she began to cry. But now was not the time for her to break down. She needed to get the truth. To understand what had happened to lead her son to kill her husband.

Jessica steadied herself and told Owen that nothing he said would stop her and Wayne from loving him, and from doing everything they could to keep him out of jail. But she thought that the least he could do was tell her what happened. She hoped that by her tone, he realized that she expected to hear the truth.

This time, Owen got the message. After taking a moment to collect himself, he began to explain.

"I heard James talking to that Allison lady on his phone that morning," he said, speaking softly but deliberately, as if he'd fully thought through the sequence of events he was describing. "He said he was meeting her at four that day, and it sounded like they weren't just friends or whatever. He said he loved her. So, after school, I went to his office. I was just going to tell him to stop it. I swear to God. That's all I was going to do. Just make him stop cheating on you. But when I got there, the lady was leaving. I passed her at the door, and I was sure it was her because, you know, she was short-haired and skinny, the way that guy who called you said. When I went inside, James was in the shower. I could tell that he'd just finished having sex with her. The sheets were all smelly . . ."

Owen was crying now. Sobbing between words. Jessica didn't attempt to console him. She didn't want to do anything that would stop his confession.

"I was so angry . . . It felt like every bad thing that had ever happened to me—getting sick, you and Dad getting divorced, everything—just built up in me all at once. I started yelling at him, cursing at him, actually. He kept saying I didn't understand, but I kept screaming at him that I *did* understand. That I had seen this all happen before, and I wasn't going to let him do this to you. To us. Not again.

"I was going to leave. I actually started running for the door. He followed me out into the living room and grabbed me."

"Was that when you hit him?" she asked, knowing there could be only one answer coming.

"I don't even remember it. I must have, but . . ."

Owen shut his eyes and stopped for a long moment.

"The next thing I remember was that blood was pouring out of him. I pulled him away from the table, like that would help, and . . ."

Owen stopped. Jessica didn't say anything in case there was more he wanted to say.

The sobbing consumed him now. Fighting every motherly instinct she possessed, she prodded him for more. "Then what did you do?"

"I knew he was dead. I just knew. I swear, if I thought I could have saved him, I would have called 911. But there was nothing I could have done, so I ran out of there. I went to the park. I don't know why. Just somewhere to be by myself. I sat there for . . . I'm not sure how long. I remember it was cold out, but I didn't feel cold. No one else was in the park. When it started getting dark, I went to Dad's."

He looked like he wanted to be held. Her seventeen-year-old son, who had rebuffed virtually all physical intimacy from her for the past few years, wanted to hug his mommy. And in yet another of life's great ironies, it was the last thing Jessica wanted in that moment.

"Owen, you could not be more wrong," she finally said. "About everything you just said. James was not having an affair. The woman you saw, the woman who called James that morning, Allison? She was an FBI agent. She was investigating James, not sleeping with him. The sheets smelled the way they did because I was with James the day before. Remember? After we had the doctor's appointment? You went to lunch with Dad, but I didn't go because I said I was meeting James."

Owen's eyes were as big as saucers. Jessica had spent a lifetime trying to protect her son. Now she watched as the magnitude of his mistake began to take hold.

"James died for nothing," she said evenly. "He was the love of my life, and he died for no reason at all."

29

Gabriel was sitting in Captain Tomlinson's office with Asra. They were joined by ADA Joe Salvesen, who had called the meeting. The purpose was to tell them that he wasn't going to indict Owen Fiske.

After Salvesen had walked them through all the difficulties in the case, Gabriel said, "It doesn't matter that the DNA isn't a match. We know the blood at the scene came from the boy."

"I know you do," Salvesen said. "And if we took this case to trial, we could put on a medical expert to explain how the boy's DNA changed because of the treatment. But juries hear 'match' or 'no match.' And once they hear 'no match,' the reasons don't matter. He's not a match to the DNA at the crime scene. That's the reality."

"But he's the only one who possibly could be," Asra said. "We know that it came from a blood relative of Howard Fiske. And we know it's not Wayne Fiske. That leaves only Owen. And we know the reason why the DNA doesn't match. That's virtually the same *as* a match."

"Let's not drink our own Kool-Aid here," Salvesen said. "At each step, the defense is going to have a field day. All the DNA evidence stands or falls on the fact that Howard Fiske is a blood relative to the person who left blood at the crime scene. But that may not even be right."

Gabriel was a bit surprised at how much better prepared Salvesen was for this meeting than he had been for court. But it made sense that the ADA would spend his time getting out of work rather than creating it for himself. It would probably be another decade before Salvesen pulled a murder case against someone with a privately retained lawyer who would fight him at every turn, so he was working hard to secure a future of nine-to-five workdays going up against public defenders that would likely carry him to retirement.

"That's what the website told us," Asra said.

"Oh, the infallible website," Salvesen said. "Can you imagine what it's going to be like to have a representative of a genealogy website on the stand explaining their process? You think they're going to say they never make mistakes? Acknowledging even one mistake is reasonable doubt, right there."

"C'mon, Joe," Gabriel said. "Do you really think they'll claim they made a mistake that just happened to give a false positive of some guy in Oregon who just happens to be related to the stepson of a murder victim?"

"Okay, okay. Let's assume for the sake of argument that we convince the jury beyond any reasonable doubt that the blood at the crime scene was left by Owen Fiske. Where does that leave us? Now we have evidence that the man's stepson was in his place of business. No surprise there. You have evidence that he left some blood. That he scraped a knuckle. He's a teenager. When my boy was Owen's age, he was bleeding everywhere all the time. A regular Chuck Wepner."

"Who?" Asra asked.

"He was a boxer in the seventies," Salvesen said. "The Bayonne Bleeder, they called him. Knocked down Ali. But my point is that the defense will say he could have had a bloody nose that morning when he visited his stepfather before school. Or even after school, before the FBI agent brought James Sommers back to his office. So the blood doesn't really move the needle that much. It's not like the murderer had to leave blood at all. In fact, it's perfectly possible that the murderer didn't leave his own blood at the scene."

"The ME will say he did," Asra argued. "And the scratch on Owen's hand is exactly where Erica Thompson said it'd be if he'd punched James Sommers in the jaw."

"The scratches could be from anything. And could have occurred days before or after the murder. On top of which, I spoke with the ME. The best she can say is that the killer *might have* cut his hand with the punch. That's not *did*. In fact, to a jury true to the reasonable-doubt standard, it's *probably didn't*."

Gabriel caught Asra's eye. He had little doubt that she was thinking exactly what he was at this point—that Joe Salvesen's picture should be next to the word *coward* in the dictionary.

"And let's not forget that even if everything broke our way at trial, a conviction is going to be difficult because of the crazy ex-wife," Salvesen continued. "The trial will be all about Haley Sommers. And she's about as unsympathetic to a jury as a witness could possibly be. She's a god-damn investment banker turned stalker. She had a restraining order out against her. She crashed their anniversary party. Just think about that for a second. The defense will call fifty witnesses to testify to the fact that this crazy lady snuck into James Sommers's home—even though she was legally prohibited from doing so—for the sole purpose of calling him out in front of his friends. Who does that? Not only that, but they'll also be able to place her at the crime scene. Or at least in the restaurant next door. She has no business being there. And she's there a *lot*. And then there's the voice mail. That's the nail in the coffin. You heard what it sounded like when it was just read it in court. At trial, they'll play the recording for the jury. Over and over again. They'll have Haley go through what she was thinking when she left it, ask her to explain why she chose each and every word. You ever hear someone try to explain to a jury that they're not crazy when they've left a paper trail that only a psycho could create? It's not pretty, believe me. So, when all is said and done, with the evidence you have, our absolute best-case scenario is to give the jury a choice between convicting a kid with cancer or a woman who acts like *Fatal Attraction*'s batshit sister."

It was all too clear to Gabriel by now that nothing he or Asra said, or even the pressure from their captain, would cause Salvesen to grow a pair. And certainly not following a long balls-free career that had served the ADA just fine.

———

That night, for the first time in nearly two weeks, Gabriel came home before dinner. He hadn't called to alert Ella, wanting to see the surprise on her face when he walked through the door.

He wasn't disappointed.

Ella literally ran to the front door to greet him. After a long embrace, she asked, "Did you go over the wall to escape?"

He laughed. "No, the case is over."

"Congratulations," she said, clearly assuming that it had ended with an arrest.

"No. Like you'd say, we came in second."

"Salvesen too scared to take on Alex Miller?"

"That was the subtext. What he actually said was that we should wait for the boy to confess or for his parents to turn on him."

"Yeah, those are some sound prosecutorial tactics," she said with a laugh. Then: "You okay?"

"Hard to lose sleep over not putting a teenager with leukemia in jail for something that probably was more of an accident than a pre-meditated crime. Especially when there's no family demanding justice."

"So maybe you came in first, after all."

Gabriel made his way to Annie's crib. She was staring up at him, chewing on a rubber pretzel she held in her hand. When she caught sight of her father, Gabriel could have sworn his daughter smiled.

"Sure did," he said.

———

Alex Miller told Wayne that no arrest would be forthcoming. "Of course, that could change," the lawyer said. "New evidence could be found, or a new DA comes in and he or she decides to go for it. But usually that doesn't happen. If they don't think they have a strong enough case to take to trial now, time rarely improves the situation."

"What if Haley tells them what she saw?" Wayne asked.

This had always been Wayne's fear. There was an eyewitness, after all. She had seen Owen enter James's building, then flee the crime scene with blood on his hands.

The cops still didn't know about that. And for all Wayne knew, James's death hadn't soothed Haley's desire to ruin Jessica's life. If anything, it might have exacerbated it.

"I really don't see that making much of a difference at this point," Alex said. "Don't get me wrong—it would not be a positive development, but the police would still be left in the same spot. At trial, it'll be a choice between her or Owen. Most people are much more apt to believe that a woman who has threatened her ex-husband is a murderer ahead of a teenage stepson. Especially a sick one. Besides, Haley Sommers strikes me as pretty smart and having a heightened self-preservation instinct. The status quo suits her just fine. And I suspect now, with James gone, her thirst for revenge has probably lessened. I don't see anything in it for her to reach out to the police."

Wayne knew that it was unseemly for him to be so pleased at the prospect that his son was getting away with murder. Even if that someone was James Sommers. And even if Owen never intended for James to die, as Jessica had explained was the case based on Owen's confession to her.

Nevertheless, what he'd always told Owen was true—the love a parent feels for a child is unconditional. With his treatment seemingly a success, Owen had a long life ahead of him now, and the last thing Wayne wanted was for his son to spend a moment of it behind bars.

He also couldn't deny that he was happy that James was gone. He would have preferred that Jessica left James, rather than the man dying, but what Wayne really wanted was a chance to get his family back. How that opportunity came about was far less important.

He'd have to proceed slowly with Jessica. She was still grieving, after all. But he knew how much she feared being alone, and she wasn't getting any younger. She'd come back to him in the end. He knew she would.

———

When Jessica told Owen that the police had effectively closed the case, her son displayed no emotion whatsoever. He barely reacted to the news at all.

"This makes your father and me very happy," she told him. "It should make you happy too, Owen."

"Why?" he said in a defiant voice.

"Because it means you're going to get to live your life. Go to college. Get a job. Get married, if you want. Have a family of your own someday. I know that you're going to have to live with what happened for the rest of your life, but there's no reason that you have to suffer for the next . . . seventy years."

"But shouldn't I? Suffer, I mean. What I did was the worst thing that someone could do to someone else. I deserve to suffer."

Jessica thought about how many times over the past four years she'd feared this day would never come. Now that she'd finally get to see Owen graduate from high school, her pride in his accomplishment was inseparable from her guilt.

It had been less than three months since Alex Miller had told her that he thought Owen was out of criminal jeopardy. Ironically enough, Owen's escape from prosecution reminded her of his medical status—how Dr. Cammerman had told her that Owen's cancer was "in remission," but that he couldn't guarantee that would always be the case.

The two prognoses—about Owen's freedom and his health—occurred within a few weeks of one another. Alex Miller said their son would be allowed to return home after he left the hospital, and then Dr. Cammerman discharged him.

After that, Owen had gone back to school and resumed his daily routine. At times, Jessica wondered how much James's death weighed on him. But more often than not, that question was answered by the look in her son's eyes. In those moments, she knew what he was thinking as clearly as if he'd voiced it. But he never uttered a word.

She suggested he see a therapist, but he declined.

"Maybe when I get to college," he said.

College was SUNY Buffalo, his father's alma mater. It was a good fit because Owen wanted to leave New York City, and the family finances were such that private college tuition was not within their reach.

"I loved it there, O," his father had said. "And I promise that, unlike my old man, I'll let you attend Harvard Medical School if you want."

"The last thing I want to be is a doctor," Owen said quickly.

Jessica had always refrained from *What do you want to be when you get older?* types of questions. Largely because Owen's survival had long been in such doubt. As a result, she had no idea where her son's interests lay, aside from video games and the violin. Apparently, she could cross *doctor* off the list of his future career choices. Not that she blamed him. He had already spent enough time in medical facilities for one lifetime.

Owen suggested that he might study art history, which was a little odd. He'd never before expressed an interest in art. Music, yes, but not art. Jessica thought she knew why he'd had that sudden change of heart. It was a form of penance.

"Don't do that," she said.

"Why not?" Owen asked.

"Because you can't bring James back. So trying to do things that you think might've made him happy is just a recipe for disaster. It's best that you come to terms with that now. Because if you don't, you're going to spend your life on a wild-goose chase."

"You say that like it's a bad thing," Owen said.

He wasn't smiling, but he often chose to pretend to be serious when he was joking.

"I'm only sharing some hard-earned experience. Don't live your life in any way that isn't designed to bring you, or the ones you love, happiness."

"I had no idea you were so selfish, Mom." This he said with a smile.

She wasn't ready to break from the serious nature of the discussion, however. "I'm not saying don't care about other people. Or that you shouldn't devote yourself to helping others. That's all great. But I am saying don't do it unless it's what *you* want to do. Not because your father or I want it, and certainly not because you think it's going to soothe your guilt over James. The surest path I know to unhappiness is to live your life to meet someone else's expectations. Especially if that someone else is dead."

Owen sighed. "I don't know how I'm going to be able to live with this."

"You will, Owen. If for no other reason than you have no choice in the matter."

———

Owen's graduation ceremony was held in the Metropolitan Opera House, the anchor of the Lincoln Center complex. The theater held close to four thousand, and still tickets were limited to four per family.

Jessica's family needed only two. One for her and a second for Wayne.

Wayne sat beside her, midway back in the orchestra section. His face betrayed no trace of misgiving about the path that had led them to this day. If anything, he seemed like a man who had just ended a long journey and was satisfied his destination was worth the trip.

In the past few weeks, Wayne had become bolder in expressing his hope for them to share a future together. Jessica thought she'd made it clear that was not going to happen, but every so often he would say or do something that suggested the message hadn't been fully received.

"He made it," Wayne whispered to her in between the speeches offered by the valedictorian and the salutatorian.

She smiled but couldn't confirm his assessment. If Owen had made it, it was only in the most literal sense. He wasn't the same person he had been before. Even being sick had never so fundamentally changed him as his guilt did. You could get well after having cancer, but she knew all too well that there was no escaping living with the bad things you had done.

Perhaps that was only the pessimist's view. After all, Owen was graduating from high school and heading off to college soon. Which meant that he would be free to live the life that they'd dreamed he would. Not so long ago, they'd have gladly sacrificed their own lives to give him that chance.

So maybe Wayne was right. Owen had made it.

The graduating class included more than eight hundred students, and they were called up by major: drama, dance, tech, art, instrumental, and voice, in that order. The applause for any individual graduate had fallen precipitously after the first few crossed the stage, so that by the time Owen was called to receive his diploma, Jessica thought that she and Wayne might have been the only ones clapping.

Owen's hair had grown back, at least to the extent that he no longer looked like he had ever been bald. Jessica had asked him whether he planned on growing it out again.

"No, I don't think so," he had said. "Seems like tempting fate."

Upon receiving their diplomas, some of the graduates turned to the audience, either holding up their arms in a prizefighter victory stance or engaging in some other gesture of joy. Not Owen. It was difficult to tell from so far away, but Jessica didn't think her son even smiled in his moment of triumph. He took the diploma from the principal, shook his hand, and walked across the stage.

For the longest time, Jessica had been convinced that leukemia would shape her son's life. Perhaps that was still the case, but she no longer believed it would be paramount in molding the type of person he'd become. His curse would be to live out his days with the knowledge of what he'd done. Ironically, escaping legal retribution for his mistake would be his lifelong punishment.

It was a sentence she knew all too well. When she'd left Wayne for James, she had felt, in some small measure, like she had gotten away with it. She had cheated on her husband, broken his heart, and left him without having to face his anguish. And what was her punishment for violating one of God's own commandments? Bliss with another man.

Of course, there was no refuge from a self-imposed sentence. But she knew she'd gotten off lightly. A slap on the wrist, most people would have said.

Jessica had never believed in any afterlife. The existence she had now was the only one she ever would. She could make it heaven or hell. For her—like many people, she assumed—it felt like both at different times.

She wished she'd never been so naïve as to believe that she and James would live happily ever after. Not after what they'd done, the people they'd left hurt in their wake. How much they loved each other was irrelevant to others, after all.

Nothing born of sin ever ends well.

Watching her son leave the stage, Jessica hoped above all else that it was possible that he could live with the guilt and still find happiness. She'd managed that, however briefly. Perhaps Owen could as well.

And if he could, maybe she could too.

ACKNOWLEDGMENTS

Thank you very much for reading *The Perfect Marriage*. While I am writing a book, I feel very connected not only to the characters but to my readers as well. Then, when the book is finished, that connection abruptly breaks. So that we can reconnect, I encourage you to email me at adam@adammitzner.com and share your thoughts. I promise I will respond, and more than one reader in the past has won a bet against a dubious friend that they'd ever hear back from that author they emailed.

Although my readers always deserve my first thanks, a great many people contributed to *The Perfect Marriage* before anyone turned the first page. *The Perfect Marriage* is my fifth book with Thomas & Mercer (and my ninth overall), and I have immensely enjoyed working with them. Throughout that time, my team has been rather fixed, and I wouldn't have it any other way: Liz Pearsons has been my editor and friend since the beginning. Ed Stackler, who almost fifteen years ago read the very first thing I thought could be seen outside my family, still provides insightful suggestions that make everything I've published that much better. Laura Barrett, Ashley Little, and Robin O'Dell copyedit and find errors that I would never in a million years spot. Sarah Shaw is always there to help if I have any thoughts or questions.

My agent, Scott Miller, has also been with me since day one, and I'm grateful for his guidance and friendship. Scott's colleague Logan Harper has always been just an email away.

As I write this, a narrator for the spoken version of *The Best Friend* has not yet been selected, so I cannot thank anyone by name now, but I know many of my readers are really listeners, and that couldn't happen without all the great people at Audible.

My friends and family who read drafts and provide valuable insight are also almost unchanged since my first book a decade ago, and I continue to owe them more than I could ever repay, not just for their help in making my writing better but for making my life better. A heartfelt thank-you to Jessica and Kevin Shacter, Jane and Gregg Goldman, Bruce and Marilyn Steinthal, Margaret Martin, Lisa Sheffield, Jodi ("Shmo") Siskind, Ellice Schwab, Lilly Icikson, Bonnie Rubin, Clint Broden, and Matt and Deborah Brooks.

A special thank-you to my colleagues at Pavia & Harcourt, especially George Garcia and Jennifer Fried.

You cannot write a book about a blended family without spending a lot of time thinking about your own blended family. And though I assure you that the characters you just read about are not me or my family, my children—Rebecca, Emily, Michael, and Benjamin (who offered his usual spot-on *constructive complaints*)—are perfect in every way and have enriched my life beyond my wildest dreams.

And, of course, you cannot entitle a book *The Perfect Marriage* without thanking your lucky stars every day that you are in such a marriage. To my wife, Susan: a thank-you in the acknowledgments is all I can do in this format, but I'm trying every day to be worthy of your love and bring to you the happiness you've brought to me.

ABOUT THE AUTHOR

Photo © 2016 Matthew Simpkins Photography

Adam Mitzner is the acclaimed Amazon Charts bestselling author of *Dead Certain*, *Never Goodbye*, and *The Best Friend* in the Broden Legal series as well as the stand-alone thrillers *A Matter of Will*, *A Conflict of Interest*, *A Case of Redemption*, *Losing Faith*, and *The Girl from Home*. *Suspense Magazine* named *A Conflict of Interest* one of the best books of 2012, and in 2014 the American Bar Association nominated *A Case of Redemption* for a Silver Gavel Award. A practicing attorney in a Manhattan law firm, Mitzner and his family live in New York City. Visit him at www.adammitzner.com.